COLD COUNTRY

COLD COUNTRY

— A NOVEL —

RUSSELL ROWLAND

DZANC
BOOKS

DZANC BOOKS

5220 Dexter Ann Arbor Rd.
Ann Arbor, MI 48103
www.dzancbooks.org

Library of Congress Cataloging-in-Publication Data

Names: Rowland, Russell, author.
Title: Cold country : a novel / by Russell Rowland.
Description: First edition. | Ann Arbor, MI : Dzanc Books, [2019]
Identifiers: LCCN 2019013630 | ISBN 9781945814921
Subjects: | GSAFD: Mystery fiction.
Classification: LCC PS3618.O88 C65 2019 | DDC 813/.6--dc23
LC record available at https://lccn.loc.gov/2019013630

First Edition: November 2019
Cover design by Steven Seighman
Interior design by Michelle Dotter

Printed in the United States of America

10   9   8   7   6   5   4   3   2   1

*To my sister Collette Rowland, a calming influence from the day
she foiled my career as an only child*

PROLOGUE

ROGER LOGAN FOLLOWED HIS FATHER Carl, stepping out into the cold dead of Montana winter. It was midnight, and the dry air was black and odorless, cut by a thin slice of moon. The snow gave the ground an eerie glow. Roger slipped a little, the black loafers that were the only shoes he owned sliding on the snow.

"You got the flashlight?" The snow crackled under Carl's boots.

"Got it right here." Roger lifted the light, showing it to his father, who didn't bother to look back.

"All right. Let's go see if we got any new babies out there."

Carl wiped the moisture from his nose and opened the gate, a mounted wagon wheel, into the small pasture behind the clapboard farmhouse. Roger shivered beneath his insulated coveralls. His small button nose was bright red with cold. He pulled his scotch cap lower, over his eyes. But when the hat moved forward, he felt the cold air against the back of his neck, and he tilted the cap back again, so that the neck band touched his collar. To the west, the Gallatin Mountains hovered black and solid along the horizon. The Absarokas looked a little brighter to the east, reflecting the moon. They looked to be holding up the sky, which eased into the color of oily blue steel as Roger's eyes adjusted to the dark.

"Turn that puppy on, son." Carl waved his hand back toward Roger, who pressed the button on the flashlight, sending a silent beam across the pasture. A startled cow blinked into the light, her eyes big, her nose wet and steaming.

"Evenin', sweetheart," Carl said. "You dropped your load yet?"

The cow glared at them, angry at the intrusion, which had occurred several times a night for the past three weeks. Roger shined the light on her tail and on the ground behind her, neither of which revealed any sign of new life.

"You stubborn old maid," Carl said. "You're going to be the last one to calve, sure as I'm standing here." He slapped her flank, softly, and the cow twitched and mooed. "Yeah, I know what you mean," Carl muttered. "Waiting is hard."

Roger watched his father's affectionate banter with the cattle. It was here, with the animals, that his father seemed comfortable, happy. And Roger felt hopeful, for the hundredth time in recent weeks, that this would be the time his father talked to him about everything that was going on in this new place, and about the murder of Tom Butcher.

Roger wanted to know why people were saying that Carl had committed the crime. And he wanted to know why his mother left— whether it was because of anything Roger had done. And he wanted to know whether she would be coming home for Christmas.

But in the moments when they were alone, his father's look was always far away, as unreachable as those beautiful blue mountains.

"Dad?"

"Yeah, son," Carl answered absently.

"How many are left?" Roger scanned the pasture and let the beam settle on another solitary, blinking cow.

"How many?" Carl walked on, head bent low, two paces in front of Roger. "How many what?"

"How many that haven't calved yet?"

Carl sniffed. "Twenty-three."

Roger watched his father's blue silhouette saunter across the pasture, his rubber boots breaking the crusted snow. It was so cold that there were no smells other than those close to his face, the scarf wrapped around his neck, the smell of his leather mitten when he wiped his nose.

"How long's it been since you came out with me?" Carl asked.

"A week ago. My birthday."

"That's right. I remember now. So we must have had about thirty-five left then, huh?"

"Forty."

"Mm." Carl scratched the back of his head, his gloved hand rubbing furiously against his plaid wool cap. "Oh, boy. Check that mamma right there." He pointed.

Roger aimed the flashlight in line with his father's arm. The light revealed the hunched figure of a cow in labor, her back bowed, her tail in the air, her rear legs spread awkwardly.

"Bingo." Carl's quiet exclamation stopped dead, knocked down by the cold.

From beneath the cow's tail, the bowling pin shape of a calf's skull hung limp and wet, rising slightly as the cow began to push.

Carl rushed over to the cow, his elbows sticking out like chicken wings, as if he was attempting to be comical. But this was just the way he ran, and Roger followed, trying to hold the light steady on the cow.

Carl pulled off his gloves, tucked them into the deep pockets of his coveralls, and lifted the calf's head. He rested one hand gently beneath it, as if it would shatter if dropped.

The cow swung her head, looking at this sudden, uninvited interruption with a wild, glowering brown eye.

"Easy, girl. Easy, boss," Carl murmured, almost whispering. "Give her all you got. Give her everything you got, sweetheart."

The cow's back arched. She moaned, then let out a cry, lifting her head, then another low moan. Roger watched the calf's head move only a few inches further, then stop even when the cow continued pushing.

"Damn," Carl shouted. "God*damn*." His voice rose in volume until it scared Roger.

"What?" Roger asked breathlessly.

Carl didn't answer, but placed one hand against the cow's flank and slipped his fingers beneath the skull, into the birth canal.

"She got a leg caught up?" Roger asked.

Carl pulled his hand out and unbuttoned the sleeve of his coveralls, and his shirt sleeve, then rolled them both up as far past his elbow as he could. One of his gloves fell from his pocket, onto the ground. He slipped his hand back into the canal, leaning toward the cow so he could get his whole arm inside.

Roger held the light steady, knowing that the calf's front leg must be folded back but wishing his father would tell him, just so he could hear him say it.

Carl strained and grunted, as did the cow, although she had stopped pushing. Carl twisted his body, and the bill of his scotch cap bumped against the cow's flank, tipping the hat back on his head. His brown curls poked out from beneath the bill. His teeth clenched.

"You got a hold of it?" Roger asked.

Carl swore and slowly pulled his arm from inside. The arm was streaked with thick blood and afterbirth. Carl shook the limb, then held it out and massaged the forearm muscle with his other hand, trying to squeeze out a cramp. "Why in the hell does Kenwood have to be the only rancher in Paradise Valley to calve in the middle of goddamn winter?" he said to himself.

Roger flipped the beam toward the cow's head. The tip of her tongue hung from her steaming mouth, her eyes wild and scared when she swung her heavy skull around to gaze into the light.

"I need that light, son," Carl said sharply.

"Sorry." Roger rotated the light back to his father, who formed a point with his fingers. He had just inserted his hand inside the cow again when she shifted suddenly. Carl whipped his arm out as the cow dropped to her front knees. She landed on her side, crunching the snow.

"Goddamn, girl, you trying to break my arm?" Carl muttered. He lowered himself to his knees. "This isn't going to make my job any easier."

Roger felt his own arm begin to cramp, and he shifted the heavy flashlight to his other hand, trying to hold it steady on the cow.

Carl was leaning on his elbow, nearly lying on the snow, and he slid his arm as far as he could inside the cow. The angle was awkward, and the strain twisted his face, which was red and sweaty under the black curls pasted against his forehead.

The front hoof of the free leg now protruded under the calf's head. The hoof lay against the bottom jaw, as though the calf was scratching its chin.

Roger felt his toes stiffen with cold, and he bent his knees, one at a time, running in place without lifting his feet from the ground. "Did you find the other leg yet?"

Carl strained and groaned, finally lowering himself onto his side on the ground. Roger thought he saw his father give a quick nod.

Roger continued to shift his weight and rotate the light from one hand to the other, and open and close his free hand to fight off the cold. His cheeks went numb.

The cow mooed, and her body clenched into a contraction every so often, and with each push her effort weakened. Carl's arm finally started to emerge from inside, slowly. Halfway out, it stopped, and he began tugging, bracing himself against the cow's flank with his knees and his other hand, pulling with all his weight.

Each time he tugged, he groaned—a low, throaty growl. And at last, with a heave, the leg came loose. Carl fell backward, and the calf's torso followed his arm and its own leg, sloshing out into the cold night air, spilling blood and afterbirth onto the snow. The cow moaned, and her side collapsed. Carl lay on his back, panting, still gripping the tiny hoof.

"Yahoo!" Roger shouted. His voice sounded suddenly high and boyish, and he was embarrassed about yelling. He walked toward the calf, shining the light down on its face, and when he saw the eye, he stopped, feeling a sudden chill.

He looked over at his father and knew from the look on Carl's face that his suspicion was right. His heart seized as though it had suddenly been exposed to the icy air, and his eyes teared up, but he fought it off.

Carl stood, rising suddenly. He fished inside his coveralls, found his pocketknife, and flipped the blade open. He wordlessly cut the umbilical cord, put his knife away, then grabbed both of the calf's front hooves and started dragging the carcass across the snow, leaving a thick red trail.

Roger followed, assuming his father was going to throw the calf behind the barn, where three other dead calves now lay frozen. But Carl walked instead to the barn door, swinging it open. He reached inside and flipped on the light, then dragged the calf from the snow onto the straw-covered barn floor.

Roger stepped over the four-by-four threshold and pulled the door closed behind him. "What are we doing, Dad?" He tried to speak in a low voice, to sound more like a man, but the ten-year-old boy voice echoed through the barn, and he knew his father probably wouldn't answer.

"Just follow me," Carl said, and Roger skipped for a couple of steps before catching himself.

The smell of iodine and straw filled Roger's nose, and the bright yellow of the incubator just inside the door warmed his face. It felt so good. A newborn calf lay curled up inside, sleeping, its long eyelashes resting peacefully against its face. The barn was huge, and although it was no more silent than the outdoors, it seemed much more still. Roger always felt like shouting when he first entered the barn, to break the stillness apart just for a second.

Carl walked down the aisle between the stalls, and the dead calf's head hung loose between its legs, bobbing with each step.

Carl stopped in front of a stall, dropping the calf to the ground, where its skull settled into the dusty straw. Roger saw that the stall held another calf, a new one, probably only a day old. Two inches of the twisted black remains of the umbilical cord hung from the calf's belly, and its coat was still matted with dried afterbirth.

"Where's his mamma?" Roger asked.

"She didn't make it." Carl flipped the hook from its mooring and swung the gate open.

"Make sure he doesn't get out," Carl said, and Roger stepped inside the stall, holding his arms out to keep the shivering calf from rushing past him. The calf lowered his head and backed into the corner, eyeing Roger.

Carl dragged the dead calf into the stall and swung the gate shut, replacing the hook. He took off his scotch cap and wiped his forehead, pushing his curls back, leaving a streak of blood across his forehead. He thought for a minute, staring off, past Roger, way past him, so that Roger felt as if his father wasn't in the same place, the same building. Then Carl turned and left the stall, shutting the gate behind him and leaving Roger with the two calves, one dead, one curious and frightened. Roger laid the flashlight down, then thought better of it and picked it up. He reached through the rails, placing it outside the stall, out of the way.

He studied the dead calf, staring at its eye, lifeless but dark brown and shining, seemingly ready to blink at any moment. He wondered if a human eye looked the same when the person was dead. Whether it had the same bright stillness. He wondered whether the person who killed Tom Butcher three months before had studied his eyes after he died. And finally, he wondered what color Tom Butcher's eyes had been— whether they were the same dark brown as the calf's, or steely blue, or maybe green. And he thought how strange it was that a man he'd never met had changed everything in his life. Ruined it, really. Just by dying.

Roger turned back toward the living calf, which was still eyeballing him, his head low to the ground. Roger wondered whether the calf would be less afraid if Roger was a cow.

"Mooo," Roger said. "Mooooooooo."

"You ready?"

Roger jumped. His father was behind him now, entering the stall, and Roger was embarrassed to be caught mooing, although it was impossible to tell whether his father even noticed. Carl carried a bundle of tangled twine and his pocket knife.

"Yeah, I'm ready," Roger said, although he didn't know what he was ready for.

"All righty," Carl said. "We're going to give this little fella a new winter coat. He'll be the only one in the valley with his own fur coat."

Carl grabbed one of the dead calf's hind legs and rolled it onto its back, then crouched next to it and slit its belly. The hide fell away, spilling blood and innards onto the fresh straw. Carl ran his knife up to the rib cage, where he started sawing. He split the calf's chest in two, then allowed the carcass to fall onto its side. The heart that no longer beat lay still and useless inside the gaping chest cavity. The smell of blood was overpowering.

Roger watched in fascination as his father sliced away, separating with deft strokes the calf's hide from its meat. Carl skinned the animal, legs and all, preserving the hide's shape. Roger had never seen his father skin anything, and he was impressed.

"You know what's going on here?" Carl asked.

Roger didn't, but he nodded. "Sure."

His father smiled at him, knowing. The blood on his forehead had dried and it looked like a streak of dark soil. "All right, let's get to it."

Carl stood, then reached down and hefted the hide up over one shoulder. "First thing you gotta do is catch that little bugger." He indicated the live calf with a nod.

"Okay." Roger crept toward the calf, which lowered its head again, studying him with wide-eyed suspicion.

Roger veered toward one side, and the calf leaned toward the other, ready to run. When Roger was a few feet away, he rushed the calf, throwing his arms around its neck and bracing his feet forward, pushing his weight back to keep the calf from running.

The calf was small but strong, and Roger was surprised how easily he managed to get it under control—but not without feeling a tromp on his foot. Roger gritted his teeth, holding back a cry of pain.

Then he realized why catching the calf had been so easy. His father had the calf by its spine, a foot from its hips, one strong hand gripping the narrow flank. With the other arm, Carl flipped the hide off his shoulder, onto the calf's back. One leg of the thick hide brushed Roger's head, knocking his scotch cap to the ground.

Roger held the calf as steady as he could. His legs felt strong. The effort warmed his blood.

Carl adjusted the hide, aligning its legs with the calf's. Then he picked up his knife and poked two holes in one of the hide's legs. He cut a short length of twine and laced it through the holes. He tightened the leather around the calf's leg, stretching the corner of the hide.

Carl did this with each leg, and Roger felt his own legs and arms weaken with each minute. As his strength waned, the cold seeped back into his bones, and he felt stiff. His foot ached, and he shifted his weight.

After Carl finished with the legs, he poked three holes in each side of the skin's torso and laced more twine under the calf's belly, back and forth like a shoelace. He tightened the twine and tied it securely. Roger's leg muscles burned.

"All right," his father said. "Let him go."

Roger did.

The calf ran the ten feet across the stall and kicked his heels, coming down on the dead calf's hip. He kicked again, and once more, but the hide did not budge. The calf stopped and glared at them.

Roger looked at his father, unsure why they'd done this, or whether they'd finished, or what to expect next.

"Well," Carl said, rubbing the back of his head. "Let's go get that cow in here." He bent down and picked up Roger's cap, absently handing it to him.

"Thanks," Roger said.

Carl grabbed the carcass by one hoof and dragged it outside. Roger shined the flashlight out into the blackness, in the direction where the cow had given birth. And suddenly he knew what they were doing, and he had to contain his excitement about figuring it out for himself.

He looked up at his father and smiled, pleased with the plan and wondering whether his father had thought of it himself. Then he wondered something else, and wanted to ask, but couldn't bear the thought of his father not answering him again, especially about something so important. He walked beside his father, trying to keep as close to him as he could, taking three steps to every two of his father's, and the not knowing finally got to him, and he had to ask.

"What happens if the cow doesn't take the calf? If she knows it isn't hers?" He studied his father's placid, pink face.

Carl turned his head away from Roger, into the dark night and the cold, toward the Gallatin Mountains. "He'll die."

BOOK ONE

A PAIR OF LOAFERS

CHAPTER ONE

TWELVE WEEKS EARLIER

ROGER LOGAN STOOD IN THE entrance of a small, thirty-foot trailer that housed the upper three grades of Slack School, the last one-room school in Paradise Valley, Montana. Although technically it was two rooms, with the trailer reserved for grades four through six and the original schoolhouse for the lower three grades.

Roger held a thick loose-leaf binder tightly against his thin frame as he looked around at the feet of the other seven children. The boys all wore boots. Roger looked down at his own feet, at the nearly new black loafers he had persuaded his mother to buy earlier that summer, before their unexpected move to the country.

Roger's feet were skinny, and he'd endured plain black oxfords, which came in narrow sizes, for the first nine years of his life. But when Gorem's Shoes in Bozeman finally ordered loafers in narrow sizes, Roger's mother Laurie had agreed to buy them. When Roger tried them on, he curled his toes tightly to hide the fact that they slipped in the heel. His mother didn't notice. Now Roger regretted that day as he shuffled toward a desk in the corner, trying to shield his feet.

One of the older boys, a freckled kid with a severe cowlick, stepped forward.

"What grade you in?" he asked Roger.

Roger swallowed. "Fourth."

The freckled kid turned to a stocky boy with ears that stuck out. "There you go, Scooter. You finally got yourself a classmate."

Scooter grinned, a pointed V of a smile, and the others pushed him and showered his arms with light punches.

The freckled kid turned back to Roger and shook his hand. "I'm Bobby Kirby."

Bobby pointed out each of the other kids, four boys and two girls. Roger glanced at each face, forgetting the names as soon as they were spoken. Through the gaps between them, he took in the classroom, which smelled strongly of old wood and chalk.

Eight wooden desks in two neat rows filled most of the small trailer, along with a large, chipped desk up front. A blackboard stretched along the side wall, covering nearly its entire length, and on the front wall hung pictures of Presidents Washington and LBJ. The picture of President Johnson was upside down. There were only two windows— very small ones—on a door at each end of the trailer. Despite the glow of fluorescent bulbs, the room was dark.

"What's your name?"

"Roger."

"Roger what?"

"Roger Logan."

Bobby walked over to Scooter. "Scooter here is the only other fourth grader in the school. I'm in sixth. So's everyone else here, except my brother Craig." He pointed to another freckle-faced kid. Craig also had a cowlick, more severe than Bobby's. "Craig's in fifth."

Roger nodded, looking at Craig, who sniffed, then wiped his nose. Roger shuffled back behind a corner desk. He laid his notebook on the desk and thought about sitting. But the others were still standing.

"Your dad's managing the Kenwood place?" Bobby asked.

"Yeah," Roger answered.

"My dad grew up on that ranch. Now he owns this place just down the road," Bobby said. "The first one going east." He pointed. "You passed it when you rode the bus this morning."

Roger nodded, smiling at the thought of the "bus," which was really a van with three bench seats, just big enough for the seven students who lived too far to walk or ride their bikes to Slack School. There were about twenty students in all, most in the lower grades.

"We're getting a new teacher today," one of the other boys said. "The lady that married Spider Moses."

"He doesn't know who Spider Moses is," Craig said. Then he turned his round head toward Roger. "Do you?"

Roger shook his head.

"He's one of the old-timers," Bobby explained. "One of the rich guys. Not as rich as Tom Butcher, though. Or Kenwood. But since Kenwood doesn't live around here, Butcher is the richest rancher around. Then Spider."

"The old teacher got fired 'cause she was drunk!" one of the girls exclaimed. Roger remembered that her name was Susan, a pretty girl with dark curls.

Roger's mouth opened wide.

"It's true," Bobby said gravely. "Mrs. Ruth doesn't hold her liquor real well."

"My dad said Babe has been sleeping with Tom Butcher," another kid said.

"Oh shut up, Larry," Craig said. "Everyone knows your dad's a liar."

The other kids laughed.

"Her name is Babe Ruth?" Roger asked.

Bobby nodded. "Pretty funny, huh? She married ol' Lester Ruth after his first wife died."

"Was she drunk in school?" Roger asked.

The other kids all looked at Bobby, who turned his eyes down at his boots. "Well, she fell asleep during class. A couple a times."

"Wow," Roger said.

"Now we have Mrs. Moses. Mrs. Moses is as big as a bear," Susan said, holding her hand high above her head. The other kids laughed.

"She's tall, all right," Craig said. "Kinda scary."

"She used to be a professor at the university up in Missoula," Bobby said.

"Yeah, then her husband died, and she married his brother," Larry said. "Right after the funeral."

"Shut up, Larry," Bobby said. "It wasn't right after the funeral." Bobby turned to Roger. "It wasn't right after the funeral."

"This last summer, at the Fourth of July picnic, she hit a home run over everyone's head," Craig said. "Sucker rolled into the creek."

Roger smiled and nodded, feeling the eyes on him. The two girls stood a bit behind, outnumbered but watchful. The mention of baseball, one of his favorite things, made Roger's heart beat a little faster. But the edges of his ears still burned. He thought of his sister Julie, over in the main building. She was wearing her patent leather shoes, he remembered, with bows. He looked at the two sixth-grade girls, at their feet. One wore saddle shoes, worn nearly all the way through. The other wore a sort of slipper, kind of like Julie's shoes, only plain leather. This made Roger feel a little better.

"How come you didn't move up here before school started?" Scooter asked Roger. "You're a week late!"

Before he could answer, the door opened behind him, and Roger turned. Just a few feet away stood the tallest woman he'd ever seen. He looked up at her as she walked past them, past the blackboard along the side wall, all the way to the back, where she corrected the picture of LBJ and then stepped back to make sure it was straight.

She faced the class, showing no sign of irritation, or amusement, or anything at all. Her eyes were as green as a Siamese cat's, and just by looking at her face, the children all knew that they should find their seats. They scurried around and past each other to their desks.

Roger settled into the desk he'd laid his notebook on, the last desk in the right-hand row, and tucked his shoes under the chair. Mrs. Moses positioned herself behind her own desk, squarely in the middle, holding herself with the supreme authority of a college professor, which she'd been before she moved to Paradise Valley to marry Spider. Her shoulders were straight beneath a mustard blazer. Her pleated skirt was colored to match. Professorial glasses rested on an impressive Roman nose, and her right eyebrow swept high across her forehead in a perpetual question mark. With the tip of one pinky finger, she scratched each corner of her mouth.

Then she spoke. "Please take out a piece of paper and a pencil."

There was a momentary pause before Bobby, who was in the front, lifted his desktop and pulled a notebook from inside. The others followed suit, their desks squawking and squeaking as they opened, like a chorus of baby birds.

"During the next fifteen minutes, I want each of you to write an essay." Mrs. Moses paced the width of the trailer, holding her hands out in front of her with just the tips of her fingers touching. "The subject will be your dreams and goals. What you would like to do with your life. What you want to be. Where you'd like to go." She pivoted suddenly and faced the class. "Begin."

Roger found himself gaping at his new teacher, unable to think. She turned and gazed out the window and cleaned the corners of her mouth again. The scratching of pencils against wood echoed through the room, and he looked around. A few of his classmates were writing, but most of them sat rubbing their heads or staring at blank pages, chewing their erasers. One hand rose.

"Mrs. Moses?"

She turned. "Yes?"

"What's an essay?"

A very slight smile formed on Mrs. Moses's face. "Oh yes. I must remember you are children. A story," she said. "Just write me a story."

"Yes, ma'am."

She returned to the window.

Roger only had to think for a moment before he began to write:

My dream is to play baseball on the Los Angeles Dodgers baseball team. I would like to play first base, or in the outfield. But I would also like to pitch. I would like to go to all the different cities where the Los Angeles Dodgers play and I would like to play in those cities, too. This is my dream. And I would also like to get married, have children and play catch with my children.

Roger studied the page and erased a sloppy letter, printing it more neatly over the grey smear. He laid down his pencil and looked up. He was the last one to finish, but only five minutes had passed. Mrs. Moses stood poised at the back door, staring through the tiny window. She did not check their progress. The children exchanged glances but didn't make a sound. Everyone in the room could feel the possible consequences of a disturbance. So they sat silent but restless, their limbs jerking with anxious energy.

After ten minutes, Mrs. Moses glanced at her watch.

"You have five minutes," she announced, still not looking at them.

Scooter looked over his shoulder and covered his mouth, stifling a laugh. Bobby reached across the aisle and smacked Scooter's arm. Scooter rocked in his chair, barely able to contain his laughter.

Susan Cayley, the girl wearing the slippers, had a sudden thought, and she lowered her head and wrote with careful deliberation. But the rest of the class sat motionless, waiting for Mrs. Moses to turn from the window. Which she did precisely fifteen minutes after they'd begun.

"Who would like to read first?" A slight smile curled one side of her mouth, but it looked uncomfortable.

No one volunteered. They all held their hands firmly in their laps.

"How about you, Mr. Cayley?" She directed her gaze to Scooter, who squirmed in his chair and scratched his head.

Scooter lifted the paper to his face and began to read. "My dream…"

"Please stand, Mr. Cayley. And face the class."

Roger's stomach dropped. Everyone else in the class was suddenly fidgety.

Scooter looked at her for a moment, perhaps hoping she'd change her mind. Then he wiggled out of his desk and turned toward the class. His shoulders slumped, and he held the paper high, covering his face.

"'My Dream,' by Scooter Cayley," he mumbled. "My dream is to buy a bunch of cattle…Herefords, and raise them on my own place. And to have a four-wheel-drive and a snowmobile."

Scooter fell into his chair, the relief showing in his shoulders.

Mrs. Moses stood unmoving, still looking at Scooter. "That's all?"
"Yes, ma'am."

Her look remained fixed on him, not angry, but steady. Scooter seemed to curl up like a potato bug. "Well…" she said. "I hope some of you managed to come up with more than just a sentence and a half."

A pall settled over the class. Scooter's shoulders curled in a few more inches. Mrs. Moses pointed to the next student, Susan, singling her out with a bony finger.

"Miss Cayley, perhaps you have more to say than your brother."

Susan stood with a cold air of confidence. Her voice was clear. She dreamed of being a teacher and moving to Billings, which was about one hundred miles east. Mrs. Moses nodded with what looked to be encouragement. But she held the knobby finger to her lips and thought for a moment.

"You're a sixth grader, are you not, Miss Cayley?"

Susan nodded, her ponytail bobbing against the back of her head.

"If my memory serves, and I believe it does, a sixth grader should know that the plural past tense of the verb 'go' is 'went,' not 'had went.'" She stopped and smiled at Susan, waiting. "Is that correct?"

Susan held her eyes firm and cold on Mrs. Moses. "Yes, ma'am."

Each child rose, voice shaking, hands trembling, and read, then stood as if awaiting a blow as Mrs. Moses paced back and forth, plucking at the corners of her mouth and adjusting her glasses. At one point, she noticed a pointer hanging by a leather string next to the blackboard. She removed the three-foot dowel from its hook as if it were an antique, studied the rubber, bullet-shaped tip, and beat it gently against her open palm, sending a shiver through the room.

Roger realized as Mrs. Moses went along the rows that he was going to be the last to read, and as the teacher found something to critique in each student's presentation, he studied his essay. His stomach churned as Craig spoke softly about his desire to become a veterinarian. Mrs. Moses wondered whether Craig knew the difference between an adjective and an adverb. He nodded, but when pressed, he could not explain.

"When you say, 'a horse that was hurt bad,' does that sound right to you?"

Craig paused, his face twisted with confusion. He shook his head.

"What do you think it should be?" Mrs. Moses asked, moving toward him. She stopped just a few feet away.

"A horse that had been hurt bad?" Craig tried.

Mrs. Moses turned her back to him. "No, no, no, no, no. Does anyone know what's wrong with that phrase?" She kept her back to them. Roger knew, but the thought of speaking almost made him wet his pants.

"Is it badly, ma'am?" Bobby finally asked.

She whirled around. "That is correct, Mr. Kirby. Thank you. Craig, maybe you can learn from your brother." She smiled at Bobby as Craig's round head tilted forward. He sat down, seething.

When Bobby read, he was the only one whose voice sounded strong. His dream was to become a geologist, and Roger thought his essay was perfect. But Bobby mentioned an uncle who was a geologist, and said he wanted to be a geologist "like him."

"That should be 'like he is,'" Mrs. Moses pointed out, but Bobby, unlike the others, did not flinch.

"Yes, ma'am," he answered in a steady voice, marking the correction on his paper.

By the time she got to him, Roger felt as if the pointer that she tapped against her palm was pounding inside his chest. He rose from his chair, trying to keep his eyes on his paper and his loafers hidden behind the chair. He felt the others turn to look. His cheeks burned hot, and a steady quake started in his knees. He read, his voice breaking and rattling in his throat. And then he finished, and waited. He looked up at the imposing figure behind her desk.

Mrs. Moses stared at him for a moment, an unnerving half-smile telling him something he didn't understand. Her head tilted slightly, and then she looked down at her desk, where she flipped open a grade book and ran a finger down the page.

"You must be Roger...Roger Logan?" She looked up.

"Yes, ma'am."

"Your family just moved to the Kenwood place?"

Roger nodded.

Mrs. Moses also nodded, and looked back down at her book. Roger stood waiting for her critique, but it never came. She lifted her head and walked around to the front of her desk. When she noticed that Roger was still standing, she held her hand out, palm up, then dropped it six inches, so he sat. He was bewildered, and bothered, that she didn't say something. He felt singled out, and he did not want this. Scooter turned and gave him a quick glare.

Mrs. Moses laid the pointer carefully on her desk. Then she spoke again.

"I don't expect you to enjoy your time in my classroom," she said, her smile as cool as iron. "This may not seem fair, seeing as how most of you also work very hard at home. But I think school is a place to learn, and at best, perhaps I can help you find some joy in that process. You will get out of this what you put into it." She smiled to herself, and it seemed to come easier this time, as if these words were more pleasing to her than she expected. Then she looked at her watch. "And speaking of joy…recess!"

•

The children filed out in a daze, not looking at each other. But once they were outside, where it was a beautiful, cloudless day, the mood shifted quickly, as if the fresh air had revived them. Silence turned to shouts, and shuffling into running in circles. Roger followed closely but cautiously, not wanting to draw attention to himself.

"Let's play baseball," Bobby shouted. He and a few others rushed into the main building and came out bearing bats, mitts, and a baseball. Roger smiled.

A dozen smaller kids spilled out of the original schoolhouse, a quaint white building with chunks of stucco crumbling from the corners, revealing patches of chicken wire. Roger spotted his sister Julie, wearing the red smock their mother had made for her first day of school. Roger smiled at her. She gave a little wave, her own smile drowsy.

"Who's the captains?" one of the younger boys shouted.

"Bobby," another yelled. "Bobby and Larry."

The two older boys began picking teams in the midst of the shouting, running, pushing, and laughing children. The warm smell of hay and grasses, which were fading to brown in the surrounding fields, made the day feel hazy and muted.

Bobby picked Roger around the middle of the pack, and after that Roger watched anxiously, hoping that Julie wouldn't be the last chosen. But she stood engrossed in watching the other children, her chocolate brown eyes round and dreamy. Her hands were clasped behind her back, but when she saw something that pleased or amused her, they jumped out in front of her, as if she was about to catch a ball. She didn't even notice when Bobby finally pointed and said, "I'll take her."

Roger approached her. "You're on my team," he said quietly.

"For what?"

"We're playing baseball, Jules. Are you paying attention? Don't you see all the bats and mitts?"

"Oh." She studied the equipment. "Do I have to play?"

"Jules, everyone's playing. You can't just stand off by yourself."

Her eyes moistened. "Why not?"

Roger grabbed her hand and pulled her toward their team. "Come on. It'll be okay. It's only baseball. You spend most of the time standing around anyway."

Bobby pitched for Roger's team. Larry, the first batter, flailed at three pitches and struck out, jeered by his teammates. Scooter went next, and he planted his feet in the batter's box, the tips of his ears still red, his eyes narrow.

On the third pitch, Scooter's cheeks filled with air and he swung hard. But he caught the very top of the ball, driving it straight into the ground. It bounced high over the second baseman's head.

Roger had positioned Julie in right field, but she had wandered toward the infield and stood just behind first base, her back to the game, staring at the sky. Roger ran from center field, yelling her name. Scooter barreled toward first, running low and solid. Just as Julie turned around, Scooter passed first base with a shout, a primal growl, running right at her. Julie screamed and covered her head. But Scooter veered at the last minute, racing on to second. He laughed, leering at Roger as Julie started to cry.

Roger retrieved the ball and threw it to third, preventing Scooter from advancing. Then he raced over to Julie, although what he felt like doing was burying a shoulder into Scooter's ribs.

"You all right, Jules?"

She sniffled but nodded. "He just scared me."

"I know. It's okay. You're not hurt, right?"

"I'm okay."

Roger gave Scooter, who was still smiling at him, a look that told him everything that was in his head. This only seemed to please Scooter more.

When Roger's team came up to bat, Bobby told him to hit third. He came to the plate with Bobby at second and another boy at first. Nervous energy made the tips of Roger's fingers feel tender against the bat, and he took a deep breath while he dug the heel of his right loafer into the hard ground.

The first pitch sailed in, and Roger swung, gritting his teeth. He missed.

"Hah. Wants to play for the Dodgers, but he can't even hit the ball."

Roger didn't need to look back. He knew Scooter was catching, and he didn't want to acknowledge that he'd heard him.

Larry wound up again, then threw.

"If I wore shoes like them shoes, would I be as smart as you, Roger?" Scooter's voice rang out as Roger watched the ball spinning toward him.

Roger's body coiled, and he swung again, trying too hard to knock the ball over everyone's head. He tipped the pitch, sending it past Scooter's right shoulder. One of the other kids chased after it.

"If you wore shoes like these, you might at least learn to speak English," Roger replied.

"Good hit, buddy," Scooter said. "Just like Mickey Mantle."

Roger didn't move, his neck as stiff and unyielding as a fence post. But the tender nerves tingled in his fingertips, and angry tears gathered behind his eyes.

Larry caught the ball, wound up, and hurled another fastball, right toward the middle of the plate.

"Well, I guess I'd rather be a dumbass than a fairy," Scooter muttered.

Roger's left foot lifted from the ground, sliding toward Larry as his elbow pushed the bat forward. But in the next instant, a voice in the darkest corner of his mind redirected his thoughts. Roger's muscles adjusted, turning him one hundred and eighty degrees on his left foot, and, with all his strength, he swung the bat directly at Scooter's head.

Already he was screaming at himself to stop. But it was too late. His arms were already in the fluid motion of a full swing, and the best he could do was to let the bat go. His fingers opened, and the bat dropped a few inches, just enough to miss Scooter's head. The bat cracked into his shoulder instead, emitting a dull, wood-against-bone thud that might as well have been a bazooka for how loud it sounded to him.

Nineteen children gasped in horror, their muscles fossilized in the middle of whatever motion they had started.

The bat fell to the dirt, harmless as a dead animal. Roger's hands also fell, lifeless at his sides. Scooter remained in a crouch, his jaw out, his right hand pressed to his left shoulder. A small, choked sound sprang from his throat.

Roger started to step forward, toward Scooter. He wanted to see whether Scooter was all right. But before he had the chance to say a word, a firm hand snatched him by the collar. His neck snapped as the hand jerked him backward and spun him around.

He found himself looking at the large, stern features of Hazel Moses, who grabbed the front of his shirt and yanked him even closer. Her brow hovered over him like a meat-eating mammal, and Roger flinched, expecting to get smacked or yelled at. But in a glance, Roger caught something in Mrs. Moses's expression. The frown and the furrowed brow that hardened her face framed two eyes that held a very different message—a message that Roger realized was meant only for him.

"Young man, you don't realize what you've done," she said, her voice breathless but firm. "You have no idea what you've done."

And despite the immense guilt that washed through him, and despite knowing that, with this single act, he had alienated himself from the entire population of Slack School, the two green eyes boring into his told Roger that someone understood.

CHAPTER TWO

CARL LOGAN MARVELED AT THE beauty of Paradise Valley as Peter Kenwood drove his Jeep Scout around the ranch. In the back seat, Kenwood's two ranch hands, Lester Ruth and Arnie Janko, sat with placid expressions, bored with the routine.

"I love coming out here," Peter said. "It's such a nice break from the business world." Kenwood lived in Omaha, home of the construction company he'd inherited from his father. In Carl's interview, he had explained that he married into this ranch, which his wife inherited when her first husband died. "Best decision I ever made, marrying a woman with a ranch in Montana," Kenwood continued. Arnie laughed as if it was the funniest thing he'd ever heard, but a quick glance back revealed a sour look on Lester Ruth's face. Lester's head was shaped exactly like a boot, with his jaw coming out like the toe and working a wad of Big Red tobacco.

This was Kenwood's first tour of the ranch since Carl took over as ranch manager, and although he'd only been at his new job for a few days, Carl was nervous. From the time he climbed into the Jeep, he had felt a tension, and he wondered whether it was in his head. He kept expecting someone to mention the incident with Roger at school, but it hadn't come up.

The tour had gone well so far. They drove out to the west pasture for a look at the yearling calves they were going to ship next month. Good moisture had produced a herd of fat, happy cattle, which put Kenwood in a positive mood.

"The south meadow?" Kenwood asked.

Carl nodded. Arnie had been cutting hay in this field.

"The place looks damn good, boys," Kenwood said. "I'm pleased."

Carl felt quietly proud, although he hadn't been there long enough to take any credit. It seemed like a good omen, although he thought it was odd there was no response from the back seat.

Arnie Janko was not a heavy man, but he had more flesh on his face than he needed, by about half. His cheeks, covered with a dark blue stubble, hung down like saddlebags, and he had bulging blue eyes that had the quality of chunks of turquoise pressed into bread dough. He also had a nervous habit of running his hand along his face repeatedly, as if he was rubbing a washcloth over it.

Peter Kenwood topped the rise just north of the meadow, and there sat the swather, smack in the middle of a half-finished field.

"What's this?" Kenwood stopped the Jeep. "Carl? What's the story here?"

Carl swallowed and craned his neck around to look at Arnie, who rubbed a hand over his face again.

"Why isn't this done?" Carl asked.

Arnie cleared his throat, loud, then rolled down the window and spat. "The swather wasn't runnin' too well. I told you about it a couple a days ago, Carl." He rubbed his face again, then dug thick fingers into his shirt pocket for a pack of cigarettes. "You don't remember?"

"No, I don't remember," Carl said. "I don't remember because I don't think you told me."

Arnie lit a cigarette, snapping his match out the window and taking a deep draw. "Well, I'm pretty sure I did."

Carl's mouth would not close.

"Yeah, he told you. I remember," Lester said, his jaw working.

"When?" Carl asked, trying to control the anger in his voice. "Where were we?"

"When we were all in the shop, over at your place," Arnie said, taking another drag. "Day before yesterday, I think."

"Well, I don't remember," Carl said. "So what have you been doing the last couple of days?"

Arnie cleared his throat and spat again. "I've been fixing that fence over by my place—that stretch you told me to take care of."

"We'll take a look at that on our way back," Kenwood said. His firm tone cut the conversation short.

They continued their tour, mostly in silence. Kenwood asked only the most basic questions in a terse, flat voice. He directed all of his questions about the livestock to Lester and all of his comments about everything else to Carl.

They checked on the cattle that had just been moved down from their summer pasture. The cattle looked at them, chewing, their jaws hinged sideways. They looked good, but this didn't seem to cheer Kenwood. Then they checked the bulls, who were in their own little world in the northwest pasture. The three bulls took one bored look at the approaching vehicle and proceeded to ignore them for the rest of their brief stay.

Their last stop was the larger hay field in the northeast corner. This one would be cut as soon as the other was finished, and Kenwood made it very clear that he wanted them both done in the next week. He looked directly at Arnie.

"I'll make sure of it," Carl said. "Even if I have to do it myself."

As with most of the bigger ranches in Montana, the Kenwood place was actually an accumulation of several smaller ranches. So the house where Arnie lived had once been a separate ranch, as had the Logans'. Only Lester lived on the same grounds as Kenwood, tucked away in the woods.

Kenwood circled around past Arnie's house, first checking the fence. There had been some mending done, but nowhere near two days' worth. Kenwood studied the fence with a pensive look and said nothing, and Carl wasn't sure what to make of that. Did he have enough ranch experience to see that this was clearly not two days' worth of work? Did he make a habit of letting Arnie get away with this crap?

After dropping Arnie off, they went by Kenwood's barn, where Lester got out. Kenwood drove to Carl's house, and Carl wondered if he should explain why he hadn't checked on the hay field, or whether he should tell Kenwood that Arnie was lying. But it would sound like an excuse, and he felt at least partially responsible.

Finally, Kenwood stopped his Jeep and turned to Carl. He took off his grey felt hat and rubbed a hand along one side of his silver hair.

"Carl, there are some things that I don't have any control over here—problems you're going to have to figure out a way to handle. Problems that have been here longer than I have."

He looked briefly at Carl, who remembered what Kenwood told him in his interview—that most of the crew had been here before he showed up.

"I trust your judgment, or I wouldn't have hired you. Normally, you would be free to hire and fire anyone you want. But in some situations, even I can't make that decision. Arnie is my wife's son-in-law." He considered Carl again, lowering his chin, looking through the top of his glasses. Carl nodded.

The implication was clear. Even the rich and powerful sometimes have to compromise with their wives.

"I'll take care of it. No need for you to worry, sir."

Kenwood nodded. "Good."

CHAPTER THREE

LAURIE LOGAN POUNDED A MASS of bread dough against the linoleum counter. She glanced outside, gauging the weather, wondering if the bank of soft gray clouds floating along the horizon would bring rain. Laurie had been raised on a ranch in one of the more desolate parts of eastern Montana and had been thrilled to marry a man who wanted to teach school, so she wouldn't have to endure the rigorous duties of a ranch wife. When Carl announced just after school started that he had taken a job as the manager of a ranch for Peter Kenwood, the owner of a construction conglomerate, it broke her heart. She was especially hurt that Carl hadn't even mentioned looking for a job.

The Absaroka Mountains filled half the window. Laurie considered lowering the blinds so that she could imagine the wide expanse of prairie she had grown up with, something familiar. But it was hard to deny the beauty of this range. In the background, a radio announcer gave the market report, then the news came on, giving an update on death tolls in Vietnam.

As she dumped the dough into a bowl and covered it with a dishtowel, she was surprised to see Carl pull up to the house. It was still the middle of the afternoon. A slight rain had started, but it wasn't enough to stop working.

Carl tromped inside, looking at the floor, chewing the inside of his lip. He pulled off his cloth welding cap and ran a hand through his wavy black hair.

"What are you doing home?" Laurie asked Carl's back as he passed through the kitchen, turning off the radio.

The Logans' youngest son, four-year-old Bradley, galloped through the dining room, singing at the top of his lungs. "Froggy went a-courtin' and he did ride, mm-hm."

"Bradley, calm down," Laurie said.

"Tom Butcher is coming by to look at a couple of bulls." Carl looked at the clock. "Fact, he should be here by now."

Laurie frowned, annoyed that Carl hadn't told her earlier. She turned back to the kitchen. "Why isn't he talking to Lester? He's in charge of the livestock, isn't he?"

"Yes, Lester is in charge of the stock," Carl answered with some impatience. "I don't know. I guess because we're closer to the pasture."

"Hm." Laurie opened the refrigerator. "Do you want something to eat while you're here? Or some iced tea?"

There was a long pause, and she lost patience, closing the refrigerator. She walked into the dining room, where Carl sat staring at the table. Bradley, who had rounded the living room, burst back into the dining room again, still singing.

"You don't think this has something to do with what happened at school?" she asked.

Carl shook his head. "No, not at all. Tom doesn't even have kids. He probably doesn't even know about that."

Laurie tilted her head. "Carl, come on…you've lived on ranches."

Bradley circled the table, his little forehead just missing the corners. "Froggy went a-courtin' and he did ride, a horse and a bible by his si-ide."

"*Quiet*, Bradley!" Carl barked. He fixed a look on Laurie. "I'm going to take the man at his word, if it's all the same to you."

Laurie held up her hands and shrugged. "Fine. I'm just asking." She returned to the kitchen. "How did the tour with Kenwood go this morning?" she called.

"Not too bad," he answered, but she heard the hesitation in his voice and made a note to ask him about it later, as a big black pickup was just entering the grounds. Laurie watched two men climb from the cab and walk toward the house. They were a study in contrast, the larger man moving in a strong, confident stride and the second man dancing along beside him, his small, wiry frame seemingly tested by the slight breeze. The door banged with Carl going out.

After Carl greeted them, the two men entered the Logans' tiny clapboard with a few obligatory glances around. The larger man removed his gold-rimmed aviator sunglasses, which bore a few specks of rain. The skin around his eyes pinched together as he smiled. He was a man who exuded prosperity somehow, just by the way he moved.

"I'm Tom Butcher." His thick, solid hand felt like wood in Laurie's palm. "Local troublemaker and fight promoter."

The smaller man chuckled, scratching at his abdomen.

"This here's Spider Moses." Tom jerked a thumb toward Spider. "His wife is the teacher down at the school."

"Oh yes…nice to meet you, Mr. Moses." Laurie shook Spider's hand. As soon as the grip had settled, he jerked his hand away as if she had a buzzer in her palm.

"You've fixed this place up real nice," Tom said.

"Thank you," said Laurie.

Carl gave a single nod, glancing at the modest furnishings and handcrafted wall hangings as though he hadn't noticed them before. "Poor man makes do with what he's got."

Behind Tom, Spider Moses fidgeted, taking a nervous, guilty look around. He wore a belt buckle the size of a butter dish, and he took his cowboy hat off quickly, as if he suddenly realized it was on fire. Tom cradled his like a baby.

Laurie wiped her hands on her apron. "Would you boys like some coffee before you head out?"

Carl looked at his watch, then to Tom, and Laurie could tell he was hoping Tom would say no.

"No, no…we won't take up your time, Mrs. Logan. You have better things to do, I'm sure." Tom smiled and replaced his hat, his fingers lingering on the brim.

"Of course," Laurie said.

•

Outside, Carl started toward his pickup.

"Why don't you ride along with us?" Tom said. "It'll give us a chance to visit some." Tom touched the bow of his sunglasses. "Plenty of room." He indicated his big Ford pickup with a sideways jerk of his head.

"All right," Carl said.

Carl followed Spider to the passenger door and ducked into the cab after Spider opened the door and stepped to one side. Carl settled in, and Tom and Spider crawled in simultaneously, nudging him with their shoulders as they closed their doors. Tom reached under his seat, feeling around for a second and swearing. When he pulled his hand out, Carl half expected to see a pint bottle, but instead, Tom held a wad of plastic. Tom took off his hat and carefully wiped the rain off, then held the hat toward Carl.

"You mind holdin' that for a second?"

Tom smoothed out the plastic, and Carl saw that it was a hat cover. Tom took his hat from Carl and brushed it off again, his big hands caressing the felt as if it were skin. Then he carefully stretched the cover over the hat. The elastic snapped, and he held the crown between his hands, pushing the air out so that the cover formed itself to the hat. He tugged it back on his head.

"All right." He looked at Carl with a confidential air. "I tend to be a bit particular." Tom smiled and started the pickup, then turned onto the main gravel road.

"So how you like it here so far?" Spider asked, rubbing the side of his nose with a finger.

"All right, all right," Carl said. "Brings back a lot of memories. We lived on a ranch in Wyoming when I was a kid."

"Where at?" Spider asked.

"Little town called Goose Egg, right outside Casper."

"Oil country," Tom said.

"That's right."

"You happen to know a guy by the name of Tanner?" Tom asked.

"Sounds familiar."

"Big oil man."

"I've heard the name. My dad was a welder and a ranch hand, so we didn't really rub shoulders with that crowd."

"Until you went to school, huh?" Tom adjusted his sunglasses, looking at Carl.

"What?"

"Didn't rub shoulders with that crowd until you went to college."

Carl hesitated, sensing something in Tom's voice. "Well, I don't think that changed much," he said. "A man's heart pretty much stays where it started beating, don't you think?"

Tom shrugged. "Could be. I suppose you educated folks think about that stuff more than the rest of us. That's why people like Kenwood hire you to manage places like this."

Carl hmmed.

They fell quiet, and Tom swung the pickup off the main road onto a pair of dirt tracks heading east. Carl studied the Gallatin Mountains through the swipes of the windshield wiper. The mountains were muscular, towering gray and hazy across the horizon. As though they were guarding something.

"They're in this northwest corner pasture, aren't they?" Tom asked.

"Right over there." Carl pointed at two figures, barely visible against the dark backdrop of the mountains on a cloudy day.

They started a bumpy trip through the pasture, and each time the pickup hit a rock, Carl's right leg slammed against Spider's left. He tensed the muscles, but he couldn't prevent the leg from jerking. His thigh began to cramp. The rain let up, until it was barely sprinkling. Tom stopped the pickup thirty yards from the bulls, and the men got out.

Tom hitched up his jeans, still leaving a significant sag in the seat. Spider blew his nose, then tried to stuff his handkerchief into his back pocket, which he kept missing. Tom sauntered toward the animals and stopped after only ten yards, but Spider was wandering off in another direction, seemingly aimless.

"Spider!" Tom barked.

Spider spun on one heel.

"Get your ass over here." Tom pointed at the ground, and Spider danced across the pasture, stopping just behind Tom. Tom crossed his arms and settled back on his heels, as if he was propped against a barstool. The bulls looked at the men, but only briefly. Then they returned to the grass.

"Wouldn't that be the life, though?" Tom shook his head, smiling. "Eat, fuck, then eat some more." He laughed, and Spider echoed. Carl smiled. "Just imagine, getting set loose with a couple hundred head of horny women, then having somebody take over once the kids are born." Tom laughed harder. He faced Carl now, looking him square in the eye.

Carl lowered his head. "That would be something."

"I could take that," Spider said, chuckling.

Tom didn't seem to notice that Spider had spoken. He stood silent for a moment, smiling to himself, but looking at Carl. Carl wiped the moisture from his forehead. Spider shifted his feet nervously.

"Those are some fine-looking animals," Tom said. "Kenwood has himself a good stock man, you know."

Carl looked at the bulls. They were Herefords, reddish brown, with the standard white face and occasional patch, as if someone had splashed bleach on them. They *were* fine animals, with thick haunches and shoulders that flexed with every movement of their heavy skulls.

"I've heard Lester is an excellent cattleman," Carl said. "Haven't had much opportunity to visit with him yet."

"Well, you will." Tom nodded. "He's good. A good man, too."

Spider's nervous shifting increased. Carl eyed him, wondering whether he needed to take a leak. Spider gave Carl a quick glance, and the alignment of their vision seemed to spook Spider. He jerked his head toward the mountains, making a determined effort to hold his feet still.

"Well, it's time to be straight with you, Mr. Logan." Tom rotated toward Carl, feet and all, and kept his arms crossed. "Carl."

Carl felt a sudden desire to take a step backward.

"Straight about what?"

"I'm really not interested in these bulls," Tom said, indicating the animals with his head.

"No?" Carl felt the heat of irritation, thinking of all the things he should be doing.

"Nah." Tom shook his thick head. "Truth is, I wouldn't buy a bottle of oxygen from Kenwood if I was choking to death." He studied Carl's response to this. Carl held his face steady. "Truth is, we just wanted to talk. And I apologize for not just telling you that in the first place. But I thought it might seem a little strange."

"That's all right," Carl said, looking away from Tom. He sensed Spider almost behind him, shifting again. Carl looked down at the ground, as if he was thinking, and rocked a couple of steps to one side, so that when he turned, the three men formed a triangle, all facing the middle. Carl shoved his hands in his pockets, hunching his shoulders against the drizzle.

"The problem here…" Tom started, then looked up at the sky and pursed his lower lip. "The problem here is that this community has a few standards. We've all known each other for a hell of a long time. We know what to expect. Everyone knows I'm going to open my big mouth and piss a few people off. And everyone knows that ol' Spider here wouldn't take a stand on something if his life depended on it. Everyone knows your man Kenwood doesn't give a damn about the people in this country—that he just has this place as a little hobby, a tax shelter, and that the place really belongs to Lester Ruth, who's poured his damn heart and soul into it."

Tom stopped for a minute, studying Carl, as if to make sure the message was sinking in. Carl held his gaze but made an effort not to indicate anything at all.

"When something unexpected happens out here, everyone gets a little nervous, especially when there's a stranger involved." Tom scratched his head, as if considering what to say next. "Are you gettin' my drift here, Carl?"

Carl swallowed. "Are you talking about what happened with my boy? Is that what all this is about?" His voice came out louder than he expected.

"Well, that's part of it." Tom looked at the ground. "Course it is. See, we don't like violence around here. We don't like violence, and we don't like educated folks trying to put on airs." He held up a hand. "I'm not saying you done that. You seem like a nice enough guy, but I'm just telling you, for your own sake. We aren't a real open-minded bunch of folks." Tom tilted his head and grinned a lopsided grin. "Plus a lot of folks thought Lester should have gotten that job. He's been waiting in the wings for a long time."

Carl held his breath, trying to calm himself, but the blood rose up in him, hot and red.

"All right, listen to me for a second now, Mr. Butcher." Carl struggled to control the tremor in his voice. "You don't have to intimidate me. I'm already nervous as hell. But that doesn't mean I have to stand here and listen to your threats. My son reacted to a bad situation just like any kid who's backed into a corner. He was wrong. I know it and he knows it. But that's no cause to get in my face. I came out here for one reason—to work hard and support my family, probably just like everybody out here."

Carl stared at Tom, breathing heavily through his nose. His nostrils flared with the rush of air.

Tom's expression did not change, but he had tilted his head back as Carl said his piece. He was looking at him this way now, down his nose. He reached up and took off his sunglasses, then rubbed his eyelids, pressing firmly against his eyeballs with a weathered knuckle. Spider was twitching and shuffling his feet to Carl's right. Tom looked at Carl, and his dark brown eyes showed a mixture of amusement and impatience.

"Well now, Carl, that was a hell of a speech." Then he looked away, across the pasture, toward the mountains. "But words are pretty much a nuisance. I'm not inclined to pay much attention to what a man says." He looked back at Carl. "You got to remember, our people got this land by stringing a bunch of words together. We know a little about how that works." He smiled. "You get my drift?"

Carl bit his tongue and tasted blood.

"I'm not trying to threaten you, or intimidate you. I'm just letting you know. I could have just let it be and let all the talk go on behind your back. You wouldn't know what we were saying, but you'd know we were talking…right?"

Carl thought, chewing the inside of his lip. The more he thought about it, the more he realized Tom might actually be trying to help.

"Just give it some thought," Tom said. "Let's go. I'm freezing my ass off out here." He started walking back toward the pickup, and Spider followed as if attached by a string.

Carl stood where he was for a moment—just long enough to feel alone, to think about how it would be if Tom hadn't told him these things. He knew Tom was right, just as Laurie had said, that people would talk—that they probably already were talking. And he wondered how many times in his life someone had taken the trouble to let him know exactly where he stood.

•

On the drive back, Carl studied Tom and Spider's hands, noticing how rough and callused they were. He rubbed a finger over his own palm, still smooth, and looked forward to working until the blisters formed, and broke, and hardened, until his hands would be immune to the handle of a hay hook. Six years in a classroom had softened him in more ways than one.

Tom pulled into the driveway, and Spider let Carl out. Carl started to walk around the front of the pickup to shake Tom's hand, but the pickup was suddenly backing up.

"Wait," Carl shouted. He strode around to the driver's door. He held out his right hand and shook Tom's, feeling that callused palm against his own. "Thank you," he said.

Tom winked. "No problem, buddy. Just keep an eye on that kid." And he winked again.

CHAPTER FOUR

"Where are you going?" Carl sat at the dining room table, scraping the last bite of pie from his plate.

Laurie grabbed Roger by the sleeve of his jacket. "We'll be right back."

Carl caught the look of dread on his son's face. A helpless fatigue flattened his muscles. "You don't have to do this," he said. "Things are fine. Tom was trying to help."

"We won't be long," Laurie said, pulling Roger behind her. She had that look, the one Carl knew too well, where she had a plan in mind and a blueprint that she knew was going to get her to a resolution. When she got like this, nothing would prevent the inevitable outcome. He shook his head.

"Don't forget we have that party to go to!" he shouted, but he knew she didn't hear him.

•

Roger crowded into the corner of the passenger seat, his head propped against the window. "Do we have to go?"

"We do."

Laurie wheeled down the gravel road until they got to the Kirby ranch, where Scooter Cayley's father worked as a hand. She pulled into the grounds and veered to the left, around the Kirby house to the smaller house thirty yards behind it. She stopped the car.

"You remember what to say?" Laurie touched his shoulder.

"It's not that complicated, Mom."

"Well, it's not going to be easy, but you'll feel much better when it's over."

Roger tucked his chin into his chest.

•

Sharon Cayley answered the door and stared at them with a dull expression. Though they had met briefly when the Logans first arrived, she clearly did not recognize them. "Can I help you?"

"Hi, Sharon. I'm Laurie Logan, from the Kenwood place. This is Roger. He's in Scooter's class." Roger stepped halfway out from behind his mother. Laurie's hand started to rise, but when there was no indication from Sharon that she was going to accept a handshake, it dropped back to her side.

"You ride my bus," Sharon said to Roger.

"That's right, ma'am." Roger twisted his hands in his jacket pockets.

They stood without speaking for a few seconds before Laurie finally said, "Do you mind if we come in? We won't take much of your time."

"Sure. Okay." Sharon stepped to one side.

Roger was shocked by the state of the house. He had never in his life seen clothes, dishes, and food scattered all over someone's living room. Dirty clothes draped over every piece of furniture, and plates with half-eaten food teetered in a stack on the coffee table. A mangy dog gnawed at a piece of meat in the middle of the floor, and there was a red stain, like tomato sauce, on the wall. A small black-and-white TV blared in the corner, playing an episode of *Gunsmoke*. Sharon showed no inclination to turn the volume down.

Roger had seen his mother panic if there were a few dishes in the sink when people dropped by. But Sharon didn't apologize or look around with any degree of embarrassment. Nor did she offer them a seat. Roger's muscles felt coiled up into springs, as if a single touch would send him flying across the room. Finally Laurie took Roger's hand and led him to the couch, where they both sat. Sharon settled into a wooden chair across from them.

"Are you folks planning to attend the party this evening?" Laurie asked Sharon.

Sharon's face was blank.

"At Peter Kenwood's house?" Laurie prompted.

"Oh yeah...that one. No, we're not going."

Roger watched his mother's mouth firm up. He knew that the party was a welcome party Peter Kenwood was throwing for his parents, and he wondered if Sharon knew it too.

"We were wondering whether Scooter was home," Laurie said.

"Scooter!" Sharon shouted.

Laurie and Roger jumped.

"What?" The belligerent shout came from somewhere in the back of the house.

"Come out here," Sharon hollered. She reached across to a small side table and picked up a pack of cigarettes, plucking one by the filter and flipping it like a pencil. It landed perfectly between her lips. She held the pack toward Laurie, who shook her head. Roger saw his mother's lips pinch together even firmer, until there was almost no red showing, the skin turning white from the pressure.

"What?" Scooter appeared as if he'd fallen from the ceiling. He saw Roger. "Oh."

A beaky, scrawny man with a face as shiny and red as a bicycle followed Scooter into the room. "Oh, howdy. Didn't know we had company," he said. "You the new folks?"

Laurie stood. "Yes, I'm Laurie Logan, and this is Roger, my son. He and Scooter are in the same grade."

"You don't say," the man said, reaching out to shake Laurie's hand. "I'm Gordon. Gordon Cayley. So you're a fourth-grader, too?" he asked Roger. "You're in fourth, right?" Gordon turned to Scooter, who nodded.

Sharon puffed steadily.

Roger watched his mother's expression become more and more puzzled, and he knew just what she was thinking. A commercial for Tide came on the television.

"So what can we do you for?" Gordon asked.

Laurie lowered herself slowly back onto the couch. "Um...did you not hear about what happened at school the other day...between the boys?"

Gordon's eyes suddenly flashed, and he turned toward Scooter. "Did you get in trouble again?"

"No, Pa. I didn't."

"No, no, no," Laurie said. "Actually, it was Roger who was in the wrong." She turned, looking at Roger, who shrank as far into the cushion as he could. "Roger, would you like to say something to Scooter?"

Everyone turned to look at him. Hot needles burrowed into Roger's face. He looked at his knees and pressed his back into the sofa, which emitted a plastic complaint. Roger felt the eyes on him, painting every inch of him, waiting for some kind of motion. In the background, James Arness drawled about justice and dignity.

"Is he gonna say something?" Sharon asked.

"Yeah, what's this all about?" Gordon added.

Roger shot a look at Scooter, and the steely glare that met him stopped his breath. The longer the silence lasted, with those eyes on him, the longer he felt as if the weight of what he was going to say was hanging over him like a fist. So he ran. He was a rabbit, and he bolted right out of the house, headed for a big tree in the front yard. The door slammed on his heels. He zigzagged across the yard and ducked behind the trunk, resting his head against the rough bark. His lungs filled with air, almost too much air. Until they hurt.

"Roger!"

He peeked around the tree. His mother stood on the stoop, right at the edge, leaning out as if she was about to dive off. Sharon came out behind her.

"What happened to him?" Sharon asked.

"I don't know," Laurie said, her tone defeated.

Laurie called Roger's name a few times, but with little conviction. Sharon smoked her cigarette and eventually said, "Maybe he didn't have anything to say."

His mother rubbed her forehead. "Yes, perhaps you're right." Roger could hear how tight his mother's voice was, and he could feel the disappointment all those many yards away.

Without another word, Sharon turned and closed the door behind her.

Roger waited a moment, then stepped around the tree, his hands locked behind his back. He raised his head, looking at his mother from the tops of his eyes.

"Well, come on then," his mother said.

She climbed into the car without speaking. Roger rounded the vehicle to the passenger side and crawled in. They drove in silence for most of the five miles back to the ranch. Roger kept expecting his mother to ask him what he was thinking or tell him he was going to be in big trouble when they got home. But just before they got to the driveway, Laurie sighed and said, "That poor boy."

Roger frowned. "What do you mean?"

Laurie looked over at him, and when her eyes met his, he was shocked at how old she looked. As if this short half hour trip had aged her years. As if nothing she said could possibly explain it to him.

To Roger's amazement, nothing more was said about their visit as his father and mother prepared for the party and the babysitter arrived from Livingston. His mother kissed him goodnight as if he was the best son in the world.

CHAPTER FIVE

THE FIRST TIME JUNIOR KIRBY met Carl Logan, two thoughts came into his head, both at the same time. Looking at Carl's open face and friendly smile, Junior had an immediate feeling that he was going to be good friends with this man. But the second, simultaneous thought was this: Carl Logan was in trouble.

Unlike many of his neighbors, Junior Kirby had never bought into the idea that Peter Kenwood couldn't be trusted. He liked Peter Kenwood. He thought Kenwood was charming and genuine for a man who had more money than the rest of his Paradise Valley neighbors combined. This also despite owning one of the largest construction companies in the world, a company that had recently begun construction of the Bay Area Rapid Transit in California. So Kenwood was gone most of the time. He wasn't the only one. There was a growing trend of ranch owners in Paradise Valley who left everything up to the men they hired, or simply bought the ranches for an escape and stopped doing ranching at all.

Junior admired the fact that Peter Kenwood made an effort to get to know the people here. Despite his phony rancher appearance—the Lorne Greene leather vest, the bolo ties, and the snakeskin boots—Peter Kenwood was pretty down to earth.

The party for the Logan family was a prime example. How many ranchers bothered to throw a party for their new foreman? He'd even asked Junior to take Carl around the party for introductions, knowing that Junior was one of the more popular ranchers and that he, Peter, was not. So it gave Carl and Laurie a better chance of being accepted.

But Junior also knew that Kenwood had a knack for finding men who would shoulder the burden of his expectations without complaint. He could see that in Carl Logan's eyes as they shook hands.

"Nice to meet you. I hear you grew up in the house where we live now," Carl said.

"That's right. My dad worked for the previous owner."

"But you have your own place now?" Carl frowned, and Junior could see him trying to imagine how a ranch hand's son could afford to buy his own place in this beautiful valley.

"Well I'm one of the lucky sons a bitches that married into money," Junior said, guiding his wife by the elbow and presenting her to Carl and Laurie. "Angie, the beneficiary of all my labor."

Angie laughed, and Carl and Laurie followed suit. "Sounds like someone's getting the short end of that deal," Laurie said.

"You can say that again," Angie said.

Junior nodded. "She reminds me every morning."

Angie was a woman whose hair had grayed at the age of twenty. This and the way she carried herself gave her an air of distinction that people automatically respected. The Kirbys were considered the host and hostess of Paradise Valley because Angie Kirby wanted it that way. Her parents had seen their role in the community in much the same way, hosting parties, welcoming newcomers, and most of all, avoiding becoming part of the sometimes nasty local grapevine.

"This is quite a place," Laurie said, scanning Kenwood's house. Junior could just imagine what she was thinking, and she wasn't the first. The elaborate Western décor, with an original Charlie Russell painting dominating one wall, thick cowhide furniture, and bronze sculptures, was much more showy than most ranchers would ever allow, even if they had the money. In one corner of the massive living room, people had gathered around a large console color television, where they watched *The Lawrence Welk Show*. Most people in Paradise Valley had TVs by now, but reception was spotty at best, and hardly anyone had a color TV. This was the kind of posturing that people often didn't appreciate.

"Oddly enough, most of this stuff came from Trudy's first husband. He was more of a spender than Peter's ever been," Junior said quietly.

Laurie nodded, though she looked a little skeptical. "I grew up on a ranch over in Carter County, so I'm not used to this. Nobody at home has a house like this."

Junior nodded. "This is unique to most of Montana, I'm pretty sure." He laid a hand on Carl's shoulder. "Someone said you were teaching school before you took this job."

Carl nodded. "That's right. I taught grade school in Bozeman."

Junior smiled. "So you wanted to work harder for less pay?"

Carl laughed, but Junior could tell by both Carl and Laurie's reactions that he'd touched a nerve.

"Truth is, I've always had a secret dream of having a ranch myself."

"A dream I knew nothing about until this very minute," Laurie added with a laugh, but Junior had a feeling she wasn't kidding.

"You guys need a drink?" Angie asked. Junior's appreciation for his wife grew, as he knew she was reading the same dynamics he was.

"Yes, that sounds lovely," Laurie said.

"Come on, Laurie. Let's get something. What do you guys want?"

The two men named their poison, and as the women moved off, Junior leaned toward Carl. "Sorry to get things off on the wrong foot there."

Carl shook his head. "Don't worry about it. Laurie didn't like growing up on a ranch. Moving out here was the last thing she wanted. So it's going to take some time. We'll figure it out."

"Course," Junior nodded. Then he lowered his voice. "Well I think you'll enjoy working for Kenwood. He's a fair man."

Carl leaned toward him. "I'm not sure everyone's happy about me getting this job, though."

Junior took in a breath. "Listen, Carl. You shouldn't say that to anyone else here."

Carl looked surprised. "Shit, I'm sorry."

"No, it's okay. I happen to agree with you, so don't sweat it." Junior tipped his head toward Lester Ruth and Arnie Janko. "But those fellas have lots of friends. So just be careful."

Carl nodded.

Junior led Carl over to Spider and Hazel Moses. "Spider, Hazel, have you met Carl yet?"

"I did," Spider said, his feet shuffling. "I don't think Hazel has."

"I'm so pleased to meet you," Hazel said, offering her hand. "Your son is a very smart boy, you know."

"Oh, thank you," Carl said. "We always thought he had potential, but it's nice to hear it from an expert."

"Spider and Hazel are newlyweds," Junior explained. "Just got married a few months ago."

"Congratulations!" Laurie said. She and Angie had returned with the drinks. "I'm Laurie. So nice to meet both of you. You're the teacher, right?"

From the corner of his eye, Junior saw Babe Ruth and Molly Janko approaching, slightly tilted toward each other, an indication that they'd already had a bit too much to drink. Junior reached out to prop Babe up as she presented herself.

"Hello," Babe said to Laurie. "I'm Lester's wife, Babe." She had almost translucent white skin, topped with frizzy red hair that floated above her head like a cloud. She was delicate in every other way as well, her bones narrow, her voice quiet, her clothes some kind of flimsy material that Junior couldn't even name.

"Very nice to meet you," Laurie replied. "You look so nice."

"Oh, you're too kind," Babe laughed. "I dressed up for once!"

Molly Janko was a contrast—tall, dark-haired, jeans and button-down shirt, olive-skinned and loud. "Welcome to the neighborhood!" she shouted above the crowd noise. "Peter's wife is my mother."

"So you probably grew up in this house," Laurie said.

Molly nodded proudly.

Just as they were finishing up the introductions, a loud knock sounded, and everyone in the room knew exactly who was there. A murmur of *Tom, Tom, Tom* echoed through the room. It brought a smile to Junior's face. Tom Butcher could own the party before he even entered.

Kenwood went to answer, and everyone's head turned in anticipation. The two men were not friends, and in fact often feuded. And it was common knowledge that both coveted a piece of land that Spider had put up for sale after the death of his brother, now that he could no longer keep up the Moses place on his own.

The hush of a slightly heated exchange echoed from the front hall, and then Tom Butcher made his entrance like only Tom Butcher could. And although Junior had watched this man make an entrance hundreds of times, he watched with his usual blend of amusement and awe.

Tom strolled in, shouted a hearty hello, then scanned the room, like a gunfighter looking for his rival. Kenwood followed behind, the distinguished millionaire hovering like a faithful butler. Tom shook hands with everyone, moving through the crowd like a car salesman, showing equal parts bravado and desperation, placing his big hand on the shoulders of the men, teasing the women about their hair, their dress, their shoes. He had a comment for every single person, something specially suited to them, something that would make them smile, or blush, or slap his arm.

Once Tom had assessed the crowd, he went for the bar, got his drink, and turned. He raised his glass to Junior, who motioned him over. "Have you met the guests of honor?" Junior asked, indicating Carl and Laurie.

"I have indeed," Tom said. "Good to see you both again!"

The Logans said hello and shook Tom's hand. Junior was surprised how glad Carl was to see Tom, as Tom wasn't known for giving newcomers a warm welcome. He wondered whether something had transpired between the two men.

From the corner of his eye, Junior saw Babe approaching.

"Hi, Tom," she said. "I didn't think you were coming!" She took hold of Tom's arm, and Junior did his best to steer her in another direction.

"Well, I wanted to come by and say hello to my new friends here," Tom said.

"But you told me you weren't coming," Babe insisted. She was unsteady on her feet, and the look in her eyes was too adoring to be comfortable.

"Babe, did you get something to eat yet?" Angie asked, intercepting her from Junior, who winked a thank you to his wife.

Babe followed Angie's lead, but she kept looking back over her shoulder, trying to get Tom's attention.

It was about that time that Junior noticed someone he hadn't expected. Harlan Glider was a man who worked for Kenwood, mostly in Bozeman, handling various business affairs. It seemed the only time he showed up at the ranch was when Kenwood had something in the works. Junior wondered if he was here to help with acquiring Spider's piece of land. The pasture was prime grazing, and it bordered two ranches, Tom's and Kenwood's.

Kenwood motioned him over. "I have someone else I want to introduce to you, Carl and Laurie. This is Harlan Glider. He usually lives in Omaha, but he does some work for me here in Montana. Mostly in town, but you'll see him out here at the ranch from time to time."

Harlan's expression had never exactly exuded warmth. Every time Junior had talked to him, he was stiff and measured. He tried to smile as he shook Carl's hand, but it looked painful for him.

"Tom Butcher, local troublemaker," Tom said, pushing his way into the conversation. "Good to see you again, Harlan."

Harlan measured Tom with a once-over. Now Junior was all but convinced that Harlan was there to make sure Kenwood got that piece of land.

"How's everyone doing with their drinks?" Kenwood asked. "Carl, you need another?"

"I'm good, Mr. Kenwood. Thank you."

Junior sidled over to Arnie and Lester. "What the hell are you two so surly about?"

He meant it as a joke and was surprised when neither of them answered, or laughed. They just stared steely-eyed at something over his shoulder: Carl and Laurie, approaching to say their hellos. Carl looked nervous, and Junior decided to try and ease the tension.

"You take it easy on these two, Carl," Junior said. "They're gettin' old."

Lester forced a chuckle, and Arnie laughed too loud and too long. But it was clear to Junior that this nerve was much more tender than he had realized.

"I'd never ask a man to do something I wasn't willing to do myself," Carl said, his voice tentative.

"Of course not," Laurie added.

"It's more than that. This is a longer story than you realize," Lester said, and he started across the room. Arnie offered a nervous nod of his head and quickly followed.

"What was that about?" Laurie asked.

"I think we've managed to step on some toes just by showing up," Carl said.

Junior nodded. "It's a long story that I'll tell you both another time," he said.

After a bit, Angie approached Junior and whispered in his ear, "How much longer do you want to put up with this?"

To which Junior smiled and said, "I'm ready when you are."

They had started around the room, saying their goodbyes, when Junior heard a slight commotion from across the way. He looked over to see Harlan Glider and Kenwood entering the living room from the hallway, with Spider Moses between them. Tom stood in front of them, barring the way.

"Spider, are those guys trying to squeeze you?" he asked through gritted teeth.

Spider shook his head, his eyes wide.

"Tom, come on now," Kenwood said. "This is a party. We're not here to do business."

"Are they trying to intimidate you?" Tom asked again, ignoring Kenwood.

"They aren't," Spider insisted.

Junior made his way over and grabbed Tom's elbow. "Tom, settle down, buddy. You don't want to make a scene now."

But Tom's face had turned red, and his body had coiled into a mass of tense muscle. "You don't need that land, Peter!" he said. "Why don't you give the rest of us a chance to make an honest living out here, huh? Just give us a goddamn chance!"

Junior leaned into him. "Tom, come on. Let's step into the other room."

Harlan stepped between Tom and Kenwood, squaring his shoulders, his hands clenched.

"And why the hell are you here, Harlan?" Tom asked. "Peter, are you really bringing in goons to help you with this shit?"

Kenwood just shook his head and chuckled. "Tom, I'm sorry, but you've gone too far. Harlan here is a businessman. You're off base, my friend. Let's just shake hands and pretend this never happened."

Out of the corner of his eye, Junior saw Carl watching this exchange with wide eyes, no doubt wondering what he'd stepped into.

•

Carl entered his bedroom, where his wife sat on the bed, shoulders down, head forward. Carl was muttering to himself under his breath.

"Stop that, Carl."

"What?"

"You were talking to yourself again."

Carl sat on the other side of the bed, silent.

Laurie turned her head, peeking at him around her shoulder. "Aren't you worried?"

"About what?" Carl threw himself onto his back, tucking in under the covers.

Laurie drew her hands to her face. "Please don't do this. Please talk to me."

"I'll talk to you, honey, but I need to know what you're talking about."

Laurie turned her face to him. "Don't start this again. You said things would be different here. You said we'd talk about things."

Carl sat up. "Laurie, not now. Not tonight. I'm tired, and it's late, and I have a lot on my mind."

He flopped back down against his pillow and rolled away from her. She sat silent, and for a second he thought that she would let it go. But he heard a soft sniffle, and he sighed, feeling helpless to provide the comfort she wanted.

"You swore up and down, Carl. You promised."

Carl flipped his legs out from beneath the covers. His heels pounded the floor as he strode across the room, pulling his pants on and draping himself in his work shirt.

"It's just more of the same," Laurie muttered.

"That's right," he said. "More of the same." And he grabbed his socks and left the room, running down the stairs on the balls of his feet so as not to wake the children.

•

Roger lay in bed, his blanket pulled over his ears. The floorboards creaked on the ceiling overhead.

"What do you think they're fighting about?" Julie's voice was soft and tentative.

"I don't know, Jules," he said. "Just go to sleep, okay?"

The front door slammed shut, and they lay quiet in the dark, listening to their mother crying again.

CHAPTER SIX

ROGER LOGAN CLIMBED INTO SHARON Cayley's bus with a sense of dread. He worried she would say something about their visit the night before, but she stared at him with the same dull expression as usual and said nothing during the drive. When they reached the school, the kids who didn't ride the bus, including the Kirbys and Scooter and his sister Susan, stood in a circle in the yard. Roger took his lunchbox inside, then came out and joined the circle.

He wished he could be somewhere else, like back in Bozeman, at his old school, with his old friends. Where he knew what to expect.

"Hey, Roger," said Bobby.

Roger nodded, and all the kids stood fidgeting and pushing their hands into their pockets.

"You do anything last night, Roger?" someone asked. A few snickers followed.

Here we go, Roger thought. He cleared his throat. "Went for a drive—visited some neighbors."

Scooter smiled his V-shaped smile. "Yeah?"

"Yeah, why?" Roger asked. "Did I miss a party?"

Bobby laughed. Most of the kids looked at Scooter.

It was a relief when Mrs. Moses stepped out onto the stoop and clanged her brass bell. Roger headed for the trailer and felt Scooter just behind him.

"So you're proud of yourself?" Roger said over his shoulder. "Making the new kid look stupid?"

Scooter snorted. "Yeah. I am. And you're crazy, running off like you did."

•

Roger had a hard time concentrating in class. He kept thinking about recess, which loomed before him like a thunderhead. Mrs. Moses gave them a math test, and when Roger brought his paper to her desk, she gave him a concerned look. He avoided her eyes.

Outside, a soft wind lifted the first of the falling leaves, which tumbled weightless along the grass. Birds swirled in the sky, impersonating the leaves, fluttering from tree to power line and back to tree.

Roger stood a short distance from his peers, staring into the thick brush that surrounded their little school. And he was a deer, bounding gracefully and easily through the bushes. His nostrils flared, and the smell of every plant and flower overwhelmed him.

He turned to his classmates, feeling cornered, and decided something. It was not a conscious decision so much as an instinctive one. He could not let these kids push him further away. He decided that if they tried to break him, he would fight back—but not with his fists. He decided that he would find a better way.

•

After the incident with the bat, Mrs. Moses had announced that they would not be allowed to play baseball for a while. At recess, Bobby tossed an orange soccer ball into the middle of the crowd.

"Same teams?" Bobby said.

In seconds they were driving the ball over the bumpy weed-covered yard toward goals marked by stones.

From the time the game began, Scooter charged around the field, pounding the ball through kids, around kids, over kids. He knocked his own little brother to the ground, skinning the boy's forehead.

"Easy, Scooter," Bobby yelled.

"Aww, he's all right," Scooter said, ignoring the younger boy's cries.

Bobby got control of the ball and began weaving through the players, popping the ball between one boy's legs, then splitting two others. The leaves whirled behind him as he ran. Roger ran a parallel path, and when Bobby spotted him, he passed. But just as the ball reached Roger, Scooter charged in and nailed it, sending it dead into the chest of the goalie, a young girl.

The girl was too surprised to bring her hands up. She hunched over as it bounced off her ribs, back toward Scooter and Roger. They tangled going after it, and Roger kicked his right leg out, trying to wrestle the ball away from Scooter.

The ball jumped into the air, and Scooter beat him to it, knocking it a foot out of the goalie's reach, through the rocks.

And then it came, what Roger had been dreading.

Scooter ran up to him, sticking his nose right in Roger's face.

"Sorry, Roger," he shouted in a mocking tone.

A couple of the other members of Scooter's team joined him, circling Roger and repeating the chant. "Sorry, Roger. Sorry, Roger."

Roger stood paralyzed, seeing only these faces, swirling and jeering. He felt dizzy. The faces began to blur.

"Knock it off," Bobby shouted, jumping in front of Scooter.

The chanting stopped. Scooter looked at his neighbor with a sneer. "What's with you?" Off to the side, Roger could see Julie crying quietly.

"Just knock it off," Bobby repeated.

"It's okay, Bobby," Roger said, stepping out from behind him. He walked toward Scooter until he stood right in front of him. He could feel Scooter's breath warm against his chin. Roger noticed a small chip in one of Scooter's front teeth.

"You sure you're sorry, Scooter?" He said it calmly, trying not to sound nervous. But he wasn't breathing. "I don't think you are." For a moment, Roger thought Scooter was going to pop him. But when a second or two passed, and it was clear he wasn't, Roger let out his breath slowly. "...But thanks for the apology." He smiled at Scooter, keeping his face calm, although he wasn't calm inside. Inside, his heart was flopping like a fish. Then Roger turned and walked away.

Then came the blow. Scooter jumped at him and popped him in the back of the head, and started to hit him again, but Bobby and Craig both got hold of him and pulled him away.

Roger turned. The punch hurt, but not all that badly, he was surprised to realize. Scooter struggled in the arms of the Kirby boys.

"Scooter, I don't know what your problem is, but I really am sorry," Roger said.

And Roger was shocked to see Scooter's body go limp, and he stared at Roger as if nobody had ever said that to him before.

CHAPTER SEVEN

Angie Kirby stood at the window, looking out into the fall night.

"What's going on out there?" Junior asked.

"I have no idea."

Several vehicles had driven past their house, many more than they were used to hearing at dinnertime on a school night.

"Did you hear about the fight at school today?" Bobby asked.

"I thought the fight was a few days ago," Junior said. "Was there another one?"

Craig jumped in, his face lighting up. "Yeah, Scooter gave that new kid a sock in the head. Punched him right in the head!"

"You mean Roger?" Angie asked.

"Yeah, he socked him right here!" Craig pointed to the back of his head, then pantomimed a punch.

Angie and Junior exchanged a frown.

"Now I want you boys to listen to me for a second." Angie held up her pointer finger. The boys slumped in their chairs and dropped their heads, preparing for a lecture. "Have you ever moved to a new town?" Angie asked.

The boys obediently shook their heads.

"So you don't know what it's like to be the new kid, do you?"

"No, ma'am," they said in unison.

"Why did Scooter hit him?" Junior asked.

Craig shrugged, but Bobby spoke up. "Scooter told me that Roger and his mom came to their house to talk to them last night."

Again, Junior and Angie exchanged a look. "And what does that have to do with Scooter hitting him?"

Bobby shrugged.

Angie lowered her chin and looked from one boy to the other. "We've talked about this before, but it's apparently time again. It's easy to follow the crowd, right?"

The boys nodded.

"You need to make those kids feel welcome here."

"But why?" Craig asked. "What if we don't like 'em?"

"You haven't even had a chance to get to know them yet," Junior said.

The boys bowed their heads, clearly recognizing the truth in this.

"I don't want to hear you boys saying you don't like those kids again until you make an effort," Junior said.

•

Later, as the Kirbys climbed into bed, Angie rolled over and put a hand on Junior's chest, burrowing her fingers into the hair. "How long do you think the Logans will last out here?"

Junior sighed. "I give it six months."

"God, I feel for that woman." Angie rested her head on Junior's shoulder. "Imagine growing up on a ranch and believing you'd never have to live that way again, only to have this sprung on you."

Junior shook his head. "I'd rather not, thank you."

Angie laughed, then fell silent. "The shame of it is, they seem like a really nice couple."

"Well, when you think about it, mean people aren't drawn to jobs where you have to work your ass off for no pay." He settled down into the pillows. "I'll invite them over for dinner as soon as we can figure out a good time."

"Yes. Good."

Just as Junior was drifting off to sleep, there was a loud knock. Angie rolled over, and Junior swung his legs over the mattress and started pulling his pants on. "What the hell?" he muttered.

"What time is it?" Angie asked.

He looked at the clock next to the bed. "It's only eight o'clock. We must be getting old."

CHAPTER EIGHT

LAURIE KISSED CARL ON THE cheek. "Hello."

Carl raised his brows, surprised by this show of affection. After their fight the night before, he'd spent a couple hours working in the shop, then came back to bed to find her asleep. Laurie was up and getting the kids ready for school unusually early that morning, so he expected there to still be a chill in the air come dinnertime.

Carl washed his hands and sat, eyeing the roast beef and potatoes. He studied his family. Julie looked dreamy as usual, her brown eyes wide and watchful. Bradley bounced in his chair, stirring his potatoes as if they were liquid. And then there was Roger. The thinker.

Carl had noticed Roger's silence since they moved to the ranch, and he wondered when it started. When he was tiny, Roger was constantly asking questions, probing, challenging all the time. Carl had seldom had the patience or energy for these questions, and he was often short with Roger, frustrating both of them. He felt partially responsible for Roger's retreat.

"So how was school today, Roger?"

Roger looked up, seemingly disturbed by the question. "It was all right."

"You like Mrs. Moses so far?"

Roger shrugged. "I s'pose."

Carl sighed. "How about you, Julie?"

Julie rubbed her hands against her legs. "Mrs. Moses isn't my teacher."

"I know that." Carl smiled. "I meant how was school."

Julie glanced at her brother, who stared intently at his plate.

"It was all right," she echoed.

Carl frowned.

"I fed a horse today," Bradley announced.

"Oh, shut up, Bradley," Roger muttered.

"Roger!" Laurie barked.

"Which one?" Carl asked Bradley.

"Old Ed," Bradley answered. "I fed him some hay, and he ate it right out of my hand."

"Big whoop," Roger said. "He's going to fall over dead any day now."

"That's enough, young man," said Carl.

Roger's eyes remained fixed on his plate.

"One more comment like that, and you'll find yourself sitting in your room with an empty stomach."

Laurie dished some more fried potatoes onto Carl's plate, then passed them on and encouraged everyone to help themselves to carrots and dark beef gravy.

"How did work go today?" she asked Carl.

"Not too bad."

Laurie looked expectantly at Carl, and he could feel her disappointment, the same disappointment he felt about the response from his own children. But how to assuage it? He turned his attention to his food. They ate in virtual silence, except for Laurie reminding Bradley to stop playing with his food.

Roger ate half of what was on his plate, then began fidgeting. "May I be excused?" he finally asked.

Laurie shook her head. "Absolutely not. You've hardly eaten."

"I'm not hungry. I can't eat any more." Roger sat hunched over his food, not looking up.

"Laurie." Carl made a face across the table.

Laurie frowned. "Eat at least half of what you have there."

Roger picked at his food, carving a very small piece off his roast and popping it in his mouth. He chewed forever, then made no effort to take another bite.

"Roger, go ahead and go to your room," Carl said.

Laurie placed her fork carefully on the table. She fixed a hard glare on Carl.

Roger pushed his chair back but didn't stand, looking from one parent to the other.

"If you're going to leave this table," Laurie said, "then you need to feed the dog, go right up to your room, and get busy with your homework."

Roger slipped silently from his chair. He went outside, taking the bag of dog food with him.

As the family finished their meal, Carl could feel Laurie's cool eyes. But he was distracted by an unusual amount of traffic passing along the gravel road outside. Roger came back through.

"You fed the dog?" Laurie asked.

"Yes, I fed the dog," he answered irritably, then tromped upstairs, slamming his bedroom door.

•

An hour later, when Laurie finished with the dishes, a car pulled into the drive. Julie and Bradley were playing in the living room, where Carl had just sat down with the newspaper. Roger had not emerged from the children's bedroom.

Laurie looked outside, where two county sheriffs climbed from their cruiser. She caught her breath.

The two men walked with slow, deliberate, swaggering steps. Laurie rushed to meet them, opening the door just as they were about to knock.

"Yes?"

One of the men was young—a tall, burly kid with a tight mustache and shining skin. The other had salt-and-pepper hair and a significant bulge over his belt. The older man spoke.

"I'm Sheriff Daryl Blinder. This is my partner, Deputy Trass. Are you Mrs. Logan?"

"Yes. What's wrong?"

"Is your husband home?"

"My husband?" Laurie grabbed her blouse at the neck. "Yes, of course. He's home."

"May we come inside, Mrs. Logan? We need to talk to your husband. And to you, too."

"Yes, certainly. Come on in. But I'd like to know what's wrong. What happened?"

Deputy Trass answered, his voice deep and authoritative. "We'll explain everything when you and your husband are together, Mrs. Logan."

"All right." Laurie stepped aside and allowed the two men to pass. She showed them through the kitchen, then the dining room, into the living room. Their heavy black boots clunked against the linoleum, and they filled the house with the smell of leather.

In the living room, Julie and Bradley had stopped playing. They sat on the floor and looked up at the two men, their necks bent like broken stalks.

"Kids, go to your room," Laurie instructed.

Julie and Bradley sprang from their places and scrambled out of the room. The sound of their footsteps rumbling up the stairs echoed through the house. Carl sat forward, greeting the men with a baffled look.

Sheriff Blinder settled into the couch and folded his hands between his knees. "Well, Mrs. and Mrs. Logan, the reason we're here is because there's been a murder, just down the road."

Laurie sank onto the sofa. She let out a small gasp.

"A murder?" Carl repeated.

"Yes. I understand you folks are pretty new to the area, but I think you know Tom Butcher?" He studied them.

"Yes," Carl answered. "Yes, we've met Mr. Butcher." Carl paused. "Was it him?"

"That's right, Mr. Logan. Mr. Butcher was murdered, either last night or early this morning."

Carl fell back into his chair.

"This is horrible," Laurie said. "You just don't hear about murders in this part of the country."

Blinder nodded solemnly. "I've been sheriff here for twenty-three years. This is the first I've seen." He stared down at his boots.

"What happened?" Carl asked.

Blinder leaned forward in his chair and propped his elbows on his knees. He placed the tips of his fingers together, forming a pocket with his hands. "Mr. Butcher was beaten to death, apparently with a baseball bat," he answered. "There was a bat next to him, covered with blood."

The significance of this fact settled heavy and dark over the Logans, and they were speechless. Carl ran both hands through his hair.

The four of them sat silent for a long, sad minute. Blinder finally cleared his throat. Deputy Trass took a notepad from his shirt pocket, along with a silver pen. He flipped the pad open and rested it on his knee, poised to write.

"We need to ask where you were last night, Mr. Logan."

"He was here," Laurie said quickly. "He was here all evening, all night." She thought briefly about the time that Carl had left the house, then immediately dismissed the memory.

Blinder looked at Carl.

"That's right," Carl answered. "I was here all last night."

Blinder then turned his attention to Laurie. "Mrs. Logan, we understand that you were at the Kirby place for a while yesterday evening, visiting Mrs. Cayley. Is that right?"

Laurie nodded, and then breathlessly explained. "Yes, I was there, but it was early, just after dinner. My son Roger and I were there from about six-thirty until seven o'clock. Probably more like six forty-five. We weren't there long at all."

Blinder nodded, slowly, thoughtfully, while Trass wrote.

Laurie continued. "And Carl was here with Bradley and Julie while I was gone. He couldn't have gone anywhere then, because the kids were here."

"Yes, well…" Blinder breathed deeply, nodding again. "The murder took place much later. And your story checks with what the Cayleys said, too." He glanced quickly at Carl, then back to Laurie.

"Did you have some difficulties with Mrs. Cayley while you were there?"

"Difficulties? No, I wouldn't say we had any difficulties. My son had…well, he got into a fight with their son, Scooter. We went over there to apologize." Laurie adjusted the sleeves of her blouse. "Would you gentlemen like some coffee? I was just about to make some."

"No thanks, Mrs. Logan. We've talked to several people, and I think we've downed a couple pots already. I don't know about Deputy Trass, but I think I'd shake right out of my uniform if I had another cup."

Laurie chuckled, nervously and too loud.

Blinder paused, thinking before he spoke again. "Now, it's important that we get the sequence of events right here, Mr. and Mrs. Logan, as I'm sure you understand. Isn't it true that the fight you're talking about, between your son and the Cayley boy, involved a baseball bat?"

"What does that have to do with anything?" Laurie asked.

"Probably nothing, Mrs. Logan. But I'm sure you understand why I'm asking. It's a strange situation, and we're just trying to put the pieces together."

Laurie's right hand clenched, resting in a fist on her knee. "All right," she said. "I'm sorry."

Blinder looked back and forth from Laurie to Carl.

"That's right," Carl finally said. "Roger hit the Cayley boy with a bat. A few days ago, on his first day at the school."

Trass scratched away on his pad.

"Okay. Now isn't it true, Mr. Logan, that yesterday afternoon you and Mr. Butcher had a discussion about that incident?"

Carl stiffened, surprised they had already heard about it. He cleared his throat. "Yes. That's right."

"And didn't you and Butcher get into it during that discussion?" This was from Trass, who got a sharp look from Blinder.

"No, not at all," Carl said, leaning forward. "We had a real civil discussion, actually."

Blinder held his palm up toward his young deputy.

"The reason we're wondering, Mr. Logan, is that we were told you and Mr. Butcher got into an argument. Someone said that you threatened Butcher, and that you nearly came to blows."

"Well, that's nothing but a goddam lie," Carl said, leaning further forward in his chair. "Who told you that? Was it Arnie Janko? Because that son of a bitch couldn't tell the truth if he had an extra mouth. The man is a liar!"

Blinder stared impassively at Carl, his look telling him, with very little room for doubt, that he should calm down. "It wasn't Mr. Janko, Mr. Logan. It was Trevor Moses…Spider."

Carl sat stunned, looking at a spot on the floor ten feet from his toes. "Why would he say that?" He thought back to the conversation with Butcher. He tried to imagine what Spider could have possibly interpreted as a threat, but nothing stood out. "I can't imagine why he said that."

"Maybe you're remembering wrong," Trass said. His voice was thick with sarcasm.

Carl bit down on his tongue, as well as his impulse to jump to his feet. Meanwhile, Blinder rose and stood in front of Trass, his back to Laurie and Carl. He mumbled something too low for Carl to catch.

"Sorry, sir," Trass said quietly. "Of course."

Blinder returned to his seat, lowering himself with a slow, careful crouch. "So you claim the discussion was not heated, that you did not threaten Mr. Butcher?" Blinder pointed at Carl. "Is that right?"

"Absolutely," Carl answered. "That's exactly right."

"Where did this discussion take place, Mr. Logan?"

"Out in the northwest pasture, where we keep our bulls."

"All right." Blinder nodded once, then took a deep breath and stared between his feet for a minute, thinking. "Now…"

"Tom Butcher was reaching out to me," Carl said suddenly. "He was trying to help."

"By warning you?" Trass asked, and Blinder shot him a steely look. The younger man clamped his mouth shut, but it was clear he wasn't happy about it.

"What do you mean by that?" Blinder asked.

"Well, actually, Deputy Trass is right. He was trying to warn me... just to let me know that you have to be careful about first impressions out here, in such a tight-knit community."

Trass looked temporarily mollified. He glanced over at his boss. Blinder made no effort to acknowledge him. "All right, Mr. and Mrs. Logan. I just want to ask you about a few more things..."

"But why?" Laurie asked. "What else could there possibly be?"

"It's okay," Carl said, and Laurie took a deep breath.

"I'm sorry," she said. "This is just so unsettling, our first week here and all."

"I understand, Mrs. Logan. We'll try and finish up as soon as possible here. We've had a long day ourselves. But we need to ask you about the party last night."

Carl nodded, relieved that there had been no mention of their time at home, after the party.

"I understand that Mr. Butcher made a bit of a scene at this party."

Carl nodded. "Not a scene, really. But yeah, he seemed a little upset."

"This party was for you folks, wasn't it?" Blinder asked.

"That's right," Laurie said. "Mr. Kenwood was throwing a welcome party for Carl and me."

"A couple of people mentioned that Mr. Butcher actually showed up uninvited for this party. Were you aware of that?"

Carl shook his head. "No, actually. I didn't realize he wasn't invited."

"So that had nothing to do with the argument with Mr. Kenwood?"

"No, that never came up that I saw."

Blinder's head rocked forward and back, as if he was sifting through all of this information and arranging it in a specific order. "So why do you suppose Mr. Butcher showed up at this party...uninvited?"

Carl shrugged. "Beats me. He and Kenwood seem to have some kind of feud going on."

"But him showing up would fit with what you said earlier, wouldn't it? About him wanting to warn you—about him trying to help."

"I guess so…I guess it would."

"It would, wouldn't it?" Laurie said, and it was the first moment since they'd arrived that she didn't look scared to death.

"So let me ask you this," Blinder said, as if the thought had just occurred to him. "Have you ever met Harlan Glider before last night?"

"No," Carl said emphatically. "Never."

"You're sure?" Blinder said, and his tone made Carl question his own memory.

"Yeah, I'm sure. I've never seen him before."

"What about you, Mrs. Logan?" Blinder turned to Laurie.

"I haven't met him before, either."

"And what about Babe Ruth? Had you met her before?"

Both of them answered in the negative again, but not before exchanging brief looks, wondering what she might possibly have to do with anything.

"Okay, one last thing." Blinder finally relaxed a bit. "I know this is not easy, and I'm sorry to have to ask, but how are things in your marriage here? How are you two getting along?"

Carl and Laurie exchanged a brief, guilty glance. "How can that possibly have anything to do with this?" Carl asked.

Blinder leaned forward again. "It probably doesn't…that's part of the pain in the butt of being in law enforcement, if you'll pardon my language, Mrs. Logan. But we just have to pursue all the angles. It's part of the deal."

"We're doing great," Laurie said. "We're starting a whole new life here, and it's good."

"Isn't it true that you were teaching before this, Mr. Logan?" Blinder asked.

"That's right." Carl felt a lump rising up into his trachea, and he had to swallow to speak.

"And why did you decide to up and leave teaching to become a ranch hand?"

Carl looked at his wife and knew that he was cornered. Lying to Blinder would create nothing but trouble. He pushed the lump back, his tongue rolling against it. "I was fired," he said, and his voice came out choked.

He heard a small gasp. But when he looked over at Laurie, she had already gathered her composure and was nodding to Blinder. "It was a big surprise," she said.

•

When Blinder and Trass finally stood to leave, Carl was almost shaking with relief that the matter of him leaving the house the night before had not come up. But the facts, the faces, the twists and turns of the last few days were thrown before them in a mass of puzzles and mazes. By the time the sheriff had wound down his questions, they were frantic inside, feeling backed into a corner of bizarre circumstances and lies. Carl felt like screaming to these men, to anyone who would listen, "Tom Butcher was my friend!" But the thought sounded absurd, even in his own mind.

"Well, get some rest, Mr. and Mrs. Logan. We still have a lot more people to interview in the next couple of days, but we may be back. We thank you for your time."

Blinder and Trass shook hands with both Laurie and Carl, then disappeared into the darkness, where the engine sound of their cruiser ground through the silence. Then their taillights faded, and there was only the silence and the darkness.

Carl and Laurie stood paralyzed, unable to speak or look at each other. Unable to think.

Carl moved first, sinking back into his chair, staring blankly out the window. Laurie left to use the restroom, then came back. Carl lifted his eyes. She looked scared. The way he felt.

"Why didn't you tell me?" she finally said.

Carl shook his head.

"You really didn't think I would understand?" Laurie stood. "Don't you think I realized how much you hated that job, Carl?"

He raised his eyes. "I guess not."

Laurie stared at him with an expression so blankly cold that it froze his heart. "We have to leave, Carl."

"Where are we gonna go, Laurie? We can't. They'll throw me in jail in a heartbeat if we pack up and leave."

Her chin dropped, and he could see that she knew it was true, and that it was killing her. She turned and walked, looking entirely defeated, through the dining room and up to bed.

•

Above them, Roger lay under the covers fully clothed, wondering how long it would be before his parents finally went to bed. When Julie told him who was there, Roger had crept down to the dining room and listened to his parents' conversation with Blinder and Trass.

If anyone had told him his life on Pine Creek could get any worse, he would not have believed them. He could not imagine facing his classmates after this. He waited for his parents' footsteps on the stairs, but it was a long hour.

When he finally felt sure they were asleep, Roger slipped from beneath the covers. His legs trembled as he slid his stockinged feet along the floor and tiptoed down the stairs, hugging his loafers. He set his shoes outside the back door, then donned his coat and his scotch cap He grabbed a loaf of bread and some apples from the kitchen counter. He noticed a knife lying next to the apples, and stuffed it into his coat pocket.

Outside, he pushed his toes into his loafers. It was cooler than he'd expected, and he considered going back to get some gloves. He didn't want to risk getting caught. Roger swung the wagon wheel gate open, stepping into the pasture behind the house. But once he closed the gate, he was hit with a sudden panic that someone could, at any moment, emerge from the house. So he sprinted toward the barn, pinning the supplies against his chest with both arms. One apple flew from his grasp, tumbling down the hill.

Inside the barn, he laid the food out in one stable while he saddled Old Ed in another. He stuffed the apples and the bread into the saddlebags. Then he led Ed outside, mounted, and pointed the big yellow palomino toward the Absaroka Mountains.

•

There comes a day in Montana, every fall, when everything turns. Every speck of color drains from its home and soaks into the soil until spring, when the pigments have rested enough to reappear in a brilliant explosion of color.

Overnight, the grass and leaves soften to a muted tan and the bark on the trees fades to grey, until the entire landscape is so overwhelmingly tan and grey that one cannot imagine it otherwise. Even the evergreen mountains, glorious and enormous, cannot save this dull season.

In 1968, this change came on a Saturday, the day after Tom Butcher's body was found beaten beyond recognition. The birds pointed their beaks south that morning, as though they feared implication. Flies dropped from the screens, piling in windowsills.

Carl Logan awoke, as usual, before dawn. He sat out in the yard, at the picnic table, with a cup of coffee. As the light leaked into the sky, Carl felt the effects of the muted landscape. He watched the mountains emerge from the blackness, and he sat thinking with some amazement how quickly his view of these new surroundings had changed. Just a couple of weeks before, this country looked so wide open and forgiving. Now he could almost hear the chatter rolling from the surrounding ranches, could almost picture the mountains moving toward him, his neighbors descending from the trees, surrounding him and his family, closing in, their fingers aimed at his chest.

Carl closed his eyes and pressed his fingers into the lids, trying to soothe his thoughts, trying not to wonder if moving here had been a selfish, horrible mistake.

Carl had just decided to make some biscuits and gravy for breakfast before Laurie got up, when she burst from inside the house, running toward him with the most frightening look on her face.

"Roger's gone!"

CHAPTER NINE

WHEN ROGER FIRST STARTED TOWARD the mountains, riding tall beneath the starry black sky, the weight of his burden began to lift. The air was cool and clean, and as he made his way west, he was a horse, his thick, powerful legs trotting, his head bobbing with each stride. He felt the strain in his thighs each time a hoof hit the hard ground.

Old Ed was in no hurry, and after a few futile attempts to get him to gallop, Roger settled for a leisurely stroll. Roger's mind wandered, thinking about his friends in Bozeman, wondering whether he missed them. He was briefly an eagle, spreading his wings. He flew the thirty miles back to Bozeman and soared above Hawthorn School, where he watched his classmates kicking red rubber balls and whacking yellow tetherballs in a tightening circle. But the scene made him lonesome, so he flew back and became a horse again.

When he and Ed reached the foot of the mountains, Roger prodded Ed to follow a narrow cattle trail that curled through the thick trees. The smell of evergreen was strong and pure, and the night was quiet, so that when Roger was within a quarter mile of Pine Creek, he could hear the rush of water. He could even smell the fresh, clean stream. The moon was full, and so bright that it brought a blue glow to every tree, every stone, as if little blue light bulbs were hidden among the branches.

They pushed into the trees, and as Ed rounded a slight curve, Roger caught the glinting reflection of the moon on the creek. He dismounted, giving Ed enough rein to stick his nose in and drink up the cool water. A flash of silver flickered in the water. Roger leaned down on one knee to get a closer look. As Ed drank, Roger watched a trout weave between the rocks. He thought of an episode of *Davy Crockett* where Fess Parker snatched a fish from the water with his bare hands.

Roger waded into the water, and the cold shimmied up his spine and sucked the air from his lungs. He stopped, waiting to get accustomed to the cold. He eased into the rushing creek, which was only about six feet across. The water furled around the base of his kneecaps. He spread his legs and leaned his elbows against his knees, peering into the black water, just as Fess Parker had done. Now he waited, watching the fish, which had worked its way upstream. It sat idle for a time, and in the blue moonlight, Roger eyeballed the slow silver undulation. The fish began a gradual slide through the clear water, curling one way then the other. Roger separated his elbows from his knees, his hands poised. He crouched lower. The fish approached, paused, and seemed to sense danger, as it suddenly darted. As it reached him, swimming directly between his legs, Roger was a bear, and he snatched, burrowing his hands into the cold. He felt the slippery flesh for a second, but he could not hold it. The fish slid between his fingers and darted downstream. He looked at Ed.

"Next time, Ed."

He ate an apple and a piece of bread and dipped from the creek with his hand, slurping the clean water. The darkness was steely cold, and the excitement of the journey started to fade. Roger walked ten yards from the creek and tied Ed to a tree. His wet pants stiffened. He rolled up his scotch cap and wedged it under his head, wrapping himself up in his coat. In a matter of seconds, he was asleep.

Roger's fatigue carried him through the remainder of a cold night, and he slept soundly until daybreak. But he awoke to a strange noise, a thin whine. He lay still for a moment, shivering, trying to remember where he was, then trying to place the noise. The whine stopped, then started again, and Roger rolled onto his stomach and rose to his hands and knees. He slid the knife from his pocket. He listened closely. He was a wolf, sniffing the air and rotating his ears. He heard Ed's shuffling hooves.

When the whine stopped and started one more time, Roger was scared for the first time since he'd left the house. But it was a good fear—an energetic, exciting fear. He inched forward on his hands and knees. The ground was cold, still covered with a light frost. The dew soaked into Roger's clothes. The fear and the dampness made him tremble.

But he was a wolf, and the cold did not bother him, and he kept creeping forward, slipping through the trees, past Old Ed, who pawed the ground nervously, snorting great puffs of air through his moist nostrils. Roger shushed the horse. Then, as a wolf, Roger bounded over a small knoll, into a clearing. Nothing there, but the whine was louder.

Roger crept toward a stand of evergreens, the knife poised, his heart beating his ribs like a wooden spoon. The whine grew louder still. He heard it starting and stopping, with a rhythm. He rose to his haunches, the hair standing on his neck, and he rushed between two of the trees and screamed as loud as he could. A man, who'd been sleeping sprawled on his back, jumped wild-eyed to his feet, the whites showing his surprise in a face grimy with dirt. The man yelled, and Roger the wolf snarled at him, and slashed at the man's arm with his knife.

The man yelled and raced through the trees, as though he had actually seen a wolf. Roger dropped to his knees, shaking, and in a rush of relief and absolute terror, he cried, the salty tears gushing from his eyes and down his neck. He realized that he had blood all over his hands, and he dropped further, hunched over his elbows. Then he rolled onto his back and sighed with each heaving breath as the tears slid into his ears and onto the leaves. And somewhere in his ten-year-old conscience lurked a knowledge that he had never felt so strong in his life.

•

Carl pushed his horse Sailor across the pasture, riding with confidence, completely irrational, that he would find Roger. He expected that Sailor would follow Old Ed's scent. But even more than that, he just had a hunch, a gut feeling, that he would ride right up to wherever his boy had decided to hide.

He gave Sailor a heel to the ribs, and the horse sped up to a half gallop. The wind whipped past Carl's ears. They reached the foot of the mountains in less than thirty minutes, and sure enough, Sailor headed directly for the cattle trail.

Carl saw the horseshoe prints and smiled to himself, patting Sailor's neck. "Thataboy. We know exactly where we're going, don't we?"

He led Sailor along the narrow trail, peering into the trees for evidence. The shoe prints continued along the trail. He followed them for an hour before he came to the creek and the remnants of a fire.

A knot formed in Carl's stomach, and he realized that it was a feeling of pride, an admiration that his son had gotten this far. But when he dropped from his horse and rummaged around, he noticed that the horseshoe prints continued in a straight line up the path. He also saw footprints, and realized that they were too big. They were adult footprints. Suddenly he thought about Tom's murder, and his heart rose up into his throat.

He mounted Sailor again, nudging him back onto the trail. A few yards further along, something brought him leaping out of his saddle. He stooped, furrowing his brow to study the trail, wondering what had stopped him. His breath pumped through his lungs when he realized that he was looking at drops of blood.

He swore, stabbed his boot into the stirrup, and kicked himself onto Sailor's back, throwing his heels into the horse's ribs. Sailor jumped, then hopped forward, but would not run, spooked by the cramped trail. They wound through the thick trees with Carl ducked forward to avoid overhanging branches.

He kept a close eye on the blood, trying to find comfort in the fact that the drops were small and not any closer together.

"He's alive," he said to himself.

He repeated this out loud, once, and then again, and once more. His stomach curled, and he was glad that Laurie had insisted he take some food. Still he ate sparingly, gnawing on a corner of a peanut butter sandwich, saving most of the food in case Roger needed to eat.

The trail wound upward through the thickening trees and an occasional clearing. Carl found another dead campfire. He hopped from Sailor's back, placing his hands over the charred wood, and he swallowed, his pulse quickening, when he felt heat. He looked around.

And then he saw him.

Thirty yards away, in a clearing, on a large rock, Roger sat cross-legged, chewing on a piece of fish. The skeleton lay on the rock beside him. Ed lingered nearby, gnawing peacefully at the thick grass.

Carl walked slowly toward Roger, leading Sailor behind him. He squeezed between two bushy evergreens and urged Sailor through the narrow opening. The rustling sound attracted Roger's attention.

Roger turned his head, without panic, saw Carl, and turned back, calmly again, to his fish and to the scene before him. The motion was so adult, so free of fear, that Carl couldn't decide how he felt about it. Shouldn't Roger be glad to see him? Wouldn't he be afraid? But Carl couldn't help feeling a little proud of how grown up his son looked.

He stood, watching Roger eat. He had no idea that Roger was a bobcat, and had found a rock to stretch out and sun himself. He was sitting there in serene fatigue.

When he finished his fish, Roger tossed the remains aside and looked back at his father. Carl took this as an invitation. He moved forward, tugging Sailor away from his grazing.

"Hey, son."

"Hi." Roger climbed down from the rock.

Studying him, Carl saw that there was no wound, no blood anywhere.

"You okay?"

Roger nodded. "I guess so." He looked at his hand.

"What's wrong?" Carl eased up to Roger's side.

"I hurt my hand a little."

"How?"

Roger looked up at him, and then sighed. "I stabbed a guy."

"You did what?"

"There was a man. And he came after me. I had a knife, so I cut him."

Carl looked into his son's eyes, searching for signs of delusion, or exhaustion. "Are you sure?"

Roger looked offended, but he nodded. He dug in his pocket and held out the knife. There was blood on the blade, but Carl thought it was probably from the fish.

"There was a man?"

Again, Roger nodded. "He was sleeping. And I musta scared him. He woke up and started to come after me."

Carl breathed in through his nose. He studied the boy closely again. Carl thought about the adult footprints. Roger's eyes were clear and calm. He looked as if he'd slept well.

"Son, what did this fella look like?"

Roger pushed his lips up toward his nose. He frowned. "I don't know, Dad. His face was real dirty. And I was mainly looking at his hands."

"His hands?"

Roger nodded. "They had blood on 'em. They were real bloody."

Carl took a deep breath, looking out into the woods. "Well."

Roger looked at him. "What?"

Carl placed his palm on Roger's shoulder and pulled him close. He shook his head. "You ready to go home?"

Roger looked down at the ground, at his feet, then lifted his head again. He nodded.

Carl stood unmoving for a moment. Then they turned as one and started walking, leading their horses behind them. Roger slipped, and Carl reached out and caught him by the arm.

"Why are you wearing those shoes?" he asked.

Roger glanced up at him, a quick look. "They're the only ones I have."

•

Laurie rushed out of the house when Junior pulled up. "Please go and find him! He took off hours ago!"

Junior scratched his head. "Well now, I don't think it would do anyone any good if all three of us was to start wandering around in the mountains. I better stay put and see what happens…he'll probably turn up any minute."

She nodded, trying to find comfort in the fact that he was there. She had first thought of calling Kenwood, but then worried that he might see this as an indictment of their family, of their sanity.

Before long, Laurie found herself at ease with Junior, and with fear and worry throwing her tongue into a run, she confided more than she normally would. Her face flushed as she stumbled through her concerns about Kenwood's expectations for her husband. She worried aloud about Roger, how he'd become so withdrawn. Junior listened calmly, his boyish, ruddy face eternally kind. Laurie's momentum carried her along.

"…and now with this murder, and some of the stories I'm sure people are spreading around, I just don't know how we're going to ever get along with the folks around here."

"Stories?" Junior lowered his chin, looking up through his brow.

Laurie suddenly pulled up inside, realizing she'd said more than she wanted to say.

They were seated at the dining room table. Junior leaned forward, folding his hands together. He fixed a soft look on Laurie.

"Laurie, you grew up on a ranch…"

She nodded.

"So you know about stories," he said. "Folks around here aren't any different than anywhere else. Some of us get riled up about stories… some of us don't."

Laurie chewed the inside of her lip. "All I know, Mr. Kirby, is that my family is in trouble. It's easy to pin a murder on a stranger… someone new. I've seen it before."

Junior nodded. "You got a point there."

"The truth isn't always strong enough to stand up to the lies."

Again Junior nodded, looking down at his hands. "I'd like to argue with you, but I don't think I can. But I hope you realize that there are people around here you can trust."

"I appreciate that," Laurie said. "I really do. I just don't know."

A few minutes later, as Laurie and Junior sat fumbling with their coffee cups, Julie burst into the house. "Mom, Dad and Roger are coming. I see 'em."

Laurie and Junior ran outside, through the wagon wheel gate, and toward the barn.

At the bottom of the sloping pasture, crossing the small wooden bridge, Carl rode a few yards ahead of Roger. Carl was fighting the reins, holding back Sailor, who danced and tossed his head.

Junior stood by the barn door, watching Laurie rush toward her husband and son.

And he took in the pure and unfettered joy of the entire family as they came together.

BOOK TWO

A RUBY NECKLACE

CHAPTER TEN

NINE MONTHS EARLIER

WHEN JUNIOR KIRBY ANSWERED A knock at his back door in December of 1967 and found Tom Butcher on his stoop, Tom's face ruddy from the sub-zero temperature, Junior assumed his pickup had broken down. Despite growing up just down the winding gravel road from each other, and being about the same age, Tom and Junior had never been close. Junior's father despised Ed Butcher, Tom's father, and as often happens in small communities, the chill had passed from one generation to the next. But in Junior's case, the feud had always felt like an obligation. There was no passion behind it. Even so, the only reason Junior could imagine Tom coming to his door was an emergency.

"Come on in." Junior stepped to one side to make room for Tom, who was a much larger man. Larger than anyone else in Paradise Valley.

Tom stomped his feet, knocking the snow from his boots, and stepped into the kitchen. He lifted his cowboy hat from his head with a careful flip of his wrist and cradled it in both hands.

"How you doin' tonight?" Junior asked.

"Good, good," Tom said, nodding his head. "Hope I'm not interrupting."

"Not at all," Junior answered. "I was just doing a little bookkeeping."

"Oh hell, then you were *waiting* for an interruption," Tom said.

Junior laughed. "Exactly. Come on into the living room. I'll get you a cup of coffee. Just made a fresh pot."

"That sounds better than just about anything right now." Tom took off his gloves, stuffing them in his lambskin coat. He rubbed his big hands together.

The two men sat with steaming mugs at their elbows. Despite not saying anything, there was a nervous undercurrent to Tom's manner that Junior had never seen before. As if some important event or news was clinging restlessly to the tip of his tongue. He glanced at Junior several times as though he was just about to say something, but each time he turned away and tipped his coffee cup to his mouth instead. Junior sorted through almost thirty-five years of undisclosed experiences, disappointments, and dreams, trying to settle on something to talk about.

Angie came in and said hello, and for a moment, Junior thought his wife would rescue him. But she apologized and announced that she was too tired to visit.

Tom stood to wish her goodnight. "No offense taken, Angie."

Junior waited for a humorous follow-up, which never came. That convinced Junior that Tom's mood was more serious than usual. After Angie retired, Junior sat quietly, waiting for Tom to reveal the nature of his visit.

"So how's things?" Tom asked.

Junior shrugged, relaxing back into his chair. "Ah, you know. Pretty busy."

"How're your yearlings turning out so far?"

"Real good, actually. I've only lost two, and we're almost done."

Tom shook his head. "I still can't believe Kenwood does his calving in the winter. Cheap sonofabitch is always looking for an advantage."

Junior nodded, his mouth turning down. "I s'spose that's how he got to where he is. How about you?"

"Oh, average. Can't complain. Thank God it hasn't gotten much colder," Tom added.

Junior nodded, and then they fell silent again, and the undercurrent swelled, sporting waves. There was a spark of fear in Tom's eyes that Junior wouldn't have believed if he hadn't been staring right at him.

Tom Butcher, the most fearless man along Pine Creek, was afraid of something.

"Did you hear that Kenwood fired his manager, Ellerby?" Tom asked.

"Did he really? God, how many is that now?"

Tom shook his head. "The man has a knack for finding guys who will take the world on their shoulders and not squawk about the weight of it."

Junior chuckled. "I wonder if Lester will finally get his chance to run the place."

"If Kenwood doesn't give Lester the job this time, I might have to go over there and shoot him myself." Tom pulled his mouth to one side, then he raised his eyes suddenly, as if a thought had just come to him. "You must hate that son of a bitch, huh?"

Junior blanched. "Who, Kenwood?"

Tom nodded.

"No, I don't hate him. Why do you say that?"

Tom scooted forward in his chair and straightened up. "Oh, I was just thinking about what happened with your dad."

"Oh, that. Well, that wasn't Peter's fault. That happened before Peter came along. Trudy, or her first husband…we never really knew who was responsible."

"Ah." Tom nodded. "That's right." He chewed on his lip, not finished with this topic, it seemed. "But Kenwood and Trudy's first husband might as well be the same damn guy, if you know what I mean. Cut from that same silk cloth…rich sons a bitches that bought up some land in Montana because they've seen one too many John Wayne movies." He tilted his head. "Doesn't that bother you, Junior? Those guys are going to take over out here."

Junior frowned. "Jesus, Tom. Maybe I'm dense, but I don't see them as the same at all. I like Peter a lot, actually. Trudy's first husband… well, he was a different type."

"Of course you like Peter. I like him, too."

Junior laughed.

"I do," Tom said. "Hell, we're just like a couple of big ol' elk, posing like we have to do battle all the time. That's not what I'm talking about. I'm talking about what they're doing to this country. Hell, they don't give a damn about Montana. They're just here to pose for pictures, you know…get a photo on their ranch, sitting on a big ol' expensive horse so they can put it on their desk in Omaha and impress their corporate buddies…"

"I know what you're talking about, Tom, but I just can't work myself into much of a lather about that. They have a right to buy land wherever they want. And I think Kenwood loves Montana as much as anyone."

Tom squinted at Junior. He seemed disappointed. Junior thought about how many of their neighbors shared Tom's resentment toward Kenwood. Tom had plenty of allies. And again, Junior wondered why Tom chose his doorstep this particular evening.

Tom twisted his neck, surveying the room. "You've got quite a few books."

Junior sipped his coffee. "Yeah, between all the books we inherited from Angie's family and mine, we're sort of the community library."

Tom nodded thoughtfully, his eyes looking into another time. "I just remembered how often we used to stop by here when I was a kid… Angie's folks' kitchen was like the local drugstore, the place everyone stopped to have coffee and chat. Is it still like that?"

Junior tipped his head. "It's a rare week when we don't get visitors, I guess."

Tom smiled. "It's funny that I forgot all about that until just now."

Junior hmmed. "You want to take a look, see if there's a book you'd like to borrow?"

"Sure." Tom stood, setting his empty mug on the end table next to his chair. "You got any of that Louis L'Amour character's books?"

"Yeah, we have a bunch of them."

Tom read the back covers of several of L'Amour's books before choosing *Hondo*, one of Junior's favorites. Junior headed back toward the living room, but Tom stopped just outside the den.

"I should probably get going," he said. "I didn't realize it was this late."

"Well, don't feel like you have to rush off."

"I have to get up early. I'm sure you do, too."

As Tom pulled his coat on, then his cap, Junior noticed a small scratch along one cheek, running from just above his ear down the length of his jaw, to the point of his chin. The blood that had dried along the scratch was still bright red.

"What'd you do, tangle with a cat?" Junior asked, running a finger down his own jaw.

"Ah, no," Tom answered, burying the scratch with his big hand. He didn't make any effort to explain, and Junior sensed that pursuing the matter any further would be unwelcome.

"Well, stop by any time," Junior said, resting a palm on Tom's shoulder.

"You might be sorry you said that," Tom said, chuckling. "I'll get this book back to you soon as I'm done with it."

"No rush," Junior said. "I think I've read that one about four times now."

"Well, you never know when you might get the itch to read it again."

They both laughed, and Tom walked out of the house. Junior watched his huge, dark figure stride across the snow, tilting to one side, then the other. Junior sat for a while, puzzling over what wasn't said during this surprise visit. As his mind tinkered with various theories of why Tom would suddenly find his way to his door, he was too preoccupied to notice that Tom Butcher sat outside in his pickup for a very long time before driving off.

•

A few days later, Angie answered another knock at the door. She led a rosy-cheeked Tom into the living room. His black hair was oiled, wrapped like skin around his skull.

"I'm back!" he announced, holding up the book.

"Well, now." Junior actually was busy this time and wasn't quite as happy to see him. "You're turning into a regular member of the family. Angie, maybe we should just set up the guest room for Tom."

"Not without getting some rent out of him." Angie winked.

Tom laughed and settled into a chair, setting the book aside. He seemed in much better spirits. The scratch on his jaw had nearly healed.

The three of them sat and visited. Tom told some stories that had the Kirbys laughing, but it seemed to Junior as if Tom was trying to make up for the previous visit. His efforts to entertain them had an almost frantic air. His gestures were exaggerated, his voice changing with each character, growling here, purring here. This was the Tom Butcher they were accustomed to seeing at the local parties. Junior was happy to see Tom feeling better. But he was curious.

●

"So when did we become such good friends with Mr. Butcher?" Angie asked.

"I don't know what's going on," Junior answered. "Pretty strange, huh?"

The Kirbys were just getting into bed. Angie nodded as she pulled the covers up to her neck. They settled in and Junior turned out the lamp.

"You know what else is strange?" Angie asked.

"What?"

"In the last few weeks, almost every time I've driven by the school after the kids are gone, Tom's pickup has been parked out front."

"Tom's?"

"Yeah."

"That is strange. I wonder why."

"Well, think about it," Angie said, looking at Junior from the top of her eyes.

"No…you think?"

"I can't imagine any other reason."

"How long's that been going on?"

"No idea."

Junior lay on his back, thinking, wondering. "What the hell are they thinking?"

"Well, I guess it's pretty safe to say they're not," Angie said.

"Yeah, I guess."

"I wonder why Tom never married that gal from Bozeman," Angie said. "That other redhead."

"Well…I heard she had a tendency to get around."

"Birds of a feather," she said, and they laughed.

•

Junior drove along the gravel road that ran parallel to Pine Creek, the ice crunching under his tires. As he passed Slack School, Junior had to shake his head. There was Tom's pickup, just as it had been almost every day   like a big black flag, announcing to the whole community that he and Babe Ruth had chosen to ignore the conventional discretion about such matters.

It was pure Tom Butcher. Like it or not, he refused to hide. Although Junior couldn't agree with his methods, especially when he thought about how much public humiliation Lester Ruth had already suffered, he couldn't help but secretly admire Tom's moxie.

But as the brutal truth of this affair sunk in, Junior's thoughts turned to Babe. From whatever angle he picked, the stakes were much higher for her. As Junior thought about her, wondering at her motivations, it occurred to him that he had not thought about her in any meaningful way for a very long time. That evening, he suggested to Angie that they invite the Ruths over for dinner.

CHAPTER ELEVEN

"YOU MUST HAVE BEEN TO town this week." Babe impaled her salad with a fork. "This lettuce looks pretty fresh." In the background, a black and white image of Lyndon Johnson drew a handkerchief across his sweaty brow, trying to explain a war to the nation.

"Tuesday, actually," Angie verified.

"God, I haven't been shopping for over a week now," Babe said. "We need everything, seems like."

Lester chewed silently, his long jaw working slightly to one side. Just after they started eating, Babe turned to Junior.

"Do you have any bourbon?" she asked.

"Of course," Junior said. "I'm sorry I didn't offer sooner. Lester?"

Lester shook his head and shot a hard look at his wife. He muttered something, then said, "Someone's got to drive" through a mouth half-filled with corn.

Junior fixed Babe her drink, then returned to his meal. "So how do Kenwood's calves look this year?" he asked Lester.

Lester answered with a quick "Fine...good."

Junior prompted him. "Have you lost many?"

Lester chewed thoughtfully. Babe threw back most of her drink in a couple of swallows. Lester glanced her way.

"No more 'n usual," Lester answered. "Lost three last night, though." He shook his head. "Bad night."

"Yes, last night was bad," Babe agreed, and Junior had a hunch that she was talking about something completely different.

"That is a bad night," Angie said. "How awful!"

"We lost three in one night once," Craig declared. "Last year. Remember, Dad?"

"Ever since the president got shot," Babe suddenly said, "I've had trouble sleeping."

There was a brief silence while everyone chewed silently, their eyes shifting from side to side.

"Four years ago," Lester muttered.

"Really?" Angie said, addressing Babe. "Why do you think that is?"

"I just don't know," Babe said. "It feels like everything's been flipped on its side sometimes."

Lester cleared his throat. "Maybe this ain't the right time for this kind of talk, with the boys and all."

"I lie in bed sometimes, and all I can do is worry about what's going to happen next. I don't feel good about it. I'm scared, is what it is," Babe said.

"Babe," Lester said. "We ought to talk about something else."

"It's all right, Mrs. Ruth," Bobby said. "We're not scared." He turned to Craig. "We're not scared, are we, Craig?"

"I am," Craig said.

Babe drank deeply from her tumbler and smiled at her husband. She tilted her head to one side, as if it was too heavy to hold up. "Lester just doesn't like to talk."

Junior realized from the bleary look in Babe's eye, and the suddenness of her condition, that she must have been drinking before they arrived, and he was sorry he had poured gasoline on the fire.

"Well, maybe we could talk about something a little less... dramatic," Angie suggested.

Babe wrapped an elbow around the back of her chair and picked at her food. At that moment, she looked old, and Junior realized how much she'd aged in recent years. Babe had been just a year ahead of Junior and Angie in high school. She had been quiet but not shy, likely to surprise people with a humorous but cutting comment.

And she was really beautiful then, in a way that was more delicate than most rural women. She always had fair skin. She couldn't go out in the sun much, at the risk of burning herself to blisters, so her work was confined to the indoors. Everyone expected her to move to a city and pursue some creative endeavor. She was an extraordinary seamstress who made wedding dresses for many of the young brides in the community. But now her pale blue eyes looked cloudy, and she had a tobacco yellow tint to her skin. The sadness in her eyes burned right through Junior.

"How's everyone's steak?" Junior asked. "Anyone need a little more fire?"

"Fine, fine," everyone said, except Babe, who didn't answer.

"Babe?" Junior prodded.

"Eating steak always reminds me of my father," she said dreamily, her eyes turning toward the window. One hand moved toward her neck, where she rested her fingers against the curve above her shoulder.

"What did you do to your head?" Lester asked Junior, touching his own forehead.

"Got kicked," Junior answered.

"Why does steak remind you of your father?" Craig asked Babe.

She blinked and looked at him. "What?"

Craig repeated the question.

"Oh, he loved steak," she replied, throwing her hand out in a graceful arch. "He could eat it every night. We did sometimes, for weeks." She went back into a dreamlike trance, staring down at her plate.

"Horse or a cow?" Lester asked Junior, his long jaw working hard on a chunk of meat.

"Cow," Junior answered.

"You don't eat horses, do you?" Craig asked, eyes wide with horror.

"What?" Lester asked.

"He was asking what your father got kicked by," Angie explained. "Not what we're eating."

"Oh," Craig said, and Babe looked at him and burst out laughing. She laid a hand on Craig's head and laughed and laughed, until Craig's face turned bright crimson and his body twisted with discomfort.

"Oh dear, that was the sweetest thing," Babe said, knuckling the moisture from the corner of one eye. "You sweet young boy, you." She leaned toward Craig until she was almost tickling his face with her nose.

Craig's eyes got round. His shoulders hunched in.

"Babe, you're embarrassing the boy," Lester said.

"No I'm not, Lester," she insisted, lifting her head. "Am I, sweetheart?" she asked Craig. "Craig is one of my favorite students, after all. They know what I'm like."

Craig shook his head.

"Just because you don't like me to get this close doesn't mean nobody does," Babe said to her husband.

Lester's jaw tightened, the chords straining across his cheek, and he stabbed another piece of steak.

"Babe, would you like some more potatoes?" Angie asked.

"Oh no. I don't think I could eat another bite," Babe answered. "But I could use another of these." She held up her tumbler, and Junior cast a sideways glance at Lester, who studied and cut and ate his food as if it was the most important thing he'd ever done. Junior grabbed Babe's glass and, against his better judgment, fixed her another, weaker, drink.

"May I be excused?" Craig asked. When Angie nodded, Craig left the table with much of his food still on his plate, something he never did.

•

When they moved to the living room after dinner, the discomfort followed right behind. Babe had polished off two more tumblers, and Lester's eyes narrowed a little each time she touched the glass to her lips. The longer the evening wore on, the more Junior regretted inviting the Ruths over.

For a while, it felt as if Angie and Junior were carrying on a discussion between themselves, their words trying to maneuver their way across the room, over Lester's heavy brooding and under Babe's unpredictable offerings.

"Do you remember Mrs. Butcher?" Babe asked at one point, apparently directing the question to anyone who felt compelled to answer. Angie and Junior exchanged a worried look.

"Tom's mother?" Junior asked.

"Yes, that's her."

"Of course they do," Lester said. "She only died ten years ago."

Babe continued, oblivious to Lester's tone. "She was such a marvelous lady…wasn't she?" She turned to Angie, who in fact did not like Mrs. Butcher at all.

"She did have some nice qualities, yes," Angie answered.

"The woman was a tyrant," Lester muttered through his teeth.

"Well, she certainly had her own style," Junior offered.

"That's it exactly," Babe said, brightening. "She had style. She had *style*." She punched the air. "More people need that—style. It's not as important as it used to be. Especially now that Jackie's not in the White House anymore."

"Maybe we should think about heading out," Lester said, not addressing Babe directly but speaking very loudly—for him, anyway.

"She handed that quality down to her son, too," Babe continued, her gaze far away.

"Yeah, I need to get some shut-eye," Junior said, standing abruptly. "I've got to get up and check on my maternity ward tonight."

"Let's go, Babe," Lester said, standing.

Babe did not argue, or say anything more, but stood unsteadily and took her husband's arm. He led her to the kitchen, where Angie met them with their coats, and they left after a terse goodnight from Lester and a slightly incoherent declaration of gratitude from Babe.

"Good lord," Angie said as they watched the Ruths' car leave the yard.

"I didn't realize she'd gotten so bad," Junior said. "How long has it been since we had them over?"

Angie began scraping the food from the plates into the dog's dish. "I was trying to remember. It's been a few years."

Junior shook his head.

"At least we can be thankful Tom didn't show up tonight," Angie said.

"That didn't even occur to me." He shuddered.

The evening left Junior unsettled. He had heard rumors about Babe's drinking for months now, but it was his nature to dismiss rumors until he'd seen the evidence for himself. That night, unfortunately, he had.

CHAPTER TWELVE

JUNIOR AND ANGIE KIRBY APPROACHED Tom Butcher's house on New Year's Eve with a bowl of fruit salad on the seat between them.

"It's none of their damn business," Junior said as they pulled into Tom's driveway.

"No it isn't," Angie agreed. "But that's not the point, is it? The point is that you spent more than we can afford."

"Well then, I'll take it back. It's simple enough to fix."

"I don't want you to take it back. I love it," Angie said. Junior parked, and they both sat staring straight ahead. "I'm just asking you to stay within our budget next time. You always go overboard."

"Well, it hasn't broken us yet. And I'm not about to do that just to keep your mother and father happy. If I want to buy you a goddamn diamond saddle, I'm gonna buy it."

Angie sat silent for a moment, as did Junior, their gazes fixed out the front windshield, as if they were at the drive-in. Then Angie started laughing, holding a hand to her mouth at first, then letting it drop to her knee. She leaned forward, shaking with laughter.

"What?" Junior demanded.

"A diamond saddle?" she said, finally turning toward him. "Of all the unlikely things you'd ever come home with." She reached over and pushed a palm against Junior's shoulder. "What on earth made you think of that?"

Junior smiled in spite of himself. "Hell, I don't know. I was trying to think of something fancy. It was the first thing that popped into my head."

Angie leaned her head against his shoulder, still chuckling. "If you buy me a diamond saddle, darling, I'll follow you to the end of the pasture. I'll ride off into the sunset with you."

"All right," Junior said, adopting a mediocre John Wayne drawl. "You got it, sweetheart. Next Christmas, you're going to find yourself a diamond saddle right under that Christmas tree."

Angie moved the fruit salad to the other side, scooted across the seat, and snuggled up next to Junior, wrapping her arms around his neck. Junior tilted his head, resting it against hers. She kissed Junior's neck.

"Maybe we should skip the party," Junior said, turning to kiss her.

•

When Tom greeted the Kirbys at the door, Junior was thrown off balance. He'd gotten so used to Tom's more private personality— the quiet, almost reflective Tom Butcher—that he'd forgotten how Tom usually behaved, his public persona. Tom's smile was childlike, it was so broad, and his face shiny red. A single strand of black hair was plastered and curled on one side of the crown of his head, like an inverted question mark.

"Junior, Angie, you handsome folks. God*damn*, you are a handsome couple. Is that real fox?" he asked, taking a lock of Angie's silver hair between his fingers.

She laughed and slapped his shoulder, then gave him a hug.

"Happy New Year!" Tom declared, and the Kirbys echoed the sentiment.

"All right then," Tom said. "I see we have the famous Kirby fruit salad. We are now officially ready to ring in the New Year."

Tom Butcher's New Year's Eve party had become legendary ever since Tom took over the Butcher Ranch in the early fifties. Tom's specialty was not décor but abundance. His party was always overstocked, with enough bottles of booze to put the whole county into a coma and a couple of sixteen-gallon kegs for the light drinkers.

Tom requested that everyone bring food, although he provided all of the meat. Each year, he roasted half a beef, as well as hunks of pork, ham, and a few chickens. The party had become such a classic that it drew people from a hundred miles away.

Also adding to the character of the party was Tom's house, which he built soon after his father died. The house was symbolic of the fifties, watershed years for ranchers, as well as a reflection of its owner. Tom designed the house himself, and it was dominated by one large room, a cavernous space with a twenty-five-foot ceiling and windows all around. The room was ideal for parties and dancing. It also served as a dandy boxing ring.

The crowd that night was the biggest Junior could remember—a testament to a mild December night and clear roads. And it turned out to be one of those inexplicable evenings when everyone had something witty to say. The smiles were broad, the laughter loud and from deep within. It was as though the entire community had been waiting for an opportunity to break out of some kind of doldrums. And once again, Tom Butcher provided it.

"Kirby!"

Junior turned to find Tom standing with a group including Spider Moses and Lester Ruth. Tom motioned Junior over, wearing a conspiratorial smile. "Spider here tells me that you said you could beat me at arm wrestling any day of the week."

Junior laughed, and Spider's smile told him that he'd made no such claim. "Well, I don't want to brag, Tom, but I think I could probably break your damn arm if I put my mind to it."

"Hah," Tom barked. "Whaddaya think, Lester? You think he could take me?"

Lester grinned, a rare expression for him. "Hell, Tom, I figure anybody in the room could take you."

"Goddamn," Tom declared, throwing his head back in mock indignation. "You guys are all betting against me, then?"

"I'd bet money against you." Spider's feet shuffled with excitement. "I'd put money on old Junior here."

"Spider, you're a damn traitor," Tom said. He turned to Junior. "You feeling strong?"

"Will you look at this plate?" Junior said. "I've eaten half a pig and a three-inch slab of prime beef. I got a whole barnyard behind me."

"All right," Tom announced. "Place your bets, folks. Let's go, Kirby. Over here."

Junior was laughing to himself as they made their way to the table, knowing he didn't have a prayer of beating Tom, who towered over him. Tom's arms were as big around as Junior's thighs. But the spirit of the moment injected Junior with energy. Junior set his plate to the side, and people pounded the men on their backs as they settled into their chairs.

"Don't hurt him," Angie muttered in Junior's ear.

"I might not be able to help myself, darlin'," Junior said.

"Bring me a beer, somebody." Tom waved an arm through the air. He glared at Junior across the table, baring his teeth and growling. Junior tried growling back, but he couldn't stop laughing. The crowd migrated toward the table, packing together like sheep in a windy pasture. Several people shuttled over cups of beer, and Tom guzzled one in a second and a half, then drank half of the second before setting it down.

"All right," he declared.

"You ready?" Junior asked.

"Oh yeah."

"You ready?" Junior asked again.

"Yeah!"

"Are you *ready*?" Junior shouted this time, and the energy of the crowd gathering around them lifted him like a wave.

The crowd started chanting their names, and they propped their elbows on the table. The men hooked their thumbs together and linked their right hands. Then they clenched their left hands together beneath this pyramid. Their eyes locked. And as their two hands wrapped tighter around each other, and the muscles in Junior's forearm tightened and the muscles in Tom's responded, a sudden competitive urge kicked in. Suddenly, Junior wasn't so sure Tom would win. Suddenly, Junior wanted to beat him.

"Start us off, Spider," Tom called. Spider stepped forward, placing his bony palm over the two fists. The men adjusted their grips, the sweat on their palms causing them to slide.

"Ready?" Spider asked.

"You ready, Kirby?" Tom asked.

"I been ready since I walked through that door," Junior growled. Their smiles were long gone.

"Go!" Spider shouted, jerking his hand away.

Muscles strained in their arms and faces. Veins swelled in the men's foreheads and necks. For several seconds, there was no movement either way, and Junior's bicep felt warm and strong. Tom's elbow slipped a bit, and the angle shifted. They both groaned, and Junior pushed harder, turning his wrist so that the back of Tom's hand tilted a few inches toward the table. The shouting got louder.

"You can't keep this up, Kirby," Tom muttered through his teeth.

"Oh yeah?" Junior clenched his jaw and tried to muster some reserve strength. But it was like digging into an empty bag of peanuts.

The two straining arms remained locked, unmoving, an inverse V of taut flesh. Junior began to wonder whether Tom was holding back. He eyed Tom, trying to measure his expression. Junior felt himself weaken, but there still was no movement either way. The shouts of the crowd surrounded them, a solid wall of sound.

From the corner of his eye, Junior noticed Angie's silver hair. She was screaming, her face red and straining and open-jawed. Tom pounced on this lapse in concentration, and in the time it took Junior to move his eyeballs, his arm was at a forty-five degree angle, backward. He tried turning his wrist, but Tom's big, beefy forearm didn't budge. Junior clenched his jaw and let out a roar, pushing with a jolt of extra strength. To his amazement, Tom's hand inched upward, to twelve o'clock, where they stalled again.

There they remained—for many long, difficult seconds. Junior's arm began to burn, searing deep down into the heart of the muscle.

The cheering increased. The sweat sprang from the men's foreheads. Junior felt the strain all the way in his abdomen.

Then, as if they'd been given a signal, both men started to groan. A slow, grinding sound rose from their throats, growing in volume as their eyes locked in an animal glare. Tom's mouth was open, his teeth ground together in what looked like a wicked smile. His eyes narrowed, and the blood colored his face.

Around them, the others got quieter, until they were silent and it was just the two of them, a picture of pure, raw combat, with no weapons, no advantage to either side. Their faces turned dark, almost purple.

The men's fists wavered to one side, then to the other. Junior's arm ached. Then the strength seemed to drain from it. His arm felt hollow. Until suddenly, Tom gave a raw, high shout and pounded Junior's hand to the table, in a motion as swift and final as the last few minutes had been motionless. Junior sighed, and then his whole body released, and he started laughing.

"Kirby, you son of a bitch, I didn't think you had it in you," Tom said, standing and walking around the table. He took Junior's hand in what proved to be the weakest handshake Junior had ever shared.

"You were holding back on me, weren't you?" Junior accused.

Tom raised his brow. "Have I ever held back on anything in my life, Junior?"

"Good point."

He slapped Junior on the back, then turned around, confronting the mass of faces behind him, his arms raised like a singer. "All right, who's next?"

Everyone laughed, but Tom stood with his arms outstretched, not smiling, and it became apparent that he was serious.

"I'll take you on," a burly guy announced.

"All right." Tom turned to settle back into his chair.

What followed for the next hour and a half was the most amazing display of strength, or stubbornness, that anyone in that room had ever seen. Tom pitted his arm against the arms of ten other men, many of them big men, and he beat every one of them, most of them easily.

Tom wrestled Spider, then Lester, who was sinewy but strong. He tangled with several young, strapping fellows and made a couple of them look like children. And Tom smiled through the entire display—savoring the attention, the competition, and probably, more than anything, the opportunity to exhibit something—something the importance of which he probably didn't understand himself.

Arnie Janko stepped forward after Tom had beaten the seventh guy, announcing that he'd once been the arm-wrestling champion at the Horseshoe Bar in Sheridan. Everyone bet against Arnie, and Tom pinned him in a matter of seconds.

The bets increased, and the momentum shifted as more and more folks swung to bet against Tom. Rather than weakening him, each bend of his wrist seemed to flex his resolve. He proved the bettors wrong time and again, draining their wallets. Arnie Janko ended up losing over fifty bucks and wouldn't speak to Tom for several weeks after.

It was during the match with Tom's ninth foe that a quiet murmur started at the back of the huge room and moved like an undulating wave toward the table. All heads turned to see what caused the stir. A silver head of hair wended through the crowd like a fish.

Tom slammed opponent number nine's hand to the table, showing only slight fatigue in the slack of his jaw.

"I ain't tired yet," Tom announced. "Who's next?"

There was no response, and it appeared as if Tom had exhausted his challengers.

"Kenwood!" somebody shouted. "Take on Kenwood."

"Is he here?" Tom asked, standing. He stood on his toes and looked around the room. Necks craned. Kenwood emerged from the kitchen, with his wife Trudy and a man Junior didn't recognize. The two men wore tuxedos, and Trudy was dressed in a sparkling evening gown.

"Oh my God," Tom bellowed, moving toward his newest guests. "What the hell is this?"

Kenwood smiled, bridging the distance between them. "We had another party in town," he explained. "So we're a little overdressed."

"A little?" Tom laughed. "Goddamn. I've never even *seen* a tuxedo in person."

Kenwood laughed, looking sheepish, and the young man with him looked downright embarrassed. He was not familiar, and Junior wondered what he must think, being assaulted by this stranger in such dramatic fashion. It was clear from his expression that he wasn't happy to be there. Trudy Kenwood wore a sour expression herself, but that wasn't anything new.

"So are you going to take me on in a little arm wrestling match, Peter?" Tom asked.

"Arm wrestling?" Kenwood, who was about a half foot shorter than Tom and twenty years older, stared up at him with a disbelieving look. "You must be joking."

"Take him on, Kenwood," someone shouted.

Trudy Kenwood turned away with a subtle snort, moving to the other side of the big room, to the food.

"Who's the big fella?" Tom asked Kenwood. He reached out to shake the stranger's hand. "Tom Butcher, local entrepreneur and strongman," he announced.

The man gave Tom a strange look before he muttered his name in a subdued voice, looking down at his shoes.

"Come on, Peter," Tom said. "Let's give it a go. Get into the spirit of the New Year. I've already wrestled about thirty guys."

"Ah, what the hell," Kenwood said, following Tom.

"Peter, you will not arm wrestle that man," Trudy said from across the room. She balanced a plate in one delicate hand.

"Oh relax, Trudy," Peter said. "You've seen the will. It's all going to you. Maybe this will be your lucky day."

While the crowd laughed, Trudy made an exasperated sound and left the room, ducking into the kitchen.

The quiet young man followed Kenwood, stationing himself just behind his chair, as if he had been assigned to guard him. Once Kenwood got comfortable, he loosened his bow tie, letting the black strip of fabric dangle around his neck. He took off his jacket, handing it to his friend. Finally, he took the cuff link out of his right sleeve and rolled the fabric up to his elbow.

Tom smiled like a hungry dog looking at a piece of meat. "You finally ready?" he asked.

"I guess I'm as ready as I'm going to be," Kenwood answered.

Nobody placed a bet. Spider again took his position as the starter and watched as Tom and Kenwood clasped hands. Tom had to cock his wrist to bring his hand, which dwarfed Kenwood's, to the same level.

Spider laid his palm on the odd pairing, then shouted "Go!" and jerked it away.

Tom muscled Kenwood's hand just a few inches from the table, then stopped and smiled. And the crowd had to admire what Peter Kenwood did next. Many men would have let their hand fall, knowing that Tom could have pounded it against the table at any moment. But Kenwood did not quit. His already flushed face dark, he clenched his teeth, grinning angrily at Tom.

Their hands did not move. Tom held him at the same vulnerable angle for long minutes, looking as if he was just about ready to take a bite out of Kenwood the whole time.

"You feel that, Peter?" he asked. "You feel the *burn*?"

Kenwood did not answer, using all his energy for one thing. Tom started laughing.

"Finish him off, Tom," someone shouted. "Quit torturing the poor guy."

This drew a round of laughter.

"I got to take advantage of every opportunity I get to torment ol' Peter," Tom said, and his smile turned wicked. More wicked. "When a man gets a chance to turn the tables, he's got to take it—got to do it with a flourish. Right, Peter?"

Again, Kenwood did not dignify him with an answer, but continued to strain against the trunk of his arm. It did not move. His face took on a purple hue, and some folks muttered in concern.

Tom's jaw tightened. He pushed just a little, lowering the back of Kenwood's hand an inch from the surface of the table.

"You can't tell me that don't hurt now, Peter. You got to be feeling that, *deep* down." Kenwood flinched.

"What the hell are you trying to prove, Butcher?" The voice was quiet but firm, and everyone turned to the stranger, who was still standing just behind Kenwood. Junior became suddenly aware of the absurdity of the situation—this man in a tuxedo standing in the midst of all these half-drunk, middle-aged cowboys, squaring his shoulders to defend his friend, who was getting the shit kicked out of him, also in a tuxedo, in an arm-wrestling match with a man twice his weight and three times his strength.

Junior started laughing. And he was met with the coldest blue-eyed gaze.

"You laughing at me?" the quiet voice asked.

Through no conscious effort on his part, the laughter caught in Junior's throat.

"Who the hell is this guy?" Tom asked, tilting his head toward the young man without looking at him.

Kenwood was so absorbed in his effort that he either didn't hear or didn't want to waste energy answering. The young man stared at Tom, giving no indication that he was about to answer for himself. So Tom went right back to the business of measuring the distance between the back of Kenwood's hand and the table.

"Stop it!" The young man barked, and the force scared Tom into slamming Kenwood's hand to the oak surface. Everyone jumped.

Kenwood let out a cry of pain, which evolved into a slow groan. He massaged his forearm. "Damn," he muttered.

Tom stood up. The smile was back. He hitched up his pants and smoothed his black, oiled hair back tight against his scalp.

"Well, friend, you seem to have more than a passing interest in this exchange."

The young man's expression did not change. He glared at Tom, his blue eyes steely and unyielding. Tom circled the table, drawn toward the possibility of conflict. He held out his massive hand.

"I didn't catch your name," Tom said. "I'm Tom Butcher. Your host." He emphasized the title.

Who knows whether the young man suddenly realized how many of Tom's friends were around him, or whether the fact that Tom was the host of the party made a difference to him. He may have seen something in Tom's eyes. For whatever reason, his face and his body seemed to ease.

"Harlan Glider." He held out his own good-sized hand. The voice was still quiet, and one side of his mouth curled up a bit.

"Were you worried I was gonna tear your boss's arm off?" Tom asked.

Harlan Glider's mouth remained tight, but he seemed to decide that he should appear to be enjoying himself. A slight, uncomfortable smile crossed his face. He put his hand on Kenwood's shoulder. "He's no spring chicken, you know."

"All right," Kenwood said, frowning. "I'm not dead yet."

"We wondered for a while there," Tom said.

Kenwood laughed, looking up at Tom from his chair. He appeared absolutely spent.

"Ten minutes!" somebody shouted.

"'Till midnight?" Tom turned to look at the clock. "I'll be damned. Amazing how fast time goes by when you're in the middle of a goddam war."

Tom hustled off to the kitchen, where he broke out a case of champagne. He enlisted a few others to help pour, and soon everyone stood holding plastic champagne glasses, their eyes glued to the clock, waiting for the last minute of 1967. They started counting down from sixty, and the volume rose, and the dancing started. By the time they reached ten, everyone in the room held their glasses aloft, bending their knees to each beat, yelling at the top of their lungs.

"Five, four, three, two, one!"

They drained their glasses. Every couple embraced and kissed. After kissing Angie, Junior looked around the room, where he saw Lester and Babe dancing close and Kenwood sharing a stiff embrace with Trudy. He also found Tom. On the countdown, Tom had been bouncing around the room, drunkenly throwing an arm around anyone, male or female, yelling, "Happy New Year." But now he stood in the corner with Harlan Glider, engaged in an earnest exchange.

Tom appeared to be trying to convince Harlan of something. Harlan frowned. Tom shook his head, repeating himself, more forcefully this time. Harlan turned his head away and held a hand up, signaling an end to the conversation. Tom put a hand on Harlan's shoulder, but Harlan pushed it off and walked away, pushing through the crowd toward the kitchen.

Tom turned his attention back to his other guests. He seemed unfazed by this exchange, although it wasn't always easy to tell with Tom.

For one night, the Paradise Valley community set aside all thoughts of stock and whatever petty grievances they had against each other. Even the Kenwoods seemed swept up in the mood, staying later than they normally would and making their way around the dance floor for a few numbers. Their friend Harlan appeared to put the disagreement with Tom behind him. He stripped his jacket and tie, and although he didn't dance, he did smile a few times. It seemed that the night would never end, and for a while they all wished it wouldn't.

But age and alcohol took their toll. After the crowd consumed a massive batch of scrambled eggs, in the last gluttonous act of the night, the exodus finally started.

It was nearing dawn. Along with Lester and Babe, Junior and Angie were the last to leave.

"Tom, that was the best party I've ever been to in my life," Junior told him.

"It was absolutely perfect," Babe added.

Lester was unsteady, holding himself up with a hand on Babe's shoulder. Junior was surprised to see that Babe was fairly sober.

"Tom," Lester said, and his eyes suddenly teared up. "I just want to thank you for everything. Everything," he repeated, throwing out a graceless hand.

"It's nothing, Lester," Tom said. "Nothing at all."

"No, no, no," Lester insisted. "I want to thank you for *everything.*"

"All right, Lester. You're welcome."

"Let's go, Lester," Babe coaxed, smiling. "Let's go on home."

She helped him to the door, bracing him with an arm around his waist.

"*Everything*," Lester shouted over his shoulder. "Thanks, Tom."

Tom watched them, his smile wide, then turned back to Junior and Angie, shrugging. "Guess *they* had a good time."

Tom and Junior exchanged a jerky handshake, and he kissed Angie on the forehead, then the Kirbys left.

•

Angie drove, as she had not indulged quite as much. They rode mostly in silence, with only a few comments about what a perfect night it had been. The moon was full, and the moonlight illuminated the snow around them so that it looked like the whole earth had crystallized.

Junior could almost feel a heat coming off the glow, and a slightly drunken smile curled his lips.

Angie glanced out her window and hummed. She smiled at him. "How's your arm?"

Junior gripped his upper arm, squeezing it like a piece of fruit. "Feels fine," he said, but the muscle was actually sore. "Hell, I wonder how Tom did that. That was amazing."

Angie smiled.

"What?"

"Nothing."

"No, what? You're laughing about something."

"Oh, I don't know. I just can't imagine what people think they're proving sometimes," she said.

"He wasn't trying to prove anything. He was just...showing what he can do."

"What's the difference?" she asked.

"He didn't have to do it," Junior said. "That's the difference. If he was trying to prove something, he would *have* to do it." Junior felt himself talking in a circle, one that even he wasn't following. Angie was laughing at him, and Junior couldn't even take offense. He leaned over and hugged her, then scooted along the seat and settled in close.

"You keep on making fun of me, I'll take that Christmas present back," Junior threatened. "And you won't get anything next year, either. No diamond saddle. Nothing."

She kissed his cheek. Junior looked up and realized they were pulling up to their drive.

"God *damn*. Were you driving like a bat out of hell, or did I sleep part of the way home?"

"Shut up and take me to bed," she said, turning off the car.

Junior carried her in, almost stumbling on the stairs. Her arms were in a lazy circle around his neck, and she kissed his jaw. Considering all the booze, and the late hour, Junior was amazed to find himself getting aroused. But they made their way up to the bedroom, and before they made some good, hard homestyle loving, Junior reached behind Angie's neck and gently removed her new ruby necklace.

CHAPTER THIRTEEN

JUNIOR'S HORSE WANTED TO RUN, and he had to keep a short rein on her. Gordon Cayley rode beside him, his horse also chomping at the bit. It had been a long, hot, hard day's ride, and although the two men were as anxious to get home as the horses were, running them would risk injury. A thick lather had already gathered around their bridles, their saddle blankets, and along the creases in their flanks.

The sky was an endless bank of soft blue clouds with solid blades of sunlight slashing down through narrow openings, casting silver curtains across their field of vision.

Junior and Gordon had spent the day moving Junior's cattle to their summer pasture, one of Junior's favorite days of the year. He loved going up into the Absaroka Mountains. The rest of the year, the mountains sat off in the distance—a steady reminder of the best things. But distant.

So a trip up into the mountains had an almost spiritual quality for Junior. This was especially true when they arrived at the summer pasture. Most of the trail up to this pasture was lined with trees, as thick as grass. But when they reached the pasture, the trees seemed to suddenly fall away. And there was a draw that ran at just the right angle down from the pasture that when Junior sat in a certain spot, along the south fence, he could look down and see their entire ranch spread out below him.

It was a view of his life and an opportunity most people didn't get, to look at things from a wondrous, breathtaking distance. It always left him overwhelmed.

Six months to the day since Tom's perfect party, Junior carried that feeling with him, anxious to get home and share it with his family. And he was anxious to be free of Gordon's company. Gordon had been Junior's hand for many years, and he couldn't ask for a steadier worker. But when Gordon opened his mouth, there was a ninety percent chance that he was going to say something negative, which left little common ground for discussion, especially on days like this one.

"What a beautiful damn day," Junior said. "Look how that sunlight is coming down through the clouds." He pointed.

"Yeah. Too bad it ain't gonna last," Gordon said.

Junior smiled to himself and held his thoughts to his vest while they unsaddled, combed, fed, and watered the horses. Gordon's comment reminded Junior of something his father used to say whenever anyone asked him, during a storm, whether the rain was ever going to stop. "It always does," he would say with a smile.

"Did you hear about Spider and his brother's wife?" Gordon asked.

"What about 'em?"

"I heard she's been staying there at his place for going on two weeks now."

Junior closed his eyes. He'd heard the rumor, as had everyone on Pine Creek, but he wasn't in the mood for gossip. "Well, I'm sure they have a lot to sort through with Tremaine gone."

Spider's only sibling Tremaine, who, like Hazel, had been a professor at the University of Montana, had died from long-term complications from a kick in the head he'd received as a young man. A horse caught him right in the temple, and Tremaine had been lucky to live. It affected his motor skills for the rest of his life: he walked and talked like a drunk, and had often been arrested for being drunk in public. Now he was dead of a brain aneurysm at the age of forty-six.

"From what I hear, there's not much sortin' going on." Gordon chuckled, slapping the back of one hand against the palm of the other. "A little comfort goes a long ways."

Junior shook his head. "Come on now, Gordon. These folks are just trying to get through a rough time. Cut 'em some slack."

"Ah, don't get your chaps all in a twist, Junior…I'm just kiddin' around."

Junior shook his head again.

"What about that piece of land they're putting up for sale?" Gordon asked. "That would be a nice chunk of grazing land."

"Yeah, it sure would…it's too damn far from us, though. I'm sure Tom and Kenwood will get into a bidding war over it, since it borders them both."

Gordon nodded. "The rich get richer."

"Something like that."

"So I'll start cutting hay in the south meadow tomorrow morning. Hope that goddamn swather is working better than it did last summer."

"It is. Those guys at Valley Motors got that little carburetor problem figured out."

"We'll see."

"'Night, Gordon. Good job today."

"All right."

Junior watched him walk away, his bow-legged cowboy stride taking him in a slow descent toward the house where Angie grew up.

•

When Junior got to the Kirby house, Bobby was sitting on the stoop outside the back door, whittling away at a chunk of wood.

"Hey, son. You ready for some dinner?"

"I s'pose." He did not look up.

"What's the matter? You miss school already?"

Bobby didn't smile. "I don't know. Nothing, I guess."

"Sure?"

"Yeah."

"All right. Well, what do you say we go have some supper?"

Bobby nodded but did not move.

"You come on in when you're ready, then."

He nodded again, and Junior rubbed his crew cut.

Inside, Junior washed off as much of the dust and smell as he could. Angie was just pulling a roast from the oven. Craig set the table.

"Good timing," she said.

"Yeah? About ready?"

"Just," she answered, setting the roast on top of the stove. She slipped her hands from the oven mitts. Junior kissed her cheek. She reached up and held his head, turning his ear to her mouth.

"Bobby wanted to go with you today," she whispered.

"Oh, no," Junior said. "Hell, I never even thought of it."

"You think he's old enough?"

"Oh, yeah. His butt would get a little sore, but he could handle it." Junior rubbed his scalp. "Damn, I wish I'd taken him. Today was a perfect day, too."

"Well, you ought to tell him then. Tell him you'll take him next time."

"Of course."

Junior was just about to go out and sit down with Bobby when Bobby came inside, folding his pocketknife carefully. He shoved it in his pocket.

"Mrs. Ruth is here," he muttered.

"Babe?" Angie turned from carving the roast.

"Yeah," Bobby said.

Junior looked at the clock, which read 6:30. "That's strange," he said. The local custom was to honor people's suppertime.

"She doesn't look too good," Bobby said.

A knock sounded at the front door, just as Junior was heading toward the back.

Junior reversed his direction. "I'll get it." When he opened the door, Junior was greeted by a frightening sight. "Good God."

Babe's face was bruised and bloody. She was crying, holding a towel to her cheek.

Junior swung the door open and wrapped an arm around her, leading her toward the den. "Angie!" he shouted.

"I'm in the middle of getting supper ready."

"I think you'd better come as soon as you can," Junior said, closing the door to the den, not waiting to hear Angie's reply. "What happened?"

Babe's cheek was purple. A cut had opened just above her left eyebrow, and both eyes were blackened. Blood oozed from one corner of her mouth. When she opened her mouth, her teeth were lined with bright blood. She wiped her mouth with the towel, then held it over her eyes. A thin wail escaped from her throat as she tried to hold back a full cry.

"What happened, Babe? Who did this?"

"I can't say," she answered, her voice strained.

Angie swept into the room, clearly annoyed until she saw Babe. Then she uttered a quiet moan and sat on the arm of the chair. She put her arm around Babe's shoulders.

"Oh, dear." Angie took Babe's head gently with both hands. She looked at her face, studying it as a doctor would.

Junior began to feel as though he was intruding. "I'll get a pan of hot water. And some bandages. Is that cut deep?"

Angie leaned toward Babe's face and looked it over. "No, I don't think it's deep enough to need stitches."

Junior left, retrieving a pan of water from the kitchen. He grabbed two washcloths and another towel.

"What's going on?" Bobby asked from the dining room table, where he and Craig had started their dinner.

"It's nothing," Junior said. "Babe's hurt. But she'll be okay. You boys just keep eating."

"Did she get beat up?" Bobby asked.

"I'm not sure," he lied.

"Sure looked like it."

"You boys just worry about filling your bellies there."

Junior returned to the den, where he heard Babe say, "It's not his fault..." She stopped when he entered, looking at him with a question of whether he'd heard. Junior set the pan down on the table in front of them, wet a washcloth, and handed it to Angie.

"Let me know if you need anything else," he told Angie. Then he returned to the table.

"Dad?" Craig said.

"Yeah, son."

"Who beat up Mrs. Ruth?"

Junior heaped a pile of potatoes onto his plate, then took a deep breath.

"Boys, there are some things that only adults should know. All right?"

Bobby and Craig both chewed thoughtfully.

"So you can't tell us who beat her up?" Craig asked.

"Boys!" Junior injected some threat in his voice, and it worked. But he almost felt obliged to give them more of an explanation. Instead he said, "So what do you boys think about coming along with Gordon and me when we go up to bring the cattle in this fall?"

Two faces turned. "Really?" Craig squealed.

"Yep. I think it's about time for you two to start pulling your weight around here. Free food, free board, free clothes…it's not right."

"Junior!" Angie called from the den.

"Yes?"

"Would you mind bringing Babe and me a plate of food?"

"Of course," he shouted. He went to the kitchen to get one more plate and a set of silverware. Then he dished up two helpings of meat and potatoes.

"You need help carrying?" Bobby asked.

Junior gave him a hard look, knowing he just wanted a peek. Bobby smiled and lowered his eyes to his plate. Junior took the food in without him.

"I'll bring you something to drink. You need anything else? Some more hot water?"

"I think we're fine," Angie answered, laying a hand on his forearm. It was a tender touch, and he understood the message behind it. He squeezed her hand.

"You feeling all right?" Junior asked Babe.

"I'll survive," she answered. "I guess I won't be in the running for rodeo queen this year, though." She laughed her airy, nervous laugh, and Angie and Junior joined in, although it was hard to find humor in the situation.

"Well, let me know if you two need anything," Junior said, and left them to their privacy.

•

"So what happened to Babe?" Junior asked.

Angie slipped her nightgown over her head and smoothed it down the front.

Junior persisted. "I heard her say 'it's not his fault.' What did she mean by that?"

Angie swiveled in her chair, facing him, her arm resting on the back. "I couldn't get her to talk about it. Something serious is going on, but she wouldn't tell me a thing."

"Well what did she mean by that?"

Angie turned back to the mirror, where she began brushing her hair. "I wish I knew."

"Do you think it was Lester?"

Angie nodded. "Yeah. I'm sure it was."

"Why?"

She turned again. "Well, who else would it be?"

"What about Tom?"

Angie shook her head. "I don't think so. You think he's going to send her home to her husband looking like that?"

Junior chewed his lip. "Well, passion isn't always logical, you know."

They sat quietly for a moment, Angie brushing, Junior's brow furrowed in thought. Then Angie turned again, very suddenly. "The one thing she did say…"

"Yeah?"

"I was kind of trying to steer the conversation over to Tom, to see whether Lester might have lost his cool over that…so I said something about seeing Tom's pickup at the school quite a few times lately…"

"Did you really?"

Angie nodded. "And she didn't even hesitate. She looked up at me and said, 'Tom and I are not having an affair.'"

"Jesus. She still thinks she can fool people into believing that."

"Well...maybe."

"What do you mean?"

Angie sighed. "I *did* believe her, Junior. I don't think they are."

"You're kidding."

But Angie shook her head. "There was just something about the way she said it."

CHAPTER FOURTEEN

ROGER LOGAN RAN UP THE front walk of the Logan house on Babcock Street in Bozeman, followed closely by his sister Julie. "First one in gets a cookie!" Roger shouted.

"Roger, that's not funny! You're way ahead of me already."

"Just kidding, Jules. Come on." He opened the door and reached for her hand, and she grasped his with a smile.

But the minute they entered the house, Roger felt something was off. There was a quiet in the house that felt sad and oppressive.

"Mom?" he called, his boyish voice echoing through the house.

"Back here!" But it wasn't his mother's voice that came from the bedroom. It was their father. "Come on back, kids."

When Roger got there, still holding Julie's hand, he found his mother curled on the bed, convulsing in sobs. Carl sat in the chair in the corner, his head down.

"What's wrong, Mom?" Roger asked. Julie started crying behind him, and she let go of his hand to climb up on the bed with their mother.

"Kids, we have some news," Carl said.

"*We* don't have any news. *You* have some news," Laurie said quietly, her voice defeated. She sat up in the bed and scooped Julie into her arms.

"Kids, how do you feel about living on a ranch?" Carl asked.

Roger stared at his parents, feeling as if there must be a world of information that was out of his reach. He was a turtle, pulling his head into his shell. When his father spoke again, his voice was muffled.

"We're going to move to a ranch about thirty miles from here. Isn't that exciting?"

"No!" Julie cried.

"Oh honey, don't worry. It will be okay," Laurie said, rocking her daughter.

"I don't *want* to move!" Julie said.

Roger had no memory of deciding to sit down, but he found himself folded up on the floor. He heard his voice as if it was echoing from miles away. "A ranch?"

"Yes!" Carl said enthusiastically, standing. "There's gonna be horses, and cows, and you kids can get a dog."

There was no response. Carl crouched down in front of Roger. "Come on, son. Stand up. It's going to be all right. You'll see."

"What about my friends, Dad?" Roger eased into his father's embrace, but part of him wanted to just stay where he was, tucked inside his sadness and bewilderment.

"You'll make new friends. Just think—you'll be meeting kids that know how to ride horses and rope calves, and fish and hunt. It will be like a whole new world."

"Why, though? I thought we liked it here."

"We do like it here," Carl said. "But sometimes people get a chance to go somewhere even better."

"Don't lie to your children," Laurie said.

The look of hurt on Carl's face was a thing Roger would remember for a long time.

CHAPTER FIFTEEN

TOWARD THE END OF AUGUST, Tom showed up at the Kirby house later than usual one night. Angie excused herself, telling Junior that she needed to do some sewing. So Tom and Junior retired to the den, where Junior fixed them each a drink.

"So you heard about this land Spider is selling?" Tom asked.

"Yeah. That could be a very good deal for you." Junior said.

Tom nodded, and a slow smile curled his lip. He picked something up from the table next to his chair and began fiddling with it, juggling it between his fingers, then shaking it in his palm.

"I want that fucking dirt, Junior," he said. "I want it bad. It would make my life a hell of a lot easier. I wouldn't have to use that rocky piece of shit pasture up against the mountain. Every summer ten of my heifers split their hooves in that pasture." Tom took a thoughtful sip of his drink. "And the grass is real thin up there."

"Well then, why don't you just buy it? Kenwood probably doesn't care one way or the other, does he? Hell, he's got more grass than he uses as it is." Even as Junior said this, he knew better.

Tom looked at him with a bemused grin. "You don't know Kenwood as well as I thought you did. He made Spider a healthy offer."

"Already?"

Tom nodded, then took a deep breath, shaking his head. "The son of a bitch always has to win, you know. I guess that's how he got to be as rich as he is."

"Yeah, well, I guess he has something in common with someone else I know then, huh?" Junior smiled.

Tom pointed at himself with a *who, me?* expression.

"So do you think Spider will tell you how much Kenwood offered?"

Tom smiled. "He'll tell me. I'll beat it out of him if I have to." He drained his drink. "You have another of these around here somewheres?"

Junior stood, taking his glass, and fixed another for each of them.

Tom seemed fairly satisfied with life that night, settling comfortably in Junior's big stuffed chair, with a big smile fixed on his face. It was the first time since their friendship started that Junior felt as if Tom might be open to talking about Babe. But he couldn't bring himself to ask.

Tom continued to roll whatever he was holding in his palm, and Junior tried to remember what was on the table next to that chair.

Tom sighed. "You know, my dad used to say...all the time, until I got sick to death of hearing it: 'We're married to this land. No other marriage counts when you live out here.'" Tom stared out the window, then turned to Junior. "I wonder what my mother thought about that." He laughed. "He used to say it right in front of her."

"I guess there's something to that, when you think about it."

"You think so?" Tom shot a quick look at Junior, then took a big drink, and turned his gaze back toward the window. "I sure as hell feel like I'm tied to this fucking dirt." He took a deep breath. "But I don't know if I'd call it a marriage. More like a damn prison sentence."

"Well, there are worse things we could be doing." Junior downed his drink in one gulp and began to feel it a little. He decided he might as well go with the feeling. It was a Saturday night, and he hadn't gotten even a little drunk for quite some time.

"Ready for another?" he asked Tom.

Tom finished what he had and held his glass out. Junior fixed two more, not bothering with water this time. Then he brought the bottle over. And the two men sat in a comfortable silence.

"I don't know, Junior. Sometimes I think there's nothing worse than what we got out here. We break our goddamn backs, all year, fighting the weather and animals smarter than we are, 'cause they sure as hell got us taking care of them." He shook his head. "And in the end, what do we got?" He held his glass out.

Junior filled it. He thought about what he had. And he thought that if he were to tell Tom what was most important, in the end, he would put his family at the top. But he didn't think he ought to say that to someone who had been alone for as long as Tom had.

"Hell, you got yourself a beautiful house out there…" Junior said, "…in a setting most people only see on postcards."

Tom waved this off and took another big swig from his tumbler. "What's that but a pile of wood."

"Self-respect?" Junior suggested. "What makes you feel better than a long week of working with livestock, watching them grow fat? How many people get that kind of satisfaction out of their jobs?" Junior leaned forward in his chair.

Tom gave him a sideways look, and chuckled.

"Jesus, Kirby, I didn't realize you were so sentimental. You sound like a goddamn greeting card."

Junior laughed and sank back into his chair. "Yeah, I s'pose I do." He raised his glass. "Here's to a corny life. Here's to a man who loves his corny damn life with his corny wife and kids."

Tom raised his glass and held it toward him. "You're a lucky man, Junior." He tipped his drink, downing it. "Let's get drunk. What do you say?"

Junior laughed and drained his glass, already well on his way. He poured straight bourbon, and they settled into inebriation, and Junior noticed again that everything felt different for some reason. It seemed that the two men had crossed some threshold of manners—that it was possible to forego the usual forbidden topics of conversation and talk about anything. And it seemed that they both knew this and needed some time to let the fact sink in. They were silent for that long minute, and neither of them touched their glasses to their lips.

Finally, Tom leaned forward in his chair. He rested the weight of his upper body on one arm, holding the drink in the opposite hand. His face was red.

"What do people say, Junior…about me?" His face had a look of gleeful anticipation.

Junior scratched his stomach and looked down at his drink, smiling. "Hell, Tom, you should have a pretty good idea. You're not exactly hard to read most of the time. You wear your heart right out there on your sleeve."

Tom laughed—a short, gruff laugh—and leaned back again.

"Yeah. I guess I can imagine. Stubborn, obnoxious, not very goddamn diplomatic."

Junior nodded. "They have a few negative things to say, too."

Tom laughed. "Thing is, Junior…I sometimes wonder whether I even fit in out here."

Junior frowned. "Seriously?"

Tom turned, and his expression told Junior that he was very surprised by the question. "Sure. You never feel that way?"

Junior didn't even have to think about it. "Not at all."

This admission seemed to hit Tom like a fist. He settled back in his chair, moody, staring at the empty bottom of his cup as if he might find there better words to explain what he meant. Junior watched him until he began to feel uncomfortable, and then he stood and fixed them another drink.

"So who have you been dating lately, anyway…anybody?" Junior asked as he handed Tom's glass back to him.

Tom sighed. "Well, you know that gal I brought to the Fourth of July picnic?"

Junior nodded. "Pretty."

Tom nodded. "Yeah…pretty. That's about it. We had conversations that lasted about four minutes."

Junior smiled. "So love 'em and leave 'em, huh?" He was beginning to feel the effects of the booze. "Another notch on the bedpost?"

Tom smiled and tilted his head. "You can't tell the quality of a bull by its bellow, Kirby."

"Ah, come on. You're not going to tell me you didn't sleep with her."

Tom shrugged and took another big gulp. "I'm just gonna drink from the bottle. Is that all right with you?"

"Long as I get my share."

Tom cradled the bottle, holding it by the neck. He tucked it between his legs, unscrewed the cap, and tipped the mouth to his lips. The liquid jumped and gurgled inside the clear glass, and Tom emptied a good three inches. He let out a long, satisfied sigh and let his head fall back against the chair.

"You probably even believe in God, don't you, Junior?"

Junior laughed, taken completely off guard. But Tom kept a steady eye on him, and Junior realized that he really wanted to know. He cleared his throat. "Hell, I don't know, Tom. I'm more inclined to worry about what I have to do to get through the week than what's going to happen when they dump dirt on my head."

"You don't think faith has anything to do with gettin' through the day?"

Junior shrugged.

"Quit dancing around the band. Give me a straight answer." Tom's brow lowered. He held the bottle toward Junior, who took it and filled his glass, spilling a little on his jeans.

"Yeah, I guess I believe in something. I don't know whether I'd call it God. But there's something I feel, when I'm up in the Absarokas especially...something that gives me a little hope that what I'm doing matters, that I'm not wasting my time."

Tom studied him for a long time. Junior didn't know whether he'd ever voiced this little bit of theology, and to have it followed by a discerning gaze, so silent, so steady, was unnerving. Junior noticed something in Tom's look that felt strange, even uncomfortable, to the point that he had to look away. Finally, Tom's eyes narrowed, then shifted across the room.

"Don't you ever wonder, Junior, whether you were supposed to do something completely different? Whether you missed a turn you were supposed to take? And now you're stuck on the wrong path. There's no chance of ever getting over to that other one again?"

Tom looked back at him. A desperation crept into his expression. It was as unsure as Junior had ever seen him. And Junior knew that what he really wanted to hear was that Junior was like him—that Junior had doubts too, about living out here, about doing the things they did, devoting themselves to the earth. About fitting in.

Junior couldn't give Tom the answer he wanted.

"Sorry." He shook his head. "I guess I'm one of these guys who was too stupid to think about anything else. I've always known this is where I belong."

"You son of a bitch. I had a feeling you'd say that." Tom reached over and snatched the bottle from his hand. "Ah, I'm drunk. Might as well go ahead and make myself sick."

He laughed and unscrewed the bottle, drinking a frightening amount in one swig. He finally lowered the bottle, replaced the cap, and slumped in his chair. He set the bottle on the table next to him, but not without some difficulty. Something caught his eye. He reached over and plucked the small object from the table again. His thick fingers held the object up to his face, where he studied it closely. It was one of Angie's earrings, a heart-shaped clip-on with fake jewels.

Tom held it as close to Junior as he could.

"You believe in this stuff, don't you?"

"What stuff?"

Tom shook the earring, the little heart dangling from his thick fingers with a tiny click, click, click. "This, Kirby. Love."

CHAPTER SIXTEEN

ONE COOL FALL DAY, JUNIOR had a rare evening home alone. He walked through a quiet house, hearing the echoes of his own footsteps. It felt strange and unnatural to know that a call through the house would go unanswered.

He stood in the doorway of each boy's bedroom, noticing the dramatic differences in personality. Bobby's room was fairly clean for an eleven-year-old boy. His books stood in neat rows along the shelves he and Junior had built the previous winter. Junior remembered how angry Bobby got when he left streaks in the finish. Bobby's bed was made, the pillow neatly tucked up inside the top quilt.

Craig's room was cluttered with every bit of clothing and every toy he owned. There were no square feet of empty space, and Junior wondered how he managed to find his way in and out of the room each morning. His blankets were half on, half off the bed, the pillow tilted against the wall, at an angle, as if flung there in a frenzied dream.

Angie had gone to town for her monthly shopping trip. She and the boys would stay with her parents for the night and come back tomorrow loaded with a month's worth of groceries.

Junior always felt a bit lost for the first hour or two of these evenings. Why it was harder to read a book alone than with family there, he wasn't sure. But it seemed that the quiet, which he loved, took on a whole different shade when there was little threat of interruption.

After wandering aimlessly through the house and making several fruitless attempts to sit down and read, Junior settled with a cup of coffee in the den, where he stared at the fire. He thought briefly of calling Angie at her folks' house, but knew she was probably in bed. So he sat, gazing at the dancing flame. Finally, their dog started barking, and when he heard a car pull into the drive, he figured Gordon or Sharon must be coming home from a visit. But part of him hoped that Tom might be making one of his unexpected calls.

When the car stopped at the Kirby house, and the engine shut down, Junior was sure it was Tom. So he got up to greet him, but instead, he heard delicate heels against the wooden porch floor.

A light knock followed, and Junior pulled the drapes to one side. It was Babe. He swung the door open. Babe's mascara had run down her cheeks in a thin black sheen, and she was desperately trying to wipe it off before he noticed. She was dressed up, in a beautiful wheat-colored cotton dress with rusty roses falling in a flowery cascade from neck to hem. She wore heels matching the roses, and although her hair was disheveled, it was done up, gathered at the crown of her head with a brass barrette. She brushed her cheeks with the back of one hand.

"Babe, what's the matter? Are you all right?" Junior put a hand to the small of her back and led her inside, closing the door and walking directly to the den, where Babe sank wearily into his big easy chair, which dwarfed her. She started crying again. Junior sat on the footstool a few feet from her.

"What happened?" he asked.

She shook her head, holding a palm over her nose and mouth, and as Junior waited for her to pull herself together, it occurred to him that this could be a long evening. So he simply sat, looking for a sign that Lester might have hit her again. But he didn't see any bruises.

"Do you want something?" he asked. "Something to drink?"

Babe shook her head again. Junior stood up. "Let me get a handkerchief. I'll be right back." He turned at the door. "Sure you don't want something to drink?"

Babe lowered her hand and swallowed, then took a deep breath. "All right."

"What would you like?"

Babe made the effort to rest her elbow on her knee, but her elbow slipped off, and she nearly toppled forward. Junior lunged, ready to catch her, but she regained her balance. She started laughing, and her eyes drooped. Her head fell to one side. Junior had smelled alcohol, but it wasn't until then that he realized she was plastered.

"Maybe I should make some coffee," he suggested.

"No." She shook her head, again disturbing her balance. "Whiskey."

He hesitated, but decided to get what she wanted rather than upset her more. Meanwhile, her laughter shifted back to tears in the time it took him to turn and leave the room.

Junior returned with Babe's drink and found her lying back in the chair, sprawled like a child who's fallen asleep in the car. Much of her hair had worked loose from the barrette. It lay across her face, a light red wave flowing down to her shoulder. Her eyes were wide open but completely vacant.

Junior set the drink on the table next to her chair and repositioned himself on the footstool.

"He doesn't want me," Babe said, her voice flat.

"Who?"

Babe stared straight ahead for a moment, seemingly forgetting what she'd just said. Then she suddenly looked at him, her eyes showing a spark. "Where's Angie?"

"In Bozeman, with the boys. They went shopping."

"Be home tonight?"

Junior shook his head.

Babe lifted her drink and cradled it unsteadily in both hands, moving her head toward the glass. She drank and set the glass back down, holding it for a second, studying it, as if making certain that it didn't move.

"Babe?"

"Hm?"

"Who doesn't want you? Who were you talking about?"

Her head flopped to one side. She coughed a little, holding a hand to her chest. "Tom," she answered, confirming the obvious. "Tom doesn't want me."

"What do you mean?"

She sighed, a heavy expulsion from deep down. "I've tried everything."

Junior held his tongue, knowing that an explanation was something he shouldn't hear.

Babe leaned her head back, resting it against the chair. She closed her eyes. Junior was afraid she would fall asleep.

"Were you at Tom's tonight?"

She didn't respond for a time, and Junior wondered whether she was asleep. The thought of her drifting off concerned him. He couldn't let her stay, or they'd have the whole community talking. And driving her home seemed just as risky, as he had no idea how Lester would respond.

"I love him, you know," she murmured.

Junior shook his head. "No, I didn't." It made him sad to hear this, because she stated it so truly, so sincerely.

"I've never known anyone like him." Babe's eyes opened, but only halfway. She stared off into space, her mind obviously miles down the road from where she sat.

"Tom is definitely one of a kind," Junior agreed. "I've never known anyone like him either."

Her gaze remained distant, dreamy, sappy. The hint of a smile tickled her lips. "Nobody knows him like I do."

Junior chewed his lip, thinking of all the other women Tom had been involved with through the years. He wondered whether they all felt this way, convincing themselves that they were the only one who had seen the real Tom Butcher.

"I know things about Tom Butcher that would curl your hair," Babe continued, and then she started laughing, giggling uncontrollably, as if she had just been reminded of a particular memory. She laughed until her eyes watered, still looking off, still imagining herself in his world, away from where she was now. She sighed, then let loose one last sigh. She closed her eyes again, letting her head pivot to one side. "He won't touch me, though. He won't come anywhere near me."

Junior turned his head, knowing this was just the kind of information he should not hear. But it also tickled months' worth of curiosity. Part of him wanted more than anything to understand the complicated mystery of these two.

"What about Lester?" he asked.

She scoffed, the sound of disgust exploding from her lips. "Lester is hopeless—more hopeless than I am."

"Babe, don't..."

She two-handed her drink again, tipping it to her lips. "He's more hopeless than I am," she repeated. "At least I remember what I used to dream about." She fell back against the chair. "Remember, Junior? Remember when I used to tell you about my dreams?"

"Of course I do. You were going to be a painter. Or a seamstress."

She smiled at him, and the smile slowly transformed into something suggestive. Junior realized she was remembering other things, and he had to look away. But she sighed again.

"Tom told me never to come back."

"Tonight?"

She nodded. "He threw me out."

"Well, maybe that's best," he suggested. "If he doesn't love you..."

She lifted her head and frowned at him, and Junior realized he'd said the wrong thing.

"You make it sound like fixing a fence." She shook her head. "Just move on to the next thing...no complications." She waved a hand through the air.

Babe closed her eyes again, a sad smile slowly curling her lips. Junior studied her delicate features, and it occurred to him that whether she fell asleep or not, she was too drunk to drive. Either way, he was going to have to give her a ride home.

Her breathing got heavy, with her chest rising higher each time she inhaled. Just about the time he was convinced she was asleep, her eyes popped open, and she pulled herself up to her elbows. A tear leaked from one eye, and it dribbled down her cheek.

"I don't know what to do, Junior. I've never been so miserable." She leaned forward, her elbows resting on her knees. Her head dropped.

Junior leaned toward her, laying a hand on her shoulder. "I'm sorry that things have gone so badly for you."

This comment opened the floodgates. She began to sob. Her shoulders heaved in a rhythm in his hands. Finally, she stood up and threw herself against him, wrapping her arms around his waist. Her head fell against his chest. Junior's hands rested awkwardly on her shoulders.

She cried hard for a good long minute. And then the crying stopped, and she took several deep breaths. Her grip tightened, and she pressed closer against him. One hand began to move up and down his back, caressing his spine. Her fingers slipped just inside the waistband of his jeans.

"You remember high school, don't you, Junior?"

"No, Babe," he said, trying a joke to dissuade her.

"You don't?"

"Of course I remember. But that was a long time ago. There was no reason to hold back then. You need to stop now."

"But we were so good at it, Junior. Don't you ever think about that? Don't you wonder sometimes if it could still be like that?"

Her hand ran back and forth, still inside his waistband. She began tugging at his shirttail, trying to pull it out of his jeans.

"Not for a long time, Babe. Not for a good long while. There's no use thinking about things like that now." Junior tried to nudge her away, but it only made her hold on tighter.

Babe started moving up and down, gyrating, slowly, her pelvic bone pressed hard against him, against his inner thigh. She swayed, then rotated, pushing into his crotch. Junior would have had to have been made of wood to not be affected by this, and the stirring that started between his legs swirled right up to his head. He closed his eyes for just a second, trying to clear his thoughts. This was as long as it took for Babe to pull his head forward and lock her lips against his. Her moist tongue slipped between his lips, and his teeth, and began tangling with his own tongue.

Junior grasped Babe's shoulders and gently pushed her away. He had to take a deep breath.

"What's the matter?" Babe tried to pull his head down to her mouth again.

"Babe, you know I love Angie too much to do anything like this. Come on now."

"This hasn't got anything to do with Angie. Being married doesn't mean anything when the passion kicks in. Haven't you heard—this is the age of free love. You've heard about free love, haven't you?"

She tried to spur him on by moving her hand from his back to his crotch. Junior grabbed her wrist. He was embarrassed by what she was saying, not so much because of the suggestive nature as by the fact that she could possibly believe he would give in.

Babe's eyes got misty, looking up at him.

"Junior, don't you understand? I'm still in love with you. I've thought about you this way you ever since those days we parked along the creek."

"Babe, come on. Now you're talking nonsense. You were never in love with me any more than you were with…with Lyndon Johnson."

"Junior, don't say that. You don't know…"

Junior felt his face redden. "Yes, I do know. I do, and so do you, Babe. We even talked about how silly it was then, how we weren't right for each other. You wanted to be a painter. You didn't want to be a ranch wife. Let's sit down. Come on." Junior led her to the chair, and her steps were very unsteady.

"How can you do this to me, Junior—tonight of all nights? Tom doesn't want me, you don't want me, my husband couldn't care less."

Her self-pity started to grate on Junior now. "Maybe you should go home and get a good night's sleep, Babe. You've had a rough night."

"I have to pee," she said suddenly.

Junior sighed. "All right. Let me take you upstairs." He bent down to pick her up, but she swatted his hands away.

"I don't need your help, dammit." She struggled to her feet. "Let me do it myself." She wobbled from the room, and Junior sank into his chair, covering both eyes with his hand.

•

Junior sat thinking about this kiss, and about how embarrassing it would be for Babe once she sobered up, and how awful the memory was going to feel for both of them.

And he knew that he could conjure up all of his persuasive powers to comfort himself with the thought that nothing happened, and that the "nothing" that happened wasn't his fault. But he knew this wouldn't work. Because something *did* happen, and he had no idea how he'd let it go that far, but it felt as if he had temporarily broken somewhere inside, as if a small part of what had always been solid had cracked.

Above him, Junior heard the tapping of heels against the wooden floor. Then they were muffled, and he assumed that Babe had taken off her shoes, which seemed smart in her condition.

But then there was another sound—a knock at the door. Junior's heart jumped. Tom? Lester? He wished Angie was there.

With Babe's car sitting out front, there was no other choice but to answer the door. Junior rose and pulled the drapes to one side. The round face of Sharon Cayley gazed at the doorknob, oblivious to his presence two feet away. He opened the door.

"Evening, Sharon. How you doin'?"

"All right, Junior. All right. Is Angie still awake?"

Junior gave a brief thought to lying, saying that Angie was asleep. But he had the presence of mind to think ahead, to how this lie would compound if the truth came out. And of course it would.

"Actually, she's in town, doing the month's shopping. You want me to give her a message?"

"Coming back tonight?" Sharon raised a brow.

"No. She's staying at her folks' house. Anything I can help you with?"

Sharon craned her neck, looking out behind her into the dark, then trying in her less than subtle way to see behind Junior, inside the house.

"I really need to talk to her. It's about…uh, the school fair." She nodded, clearly making this up as she went along. "Isn't that Babe's car?" Sharon indicated with her head.

Junior cleared his throat. "Yeah, as a matter of fact. She's here." He couldn't even come up with a story to explain Babe's presence, so he left it at that, which prompted a long, uncomfortable pause. Sharon looked up at him, and her face suddenly registered a look of surprise, then a slight smile, as if she had noticed something. Junior did his best to mask his guilt, smiling as benignly as possible.

"Well, I'll tell her you need to talk to her," Junior finally said.

"Babe?"

"No. Angie."

Sharon's eyes rolled up in thought. "Right. Okay. Thanks. 'Night, Junior."

"Goodnight."

Sharon crept away, and Junior said a silent prayer of thanks that Babe had not come down while she was there. He returned to the den. When Babe returned, he noticed she was still wearing her shoes. She seemed to have steadied herself.

"I've got to take you home, Babe. It's getting late."

"You don't either have to take me home. I will take myself home. I am perfectly capable of taking myself home."

"Absolutely not. I'm not going to argue with you, Babe. If you got hurt, I'd feel guilty for the rest of my life. Now come on. Let's go."

"Why would I get hurt? What are you talking about?"

Junior ignored her and took her by the arm, not giving her a chance to sit down. He led her squirming and arguing to his pickup. He drove her home and dropped her out front, with no desire to explain anything to Lester.

He went home and moved Babe's car into the barn, just to prevent any more unnecessary tongue-wagging. Then he turned in, relieved that this night was over and hoping that Sharon Cayley's passion for gossip wouldn't put him deep in the doghouse.

•

"Man alive, do you boys look like a million bucks!"

Junior reached out and straightened Craig's bow tie, then tried in vain to smooth down Bobby's cowlick. The boys stood with their heads down, awkward in their black dress pants, oxford shoes, and starched white shirts.

"The girls are going to be begging you boys to dance."

"Da-ad." Bobby said.

"What, you don't want to dance?"

They both laughed, tucking their hands behind their backs.

It was the night of the big back to school dance in Livingston, and the Kirbys were about ready to put in their annual appearance. Junior went to the foot of the stairs and shouted up to Angie. "You about ready, honey?"

"I'll be right down."

He went back to the living room, where Craig had already taken off his bow tie and was studying the clips, flipping them open and closed, open and closed.

"Son, leave your tie on, will you? You can figure out how it works the other three hundred sixty-four days of the year." He struggled to clip the tie back onto his tiny boy collar.

"You should have seen Roger whack him with that bat!" Craig said. "It was like Scooter's shoulder was a baseball! He whacked him good!"

"Craig, that's enough," Junior said.

"What? I'm just saying what happened, is all."

"I know. But it's not a good thing. It's not good when people get violent."

Craig frowned. "But it was so cool!"

Junior sighed, feeling the lost battle of parenthood.

The sharp click of high heels sounded from the stairs. When Angie entered the room, Junior was still wrestling with Craig's tie.

"We're all set?"

Angie didn't answer, and after a strangely silent moment, he turned. Her face was white, her mouth slack. She held her hand to the collar of her dress.

"What is it?" Junior asked. "What's wrong?"

"Junior," she said, breathless.

He stood and went to her. "What? What's wrong?"

Tears spilled from Angie's eyes. "My necklace, Junior…"

"Your necklace?"

"My ruby necklace. It's gone."

•

Three months later, Tom Butcher was dead. When Junior pieced it all together later, he found that Daryl Blinder and Rodney Trass interviewed half of the people along Pine Creek the night after the murder and the other half the next day. The Kirbys were the last ones they visited that first night, right after the Logans, and Angie said later that you could almost hear the apology in the way they mounted the stairs, as if they were trying to walk without weight.

But from the minute they walked in the door, everything about them was heavy. Blinder's shoulders sagged, and the holster on his belt hung so low that it looked as if it might pull him to the floor. The skin beneath his eyes looked shaded by pencil lead.

"How you doin', Junior?" Blinder shook his hand, and Trass followed suit.

"It's just such a shock…we're so shocked."

Blinder nodded, and the skin beneath his eyes seemed to sink further with each roll of his head. "I'm sorry to even bother you on a night like this," he said. "I understand you were Tom's best friend."

Junior couldn't even answer for a moment. "Who told you that?" he finally asked, and regretted that it came out like a denial.

Blinder raised his brow. "Well…everyone, actually."

"You were, Junior," Angie said gently.

Junior heard those words a long time after the police had gone and the night went quiet. He wondered if that had been true for Tom. He wondered just as much whether it was true for him. And then he wondered if this was what it meant to lose a best friend, to lie awake listening to the silence outside, waiting for the sound of a knock.

BOOK THREE
A BIG LIVING ROOM

CHAPTER SEVENTEEN

THE MEN HAD GATHERED IN Peter Kenwood's den. Cigar smoke drifted in great clouds. Kenwood brought out his crystal brandy snifters, which none of the men had ever seen him use in all the time they'd known him. Carl felt out of place sitting in this room, surrounded by opulence.

It was the quietest gathering of men. They sat sipping the most amazing liquor most of them had ever tasted and staring into their glasses. Most of them would never look at brandy the same again.

The women were in the living room, and there was not much talk coming from there either. Only upstairs, where the children played, did noise echo through the Kenwood house. The service for Tom Butcher had been equally somber. A pastor from Bozeman came and delivered what could only be described as an uninformed eulogy for a man all of them knew was much more interesting. Even Carl could see that this man knew nothing about him.

But now…when they were together, Carl could feel that the loss was compounded by the knowledge that the person responsible could be sitting among them, and this made Carl feel even more separate. Harlan Glider was off in the corner, intently studying his cigar. Lester and Arnie huddled in another corner but said nothing to each other. Many of the folks in the room had known each other their whole lives, men who shared the same special relationship with the land that Tom did.

"So tragic, isn't it?" Peter said, shaking his head.

Junior nodded. "The kind of thing that just doesn't make sense."

Peter pinched his lips and nodded gravely.

Wheels on gravel sounded outside.

Peter perked up a bit as he heard a knock on the door, then murmurs from the front room.

Angie poked her head in from the front hallway. "Someone's here to see Lester," she said.

The men all looked at Lester, who looked just as confused as they were. Who would be looking for him today? And how could they not know this was the wrong time?

Lester rose wordlessly and walked toward the front door. The rest remained quiet, but Lester's departure at least gave them something new to wonder about. He was gone for only a few minutes.

Carl was facing the hallway, so he was the first to see Lester when he returned. Lester stumbled back into the room and had to prop himself up against the wall. He put a hand to his throat. Carl jumped to his feet and rushed to Lester, bracing him by his elbow.

"Are you okay?"

Lester's skin was the color of a flour sack. He raised his eyes, but they were unfocused.

"What happened?" Peter asked.

Lester pushed Carl away and walked across the room, settling back into his chair.

"Who was it?" Junior asked.

Lester sat staring straight ahead for a long minute. "It was some lawyer," he finally muttered.

"Lawyer?" Peter sat down next to Lester.

"Yeah." Lester nodded slowly, turning to Peter. "He came to tell me that Tom left me his ranch."

"He did what?" Peter's voice got very quiet.

Lester just looked at him.

Peter studied the faces of the men around him, one by one, as if somebody might be able to give him an explanation. "Well, I'll be damned."

They all sat quiet for a long time. They didn't look at each other. There was nothing about this information that made any sense.

It was Peter Kenwood who finally spoke. "So what are you going to do?"

Lester's eyes got wide, as if it hadn't occurred to him that there was anything that needed to be done. "What do you mean?"

"Does this mean I'm going to lose you?" Peter said.

Lester stood as if somebody had just told him he was going to die. He started stalking around the chair, walking in a tight circle. And he never did answer the question.

CHAPTER EIGHTEEN

PEOPLE COME AND GO. THIS is not news. But these comings and goings have a much bigger impact on small communities. With so few around, the effect of a new arrival or of an old friend's departure is bound to be greater.

The Paradise Valley community had always taken a sort of quiet pride in the fact that, as far back as anyone could remember, there had never been a violent crime in their little cove, as if they all had something to do with preventing such a thing. In a sense, Tom's death meant more than the loss of the most dynamic member of the region. It was a jagged scar across the collective cheek of their identity.

The next several weeks were a time of unprecedented aimlessness. Because Tom had no relatives, they had nowhere to deliver food. There was no place they could stop to say how sorry they were, to shake their heads sadly. People walked with their eyes to the ground and found meaning in phrases they had not understood before—phrases like "There are no words" and "Things like this don't happen here." No one stopped in to visit with anyone else. They worked. They ate. They slept. And when they had the energy, they wondered.

The authorities had little to go on. Everyone in the community gave the same alibi that they would have given every other day of every other year. Everyone was at the party, and then everyone was home, and their family could vouch for them. Which left only two possibilities—either someone from the outside had come in and killed Tom, or someone was lying. And since there were no reports of any strangers in the area that night, the latter seemed the strongest possibility.

After a while, the thought that they had a murderer living among them became a lot less frightening than the idea that they were living with someone who was capable of keeping such an astonishing secret to themselves without cracking, without showing any sign at all that they weren't like the rest. The worst part was that no one could discuss the situation with anyone else, because there was no one along Pine Creek who hadn't had a run-in of some kind with Tom Butcher. It was impossible to know whether the ear they chose to confide in might belong to the murderer.

•

"Dad, I need help."

Junior looked over to see Craig holding his saddle halfway up the side of Pirate, his cow pony. The saddle was about to topple over on top of him. One stirrup had fallen across Craig's face, covering his eyes, and his knees looked as if they would buckle any second. Junior rushed over and got a grip on the saddle, and together they hoisted it up onto Pirate's back.

Junior adjusted the saddle, centering it, and shifted the blanket underneath. Craig scrambled around Pirate, working to get the strap loose and hand it to Junior under Pirate's belly. Junior crouched and grabbed the strap, then looped it through the metal ring, forming a knot until it was cinched tight and ready to go.

Junior checked Bobby, who insisted on saddling his own horse. But Junior tested the cinch anyway, to make sure it was tight enough. He didn't want to find Bobby dragging under Redhead's belly halfway up the mountain, so he ignored the dirty look Bobby shot him.

"You guys ready?" Junior yelled over to Gordon. Once it was decided that Bobby and Craig would go on this trip, Junior had to invite Gordon's kids along, too. So while Junior helped his boys, Gordon was doing the same with Scooter and Susan.

"Just about there," Gordon said. "Scooter's horse keeps blowin' himself up."

Junior heard a dull thud—Gordon's boot against the horse's ribs. Junior cringed. He had never liked the way Gordon treated the horses.

"Empty out them lungs, you stubborn old mule," Gordon muttered.

The horse snorted, and the creak of leather sounded as Gordon tugged at the cinch, pulling it as snug as the horse would allow.

"That should do it," Gordon declared. "Let me know if you feel it gettin' loose."

Scooter nodded.

"So we're off?" Junior asked.

"Think so," Gordon replied.

"You kids ready?" Junior shouted over his shoulder.

A chorus of affirmatives sounded. They mounted and headed off toward the Absarokas. The day was a picture of Montana in autumn. In the west, along the horizon, a half-dozen clouds floated pure white and fluffy, unthreatening. The air was saturated with the smells of the fruits of the harvest—sweet grass and alfalfa. More than anything, the aroma of good, clean air bathed them as they left the ranch grounds and eased into the open spaces. The kids started to take off, giving their horses a heel to the flanks.

"Hey!" Junior shouted. "Don't run those horses. We've got a full day ahead of us."

The kids groaned but pulled up to a trot. But the horses had been given a taste of speed, and they fought the reins, jerking their heads, restless to take advantage of the expanse in front of them.

Scooter's horse seemed particularly anxious to run, dancing and trotting with his knees high. The horse tossed its head and snorted. Scooter looked equally impatient, looking over at Junior several times, and after a half hour of fighting him, Scooter apparently decided that he couldn't deny the horse any longer. His legs whipped straight out from the horse's sides, then slammed against the flanks, once, twice, and three times. The horse lowered its head and took off, kicking up clouds of dust and tufts of grass, reaching a full gallop in a matter of strides.

Junior spurred his own horse, racing after them.

Scooter's horse was young and fresh. Junior was riding Eliza, his best cattle pony, who was better at cutting cattle than at racing. So despite Junior's prompting, it took a while before he could gain any ground on Scooter. Junior screamed at him, but Scooter ignored him and continued to give the horse's ribs a beating.

The wind whipped Junior's face as he buried his heels in her flank. Eliza snorted, and the moisture ran from her nose. Scooter's hat flew off, fluttering past Junior.

Junior was ten yards from Scooter when Scooter suddenly straightened up in the saddle and tugged the reins to his chest. His horse let out an angry whinny, its head jerking back. Junior went flying past, and it took him a second to react. He pulled Eliza up and whirled around.

"Goddamn it, Scooter, what do you think you're doing?"

Scooter sat staring at him with no sign at all of emotion. He breathed hard with his lips clenched, all the air racing through flared nostrils.

"I told you not to run that horse, and I had a good reason for it." Junior stared him down, looking for a response of some kind—any kind. But there was nothing. Scooter peered at him with a steely glare, a look that held meanings Junior couldn't fathom. Junior had never met such eyes. "We're going to be on the trail all day," he continued. "If you can't treat that horse with respect, you better turn around right now and go on home."

Scooter did not avert his gaze at all, nor did his expression change. His horse was still jumpy, lifting and stomping its hooves. But Scooter sat unmoving and unmoved.

"You want to keep on?"

Scooter nodded.

"Are you going to do as I say and not run that horse?"

"It ain't your horse."

"You do what Mr. Kirby says now, boy." Gordon rode up. He handed Scooter his hat. "Mr. Kirby's in charge. It don't matter whose horse it is."

"All right." Scooter nodded, but the agreement felt hollow.

The other kids trotted up, tentative. Junior's anger was still fresh enough that he felt the need to make a point. He turned to face Bobby, Craig, and Susan.

"If I have any more trouble with you kids and these horses, all four of you are going back, you hear?"

Bobby and Craig dropped their eyes and nodded. Susan turned away.

"All right. Now let's get going, so we're not making our way down in the middle of the night." Junior jerked Eliza toward the mountains. The picture of Scooter's face still had him burning up inside, and as he rode along, Junior began to feel badly about yelling at the other kids. But he was too angry to talk to anyone.

The morning passed, and the sun warmed their backs, and eventually the day was just too beautiful for Junior to keep that kind of ugliness inside. Once they'd had their lunch and were moving through the thick trees up the mountain trail, they spread out, with the kids falling behind. Junior and Gordon rode side by side, with just enough room between them to keep from running each other into the thick underbrush. The smells of soil and pine were strong, magnified on such a clear, warm day, and Junior breathed deep, feeling the good life sink into his lungs.

"Whaddaya think 'bout all this stuff with Tom?" Gordon asked, talking from one side of his mouth.

Junior sighed. He had hoped that this subject wouldn't come up. "I don't know what to think, Gordon. It's just a tragedy."

Gordon nodded, but Junior could smell the whiff of gossip. "Who do you think done it?"

"Hell, I don't know. It could have been any number of people."

"I think that son of a bitch Kenwood had him knocked off," Gordon muttered.

"Yeah?" Junior turned his head away from Gordon, pretending to search the trees for something.

"Think about it. The man hated him. Plus Kenwood is greedy as hell. Can you believe he's suing over Tom's will? He can't even stand to have Lester inherit Tom's place!"

Junior didn't say anything, but he had to admit he was as baffled as anyone as to why Kenwood would find it necessary to contest the will. Lester must have been much more important to him than any of them realized.

Gordon went on. "And Tom was always gettin' up in Kenwood's business—crashing that party the other night and foolin' around with his best hand's wife. The man was askin' for it."

Junior's inclination to keep his thoughts to himself was overcome by a flood of anger. "Gordon, now you're talking about stuff you don't know a damn thing about."

"Oh?"

"Yes."

"And how would you know that? You got the inside track on something the rest of us should know about?"

Junior shook his head, turning away again. "It's not worth talking about," he said.

"I don't see how you can say that when there's a man dead. *Dead*, for Christ's sake."

Junior wasn't sure what to make of this discussion. Junior and Gordon rarely discussed anything outside of work, and when they did, they rarely argued. He had never challenged Junior this way.

Behind them, the kids were laughing and shouting after each other. It sounded as if they were playing some kind of word game, and Junior was glad the morning's incident hadn't spoiled their day.

"All I'm going to say is that you're wrong about Tom and Babe," Junior said to Gordon.

Gordon started chuckling, and it made Junior want to knock his head off.

The kids' voices got quiet behind them. Junior figured they had drifted back a little further. But all of a sudden, the roar of a gunshot ripped through the trees. Junior jumped and let out a yell; the sound was deafening in the confined space of the trail.

"What the hell?" Gordon said.

"Scooter!" Susan yelled from behind.

Junior jumped off Eliza and ran back toward the kids, picturing the worst things a parent can imagine. A narrow, low-hanging branch caught his face, and his cheek stung just below his eye. He had to slow down for a second as his eyes teared up. He couldn't see, but he felt the rush of a huge presence race by from behind, barely brushing him.

The kids were shouting. Junior rounded a curve just in time to see Gordon punch Scooter in the head, harder than he'd ever seen a man hit another man, much less a child. The gun, a pistol bigger than Scooter's head, fell to the ground. Junior couldn't believe Scooter kept his seat in the saddle.

Without hesitation, Scooter jerked his horse around and took off down the trail, toward home. Junior looked at the other kids, and a chill swept through him when he saw Susan's face. Bobby and Craig both sat wide-eyed, about to cry. But Susan had the same expression that Scooter had shown earlier. No sign of fear, or sadness, or anything. The look injected a cold sliver into Junior's heart. He had to turn away.

A quiet, restrained cry began, and he recognized Craig's voice.

Gordon jumped down from his horse, picked up the gun, then remounted. "Damn kid," he muttered. "I told him not to bring this thing."

Gordon rode past them, starting back up the trail, shoving the gun into his saddle bag. Susan followed, her neck rigid, eyes straight ahead. Junior found himself standing alone, unable to make a decision about what to do next.

"You comin'?" Gordon's voice echoed from up ahead.

Junior looked up at his boys, whose faces were directed toward him, waiting.

"Yeah, we're coming." Then, to the boys. "You all right?"

They both nodded, although Craig was wiping his eyes.

Junior shook his head, unable to think of a single intelligent thing to say. He walked up the trail to Eliza. His muscles felt weary as he pulled himself back up into the saddle. They started toward the top of the mountain, plodding slowly along.

But in that moment, Junior's view of a world had taken a sudden twist. He had never seen any sign that Gordon practiced this kind of brutality toward his kids. Nor had he ever seen anyone hit a child with such a frightening combination of force and indifference. He couldn't remember seeing anyone hit a child at all, aside from the standard swat on the butt. Junior wondered whether he should fire Gordon on the spot. He felt weak, nauseous. The thought of even talking to him dried his gut like a raisin. He lowered his head and stared at his hands to keep from losing his composure.

The punch was all Junior could think about for the rest of the day.

Fortunately, the cattle were cooperative. His mind drifted separate from his body, somewhere between the euphoria he usually experienced on the trip up this trail and the horror of the moment Gordon's fist blasted Scooter's cheek.

Junior relied on Eliza's instincts as a cow pony and Gordon's years of experience to get the herd down the mountain. By the end of the ride, near dusk, when they unsaddled the horses and prepared to go inside for a well-earned meal and a hot bath, Junior had made a decision.

"You kids go on inside," he said, signaling to the boys. "Susan, tell your mom that your dad will be in shortly."

The boys left, but Susan hesitated until Gordon jerked his head toward their house. She strode homeward, her back as stiff and inflexible as her face had been. Gordon stood under a bright orange sky, leaning against a rail. The fresh air had cooled, but the smell of fall grass was still strong.

Junior cleared his throat. "Gordon, I can't let what happened up there pass without saying something."

Gordon eyed him, and his lips tightened, as if the anger of that moment had returned. "Yeah, well, you can be sure I'll be having a talk with the boy. I'll make damn sure it don't happen again."

Junior looked down at his boots and cleared his throat. "Actually, I'm not talking about the gun."

Junior lifted his eyes, and Gordon fixed a steady gaze on him, then turned his head, looking away. "You don't think I done right?"

"No," Junior answered. "I don't."

"Well, I guess you got a right to your opinion. But it really ain't none of your business, is it?" He crossed his arms.

"Maybe not. I don't know." Junior breathed deep. "I really don't know. But I'll tell you, if I ever see anything like that again, I'm going to ask you to leave."

"You are?"

Junior nodded. "I don't want to. You're the best hand I ever had."

Gordon turned to him, and for the third time that day, Junior was met with those eyes—cold as a winter stream, and steady. Gordon's look unnerved him.

"Just bear it in mind," Junior said. And then he couldn't look at Gordon anymore, knowing that his expression would not change. He turned to walk away, hoping like hell that Gordon wouldn't put up any more of an argument.

"You might want to think twice about this," Gordon said.

Junior turned. "What did you say?"

Gordon kicked the ground casually, as if he was looking for an arrowhead. "You might want to think twice…seeing as how you probably don't want your missus to know some things."

"Angie?" Junior frowned, taking two steps toward Gordon. "What things? What the hell are you talking about?"

"I'm talking about a certain night. A night when you were home alone, but not really."

Junior tilted his head, and in the next instant he understood. And he laughed. He laughed, but inside he wasn't laughing one bit. Inside, he knew the son of a bitch had him cornered.

"I'm not so sure Angie would think it's funny," Gordon said. "What with the lipstick and all."

Junior shook his head and allowed his smile to fade, fixing a glare on Gordon. "Gordon, I've never had a problem in the world with you, but if this comes up again, I'm telling you, you're on your ear."

One side of Gordon's mouth rose. "I don't think you've got that kind of balls."

"Try me," Junior said.

Gordon turned and walked away, and Junior had a sick feeling in his gut, a feeling that it was only a matter of time before Gordon took up that challenge.

CHAPTER NINETEEN

ROGER PUSHED HIS WAY THROUGH the thick brush, holding his dad's fishing pole close to his body to keep from getting the line tangled in the branches. It was a Saturday afternoon, and Roger had talked his parents into letting him out of the house for a couple of hours. So far, he had caught two decent rainbow trout. But he had spotted a big one upstream, and he guessed it had made its way down to a slow pool on the opposite side of Pine Creek.

The creek was narrow enough that he didn't need to cast the hook so much as just toss it in the water. He did this with an easy underhand motion, and the heavy worm plopped into the clear stream.

"Hey, kid."

Roger tumbled forward, falling into the water, which was only up to his knees. He scrambled to his feet and twirled around, somehow managing to keep his grip on the fishing pole. When the water cleared from his eyes, he saw Arnie Janko standing just on the other side of the thick brush.

"Sorry. Didn't mean to scare you."

"What are you doing here?"

Arnie rubbed his face. "Oh, your dad asked me to take a look at some of the cattle in that pasture there." Arnie pointed. "I just happened to see you over here, so I thought I'd check see what you're up to. I should have warned you a little better."

Roger had retained his crouch, his muscles taut. But he stood up a little straighter now, keeping on guard. "On a Saturday?"

"What do you mean?"

"He asked you to work on a Saturday?"

Arnie laughed, scratching the back of his neck. "Damn, kid. You better learn right now that working on a ranch, you don't get no weekends. No sirree. Six, seven days a week."

Roger studied this man, and his strange mannerisms, as he had done every man since his trek into the mountains. He looked for something familiar, any sign that this was the man who'd rushed at him that night. So far, nothing had registered with any of them. All he could remember was the hands and the grimy, dirt-blackened face.

"You cold?" Arnie asked.

"Not too bad." Roger waded slowly up onto the bank.

"I got a jacket here if you want to wrap up in it." Arnie slid one arm from his jacket.

"No, that's all right. I'm fine."

Arnie started easing his way through the brush, and Roger felt his heart beat just a little faster. Although his parents had never felt the need to warn him about strangers, there was something about this man that he didn't like, even though he'd only seen him a few times.

"You want to know about a real good fishing spot?"

Roger shuddered. "I need to go back to the house and get dried off."

"Oh, sure. I didn't mean now. But if you head downstream there, just past that fence that runs up to the barn, you know?"

Roger nodded.

"There's a spot just on the other side of the fence…the creek sort of slows down there. Lots of nice brook trout there."

"Okay. I'll remember that."

"Good. Yeah. You really should try it out."

Roger reached down and retrieved the two fish he'd caught, which were drifting in the water on their leader.

"I'll walk you partway," Arnie said, wading through the creek to Roger's side. "I'm parked over there."

Roger nodded, worried that if he said no, it would reveal his fear.

They twisted through the thick brush and eased into the clearing on the other side, then took up a slow pace across the field.

"Couple of nice rainbows you got there," Arnie said.

"Yeah, not too bad." Roger thought about ostriches, and how they could bury their heads. He wanted to be an ostrich.

"You know what they're saying about your dad, don't you?" Arnie said.

"No," Roger said.

"Oh come on," Arnie said. "You're a smart kid."

Roger didn't respond.

"He left your house that night, you know." Arnie rubbed his palms up and down his face. "The night of the murder."

Roger's wet clothes began to get colder, and he picked up his pace. "I need to get home."

"You think your daddy killed that man?" Arnie asked.

"I'm getting pretty cold." Roger started trotting.

"Hey. Kid. You don't have to be scared of me. I'm just trying to help."

Roger started running. He was ten yards away in seconds.

"Just be careful, kid," Arnie shouted.

Roger was a cheetah. He ducked his chin into his chest and ran faster than he ever had. When he got to the barn, he rounded the corner and stopped. He peeked around the edge, watching to make sure that Arnie got into his pickup and drove away. And then he turned and raced into the house.

"Dad!"

●

Minutes later, Carl ran from his house and jumped into his pickup. He started the engine, and the wheels spit gravel everywhere as the pickup fishtailed toward the main road. Then it came to abrupt stop. Carl pushed his forehead against the steering wheel. His thumbs whitened as he gripped the wheel tighter. Through the muddled, angry thoughts in his head, he had just enough presence to think about what would happen if he went after Arnie Janko.

"God dammit!" he shouted. And then he shook the steering wheel as if it was Arnie himself, his body pounding against the seat as the wheel refused to budge.

CHAPTER TWENTY

Junior and Gordon crouched over a bull that had managed to get tangled up in a barbed wire fence. The bull's efforts to escape left him with a deep gash in his hind leg. He also had several smaller cuts, including one on his scrotum. The two men had spent the better part of the morning just trying to guide the bull into the barn. He'd shown a stubborn resistance that was impressive even for a bull, taking down another fence in the process.

Once they got him into the stall, Gordon tried to untangle a piece of wire that was still dangling from his leg. A swift kick caught him right in the hand, and the sharp hoof took a healthy chunk of skin off the back.

"Guess we need to get him tied to the rails," Gordon said through his teeth, clutching his bleeding hand to his gut.

Junior nodded. "Maybe we ought to stretch him out, get him down on the ground."

"Sounds good," Gordon agreed. "Goddamn, that hurt." He shook his hand in the air, then held it close to his face, studying the wound.

"You better bandage that before we do anything else," Junior suggested.

Gordon shook his head, as Junior knew he would. "I wouldn't be much good with a big old hunk of gauze on my hand. I'll be all right."

"Well, at least cover it up. If it gets infected, you'll be crippled for a lot longer than five minutes."

Gordon refused at first, then finally wrapped the hand in medical tape, without the benefit of gauze. Junior flinched just thinking what it was going to feel like tearing the tape off.

They looped a lasso around the bull's front hoof, which proved to be another challenge. The bull charged each time one of them crawled inside the eight-by-ten-foot pen. After several tries, Gordon finally caught the front hoof while sitting on the rail. He pulled the rope snug, wrapping it around the rail twice. Then Junior climbed inside to get a loop around the hind leg.

From outside the pen, Gordon pulled on his end to tip the bull onto his side. But the bull fell on the side where the wound was. So they had to give the rope some slack until he got back to his feet. Then the two men pulled simultaneously, at different angles. The bull fought hard, but eventually fell onto the opposite side.

They tied the ropes to the rails and armed themselves with antiseptic and bandages before climbing back inside, keeping a close eye on the bull. Although he looked helpless, lying heavy in the straw, the whites showing in his eyes, they'd both seen enough to know that animals can and will surprise you.

Junior gingerly looped one more lasso around the bull's second hind leg and stretched the rope to the rails, tying it to the top rail so that the bull's legs were spread. Gordon went to work. He had more veterinary experience, so Junior watched, leaning on the top rope to keep the leg raised. Gordon examined the scrotum first, not touching it, leaning in close.

"It's hard to tell," Gordon said. "Looks like the nut's all right. The cut is pretty clean. It might heal up okay, but I really can't tell without the right tools."

"Goddamn," Junior muttered. "The last thing we need is a full-grown steer."

Gordon shook his head.

"Well, I guess we need to get the vet out here to take a look at him."

"Yeah. Not much else we can do," Gordon agreed. He started to tend to the leg wounds, and Junior watched his gentle attention closely, struck by how differently Gordon treated animals than he did his own children.

A few weeks before, Bobby and Craig reported that Scooter had gotten into some trouble at school, and Hazel had given him a swat on the butt. Hazel called the Cayleys that night to apologize, but Gordon had apparently not considered her punishment sufficient. Not only did Scooter show up for school with a shiner, but he walked with a slight limp for several days after.

"I'd like to take you out behind the barn and remind you what that feels like," Junior told Gordon when Scooter limped past them one afternoon.

"All right," Gordon said. "I'll take you down before you have a chance to even think about takin' a swing."

Junior stared him down, wanting to put a fist into his nose. Gordon had that cold look again, and for an instant Junior convinced himself that he could slap the look right off Gordon's face and wake him up to reason. Violence with violence. Despite his earlier threat, there wasn't enough cause to fire Gordon, but Junior had been watching Scooter closely ever since.

Now, back at the barn, Junior watched Gordon and his gentle touch, trying to comprehend the discrepancy.

"That looks pretty deep," Junior said as Gordon touched the most serious wound. The bull strained against the taut ropes. He let out a rising bellow.

"It looks worse than it is," Gordon said. "It spread, but it ain't all that deep."

"Good."

Gordon reached for a big brown bottle and unscrewed the lid. The potent, acrid smell of iodine filled the air. He held a square of gauze against the opening of the bottle, and then in quick, soft motions dabbed the gauze along the gash. The bull complained, and his free leg thrashed along the ground, raising a cloud of dusty straw.

"I don't think we even need to bandage this thing," Gordon said. "I think it'll heal quicker if we let it get some air. We could just leave him in the barn for a while."

"Sounds good to me," Junior agreed.

Junior heard the barn door swing open. He turned, expecting Sharon, as Angie was away that afternoon. But it was Laurie Logan who entered, tentatively, leading her youngest son Bradley by the hand.

"Junior?" she called, her voice high and thin. Her skin looked pale.

"Over here." Junior let go of the rope and stood, looking down at Gordon. "You think you can handle this for a second?"

Gordon nodded. "'Course."

Junior left the stall, closing the gate behind him.

"I'm sorry," Laurie said. "I'm sorry to bother you."

"It's okay."

"I need to talk to someone. But Angie's not home. I need to talk. I'm sorry to interrupt."

"She has bridge club today. It's all right. You don't have to apologize. What's wrong?"

"I don't know. Something's happening." She put a palm to her forehead.

"All right," Junior said. "You want to tell me about it?" He started walking Laurie down the aisle, toward the other end of the barn. He heard the low moo of the bull as Gordon continued his work. Studying Laurie's expression, he judged that they should be alone, so he led her just outside the barn.

"Everything's closing in." Laurie looked up at Junior, and her eyes got wide. She started talking, and once she started, the words flew at him like a windstorm.

"I don't know what to think, Junior. Carl won't talk to me. I don't know whether to believe him, or what to think anymore. He was gone for a couple of hours that night, and we fought, and at first I didn't think anything of it because I'm so sure he wouldn't do anything like that, but then Spider says Carl and Tom had this fight. Carl says Spider is lying. But I don't know what to believe. I thought I knew him, Junior. Now..." She walked the whole time, pacing back and forth, and Bradley tried to keep up by hanging onto her slacks. Junior reached down and picked the boy up. Bradley squirmed, twisting around so that he could study Junior's face. Once he'd had a look, Bradley relaxed, resting his arms on Junior's shoulders.

"All right, Laurie. Calm down." Junior made a deliberate effort to slow his voice, hoping this would have the same effect on her. But she hadn't been talking too fast for Junior to catch the key phrases. "Are you talking about the night Tom died?"

She nodded feverishly, and then Junior saw her expression change, as if she suddenly realized that she hadn't told anyone this, and wasn't sure she should.

"Carl was gone that night?"

Panic opened her eyes wide. "Well, he was in the garage. He was working on his truck. He didn't go anywhere. I know that for sure, because I would have heard him."

Junior put his hand on her shoulder. "It's okay, Laurie. I wasn't thinking anything like that. I'm just trying to follow."

"Oh, God. What am I saying?" She stopped suddenly. "Junior, I've been spending so much time alone, thinking about all this stuff. I've blown it all completely out of proportion in my head. That's why I needed to tell somebody. But I don't think he killed Tom. I don't think that at all."

"Of course not. I know. It's okay. You don't have to worry about telling me. I know as well as you do that there's no way Carl would do something like that. All right?" He stood right in front of her, getting a direct line on her face. "You have no idea how many people around here had better reasons to kill Tom."

Laurie looked up at him, a sign of hope in her eyes. "Really?"

"You've seen how he can get with people. He's pissed off everyone along Pine Creek at some time or another."

Laurie said "Wow" quietly, but she still looked shaken and embarrassed. "Well…" She looked at her wrist, although she wasn't wearing a watch. "I'd better get home." She reached for Bradley and took him from Junior's arms. "I should go."

"Laurie. Please don't worry," Junior said. "It'll all work out. They'll figure out who did it."

She nodded, but her face showed little sign of faith. She left in a hurry, and Junior stood for a moment, taking a deep breath.

•

That evening, Junior sat among his family, wondering what to do with this revelation about Carl. A part of him felt he should tell the authorities. This seemed like the only ethical choice. But he couldn't shake the feeling that telling someone would betray Laurie's trust.

Junior also wanted to trust his instincts about Carl Logan. This awkward show of honesty by Carl's wife made him feel even more protective of the whole Logan family. So that evening, Junior called Carl and invited him and his kids to go hunting for arrowheads on Sunday. Carl agreed, sounding pleased that he'd called.

Moments after Junior got off the phone, he got the second surprise of the day. A car pulled into the drive, and when the knock sounded and Angie went to the door, Junior heard a small exclamation of surprise.

He went out to the living room to find Daryl Blinder and Rodney Trass in the doorway. They wore grave expressions, as did Angie, her hands clasped tightly against her mouth. As Junior got closer, he realized that Daryl was holding his hand out to Angie.

"So Mrs. Kirby, I take it this *is* your necklace?"

Junior stared at the necklace draped over Daryl Blinder's fingers. A tear escaped from the corner of Angie's eye.

Trass stepped forward with his abrupt, businesslike manner and asked the next question, one which would shake them to their core for years after. The deputy cleared his throat, looked directly at Junior, and asked with the subtlety of a machine gun, "Are you aware that Tom Butcher liked to wear women's clothing?"

The question was so unexpected, and so bizarre, that Junior burst out laughing. Angie also started laughing. But this reaction brought such a cold look from Rodney Trass that the Kirbys were jolted into the realization that he was dead serious. Their laughter came to an abrupt halt.

"He did what?" Junior asked.

Daryl Blinder stepped forward, in between the Kirbys and Trass. "I'll explain this, Rod," he told his deputy. Blinder took a deep breath, then turned his head and let the breath out slowly through his nose.

"We found a large collection of women's clothing among Mr. Butcher's belongings. At first we assumed that they belonged to a girlfriend, or perhaps Mr. Butcher's mother. But we noticed that the style of the clothing was a bit more…modern than what his mother would have worn. And the women that Mr. Butcher associated with in recent years were much smaller women. None of them would have been able to wear these clothes, as they were quite…large."

Blinder took another deep breath.

"I'm sorry," Junior said. "Let's have a seat. Let's sit down."

"Yes, thanks," Blinder said. "Thank you."

They settled into the living room, the Kirbys taking the couch and the officers making themselves comfortable in the easy chairs.

"Anyway…" Blinder continued. "After piecing things together, and taking into consideration that he was wearing your necklace when we found him, we came to the conclusion that he had himself one of these strange little habits. A, a, a…what do you call it. A fetish. That's it." Blinder held his hand out. "He had himself a fetish for women's clothing."

"He was a homo," Trass said.

"Well, now, Deputy." Blinder held his palm up. "We don't know that."

The Kirbys sat dumb, staring blankly at the floor. They did not speak for a long time, until Trass cleared his throat, indicating his growing impatience.

"He was wearing my necklace when he died?" Angie finally asked, her voice breaking.

Blinder nodded. "We don't know how he got it," he said. "But we remembered the report you filed when it was stolen, and the description matched."

"He must have stolen it," Trass said.

"That is a possibility," Blinder said cautiously. "But we don't know that. We may never know."

Junior sat quietly glum, realizing the horrible truth.

"We have not revealed this information to anyone else," Blinder told them as they left. "And we think it would be best to keep it quiet, in case it will help us at a later date."

"Of course," Junior said.

"We understand," Angie added.

Blinder nodded, offering a sympathetic look. It seemed from his confidential tone that he had another reason for keeping this information under wraps, as if he was also thinking of Tom's reputation. Junior felt his respect for this man rise. But he couldn't shake the memory of Tom perched in his den, eyes eager as he asked what people said about him, and whether Junior knew what it was like to wonder if you belonged in a different life. And he wondered what Tom might have wanted known about himself, if he could choose.

CHAPTER TWENTY-ONE

LAURIE LOGAN BROUGHT A PLATTER of meatloaf to the table and set it between a bowl of mashed potatoes and another of green beans. Carl emerged from the bathroom and settled in at the head of the table.

"How did it go today?" Laurie asked.

"Fine," Carl said.

A familiar silence fell over the room as the Logan family dug into their dinner. Even Bradley had gone silent recently, after his childish behavior had drawn too many outbursts from his father.

A half hour into the meal, a truck pulled into the drive. Laurie stood to peer out the dining room window. "Looks like Lester."

Carl perked up. "Hm." He stood. "Wonder what the hell he wants." When he looked outside, he saw both Lester and Arnie climb from the pickup.

When the knock came, Carl had already gotten up to meet the two men at the back door. Laurie heard just the muffle of voices first, and then more as the volume suddenly escalated.

"You stay away from my boy, you hear me!" Carl suddenly shouted.

Laurie rose from her seat and rushed to the kitchen.

"What's the matter, Logan? You worried about getting caught?" Arnie Janko taunted.

"You dirty, lying son of a bitch," Carl muttered. He lunged at Arnie, but Lester stepped in front of him, grabbing his shoulders and pushing him against the kitchen counter.

"Carl!" Laurie shouted. "Calm down. The children."

"I will not calm down. That lying sack of shit has been spreading rumors about us, and I'm not going to stand here and take it."

Arnie started laughing, and Lester let go of Carl and grabbed Arnie by the arm. "Come on. If I'd a known you were going to start this, I never would have brought you."

"You sticking up for this guy, Lester?" Arnie said.

"Shut up," Lester said. "Sorry about this, folks. We'll get out of your hair."

Lester pushed Arnie out the door, and Laurie slammed it behind them. Then she turned the lock, something she rarely felt the need to do.

She looked over to see the children huddled in the doorway, eyes round. Laurie let her breath ride a minute until she could speak calmly. "It's all over. Go back to your meals."

Three small faces eased back into the dining room, reluctant.

"What on earth was that?" Laurie asked.

"It's not worth talking about," Carl said.

Laurie felt the crackle of something in her chest. Heat lightning, she thought. Prairie storm. "Really. Well, maybe now would be a good time to tell me what is worth talking about. Because lately, there doesn't seem to be anything on that list."

"Don't exaggerate, Laurie."

"I'm *not* exaggerating, and don't you dare try to make it out like I'm crazy for saying anything."

Carl sighed. "Honey, can we talk about this later? I'm hungry."

Laurie shook her head. "Sure. Let's talk about it later. Maybe next year. Or the year after."

Carl shook his head. "I'm going to eat," he said. Laurie sank into a chair and stared out the window at the dust rising in the driveway as the pickup peeled out.

•

Once the officers left the Kirby house, Junior and Angie both sat silent, contemplating the revelation about Tom Butcher.

"This is ridiculous," Junior finally said. "I don't believe it."

But Angie frowned. "I do."

"You do?"

She nodded, looking at her hands.

"Did you know?" Junior asked.

"No," she answered. "I didn't know, but I'm not surprised."

"But Tom, of all people."

Angie lifted one shoulder in a shrug that said "Why *not* him?"

"Why aren't you surprised?"

Angie sighed, puffing her cheeks. A tear trickled down one cheek, which she quickly brushed away. "Babe said he was impotent."

Despite his best instincts, Junior laughed. "Oh, come on…Tom? He's been with more women than the rest of the men in this valley combined."

"Well, I'm just telling you what Babe said. But still…how do you know that?"

"What do you mean, how do I know? You've seen him. You've seen all those women."

She nodded. "Just because he was with them…" She paused, then shrugged again.

Junior fought it. He fought it hard. But thoughts began to creep in. Memories of things that didn't make sense at the time. The fact that Tom had never been married. Never even a girlfriend that stuck around for more than a few months. And Tom's discomfort the night Junior tried to talk to him about the last woman he dated. And it suddenly became clear that Junior needed to get some things off his chest.

"I think I know who took your necklace," he told Angie.

"You do?" Angie sat up straighter. "Was it Tom?"

Junior shook his head. "I don't think so."

"Well who, then?"

There in the soft light of the living room, Junior finally unburdened himself of the secret of Babe's visit. He did not mention the kiss, thinking that it would needlessly hurt Angie's feelings, and that his inability to understand how he had allowed things to go that far would make it impossible to explain.

Angie listened, and the more Junior talked, the more troubled her expression became. Even after he finished, she sat looking at the floor, her brow low over her eyes. "I'm sorry, Junior, but it feels like there's something missing." She raised her eyes. "Do you know what I mean?"

Junior shook his head, barely able to meet her gaze.

"You kept this from me all this time...why?"

"I didn't think it was worth worrying you, especially with the history between me and Babe."

"But your past with Babe has never bothered me. That was high school, for God's sake."

Junior looked down, unable to respond.

"And did you ask Babe?" she asked. "After the necklace went missing?"

"Yes, I called her about it."

"And?"

"Well, she denied it," Junior said. "But she didn't seem surprised that I asked." Junior shrugged. "I had no proof. So I kept an eye out, thinking I might catch her wearing it."

Angie kept her back to him for quite some time. Junior sat in torment, transporting himself back to the scene, as he had many times before, and imagining himself pushing Babe away sooner, when she first put her arms around him. When he first got uncomfortable. If Junior had only followed his instincts, the whole situation would have passed weeks ago. Finally, Angie turned to him with a puzzled expression.

"So you think Babe stole the necklace to give it to Tom?"

Junior shrugged. "Looks that way."

Angie shook her head. "How sad," she said. "That is so, so sad."

CHAPTER TWENTY-TWO

Junior and his boys were late getting to the Logans to hunt for arrowheads that Sunday. The vet came out to look at Junior's bull in the morning, and it took longer than expected. Thankfully, there wasn't any permanent damage to the testicle, so Junior approached the Logan house with a mixture of relief, embarrassment, and confusion.

The confusion was a result of Bobby and Craig's reaction to their plans for that morning. When Junior told them to get ready, the boys dragged themselves down to the kitchen and slumped into their chairs, picking at their lunch as if they had hangovers.

Finally, Bobby mumbled, "Do we hafta go, Dad?"

Junior stopped in the middle of his own bite. "You guys love hunting for arrowheads. What's going on?"

Bobby shrugged, scratching at his cowlick. Craig stared at his brother, following Bobby's silent cue. Junior put down his fork.

"What's the deal, boys? Is it the Logans? You told me that you really like those kids." A pause, with no response. "Right?"

Neither of them budged, and their pace retained its slow beat until Junior practically had to drag them by their ears to the car.

Junior pulled into the Logans' driveway an hour later than he told Carl they'd be there. The boys straggled. Craig's guilty conscience seemed to be getting the better of him. But his loyalty was clearly torn, as he kept looking at his brother, then at Junior, like a baseball player caught in a rundown.

"Come on, guys, we're later than heck."

When Junior knocked on the front door, there was a long pause before Carl answered the door, and the look he gave Junior told him that he'd completely forgotten. "Afternoon, Junior. How's it going?"

"We came by to search for arrowheads with the kids. Is it a bad time?"

Behind Carl, in the dining room, Roger and Julie sat at the table.

"Oh damn!" Carl stepped back. "Come on in. I'm sorry. I forgot."

"We can go another time," Junior offered.

Carl's eyes brightened. "No, no. It's just…"

Junior and the boys entered to see Roger and Julie sitting at the dinner table as if they'd just been given a scolding. They stood, but looked listless. Junior scanned the house, realizing there was no sign of Laurie. "You sure?" he asked again.

Carl led him to the living room, away from the kids. He sighed. "Listen, Laurie left this morning. She went to her sister's—just for a couple of weeks, maybe, until…well, until…" He stuttered, looking at his feet.

"Things blow over?" Junior offered.

Carl nodded.

"What about the kids?" Junior asked.

"She took Bradley with her," Carl explained, "but we don't want to disrupt the school year for the others. It's hard enough, you know, switching schools once…"

Junior nodded. "Are you sure you don't want to reschedule? It wouldn't be any problem. We could do it next weekend."

"No, no, no," Carl insisted. "It's fine. It will be good for them to have something to do."

Carl led Junior back into the dining room, where all four kids sat at the table now, saying little. Roger looked very upset, although he tried to hide it. He looked scared.

"Coffee?" Carl asked.

"Sure, if you've got some made," Junior said.

"Yeah." Carl went into the kitchen. "Damn," Junior heard him say. "I guess we don't."

"That's okay." Junior rose to go into the kitchen. Carl was standing at the sink, his hands resting on the counter, his shoulders hunched, his head tucked down between his upper arms. He didn't hear Junior come in, so Junior backed out quietly and sat back down at the dining room table. Roger and Julie had gone upstairs, after Carl told them to get their boots on. Bobby and Craig went with them.

Junior considered insisting that they come back the next weekend. But when he peeked into the kitchen again, Carl had composed himself. He looked at Junior with a big smile.

"So?" Junior asked.

"Yeah," Carl replied, hitching up his jeans. "What a day, huh? It's beautiful out there."

"Sure is. Beautiful day."

"Yeah. It'll be good to get out there, soak up some sun."

The kids rattled down the stairs, shouting and laughing, and Junior marveled at how quickly things shift in the world of children.

"You kids ready?" Carl shouted.

•

The pasture was a short distance from the Logan house, just before the turnoff to Kenwood's estate. Junior drove, and Carl popped out of the passenger door to open the gate. It was indeed a nearly perfect fall day. One half of the sky was crowded with clouds, but they were as fluffy as a bowl of popcorn. The sun sat alone on the cloudless side, tossing a casual, dry blanket of heat over the browning fields.

The kids sprinted into the pasture, and before Carl and Junior had a chance to stretch their tired legs, Julie was racing back toward them, her pageboy haircut flaring out from her head like a dying dandelion.

"I found one!" she shouted, holding a pudgy fist above her head.

"Already?" Carl asked. "Let me see that, pumpkin."

Carl crouched, and Julie held out her hand. She was panting, and her hand trembled with excitement. In the middle of her tiny palm sat a black, triangular chunk of shale. Carl and Junior both started chuckling.

"What?" Julie asked. "It's a arrowhead."

"Well…" Carl shook his head. "It looks a little bit like an arrowhead. But you have to look for rocks with sharp edges." Carl took the triangle from her and held it between his thumb and forefinger. "The Indians would take another rock and chip away the edges, here…" He acted out the motion. "…so that the edge would be sharp, you see?"

Julie's eyes teared up, but she nodded. She threw the rock to the ground and raced off to try again. Carl rose slowly to his full height. He had a slight grin on his face as he watched his daughter run, but there was also a sad, faraway look in his eye.

"What are you going to do with these kids?" Junior asked him.

"What do you mean?"

"How are you going to take care of them? What are you going to do with them after school?"

"Oh." Carl paused, looking back out across the pasture. It was clear that this had not occurred to him.

"We'll get by," Carl said. "I'll knock off a little early."

Junior sighed. "Come on," he told him. "You know better. Especially with all this shit that's going on with Lester. You tell those kids to come over to our place after school."

"Oh, no. We couldn't."

"Carl, shut up. I'm not listening. You can't afford to quit working at three thirty, and you know it. And you can't leave these kids alone. I won't hear another word about it."

"What about Angie?"

"I don't even have to ask. I know she'll feel the same way."

Carl dipped his chin. He closed his eyes, and Junior looked away. But when Carl said "Thank you," his voice was strong and steady. "I won't forget this, you know."

Junior nodded. "How *is* Lester?"

"I never see him."

"Is he working?"

Carl nodded. "He seems to be working harder than ever. Arnie's taking it more personally than Lester is."

Junior laughed. "That makes sense."

"Yeah, in Arnie's head, I guess it does." Carl shook his head.

They watched the kids for a while. They were all hunched over on their knees, like monks in prayer, plucking objects from the ground, studying them, flinging them away. There was little talk. They took the job seriously.

"Just out of curiosity, why'd you leave teaching?"

"Hell, I never wanted to be a goddamn schoolteacher." He shook his head. "When I married Laurie and found out how much she hated growing up on a ranch, I tried putting the idea of having my own ranch out of my head. I thought a respectable job would help me forget. My dad worked as a ranch hand and always dreamed of owning a ranch, and I inherited that love of the land. He had it deep in his bones." Carl paused, looking at Junior. "I didn't forget," he said. "I got fired because I've been asleep at my job for at least three years. I started stacking hay in the summers, and when the school year rolled around again, it took every ounce of my willpower not to stay out in that hayfield."

Junior nodded. "I know what you mean. I'm the same way. But what about Laurie?"

Carl shook his head. "I don't know if she'll ever be ready to come back to this." Again, he shook his head. "I can't leave." Carl started walking, his fists digging deep into his pockets. He walked slowly, sort of rocking from foot to foot. "I got nowhere else to go," he said.

"I found one." Roger held up his hand, then immediately stuffed the find into his pocket and began searching again, as if he was wasting valuable time.

Carl laughed. "That kid kills me," he said, shaking his head. "Everything's a competition."

"How's *he* doing?" Junior asked.

Carl watched Roger for a second, taking a deep breath. "I don't know for sure," he said. "He's like me—doesn't give you much to go on. He seems to be doing all right. Sure likes that teacher, Hazel. He thinks she's the greatest."

"He's got good taste," Junior said.

The two men walked around the pasture, kicking at rocks. The kids found a few more arrowheads, or pieces of them. All except Julie, whose frustration began to show. Junior watched her for a minute and realized that she was merely following her brother around the pasture.

Junior walked over and bent down close to her. "Julie, you're not going to find any if you keep looking in the same places where Roger just looked."

She looked up thoughtfully, her mouth in a tiny O. Then she rushed as far from the others as she dared, squatted down and started digging. Junior walked back over to Carl, who was smiling.

"I was going to wait and see how long it would take her to figure it out," Carl said. "But I'm glad you did that."

Junior nodded.

"Listen, Junior. I know Laurie came and talked to you. I'm not exactly sure what she told you. Maybe it doesn't matter. Everyone's going to believe what they're going to believe. Nothing I say is going to change anything."

"Well, maybe not." Junior kicked at a chip of rock and bent down to inspect it. The pink, flinty point of a small arrowhead. "But I think if I knew everyone was talking…I think I'd want to have my say."

Carl shook his head. "I don't know. It just seems that the more noise you make, the more attention you draw to yourself. That doesn't seem like a good idea right now."

Junior chewed the inside of his lip. They heard a din of tiny thunder coming up from behind. Then a breathless, panting voice crying, "Daddy, Daddy." They turned to see Julie racing toward them. She held her right hand high, triumphant, clenched. Her little boots raised puffs of dust from the dry ground. "I found one!"

Carl got down on one knee. Junior stood behind him, bending over his shoulder. Julie held out her hand, and again it trembled with her childish excitement. Carl placed a hand on her arm, and Junior could see that the shiver immediately subsided in her, replaced by confidence and pride at the discovery resting in the middle of her palm, a perfect grey arrowhead.

CHAPTER TWENTY-THREE

Spider Moses pulled a branding iron from inside a fifty-gallon barrel filled with burning coals. With his unique, jerky deftness, Spider took a half-turn, then slid the iron through the bars of the branding chute and carefully pressed the orange-hot Lazy B brand against the flank of a fat calf. Junior leaned against the lever that pushed the side panel against the calf's ribs. The calf bawled, kicked, and twisted, trying to escape the searing pain in its side. The smell of burning hair and flesh filled the air.

Lester Ruth cut a notch from the calf's right ear, while Arnie Janko crouched next to the chute, checking the calf's sex.

"Let her go," Arnie shouted. Spider pulled the iron away and tucked it back into the barrel. Junior cranked the lever, opening the side panel and lifting the front gate, releasing it from where it rested on the calf's neck. Arnie gave the calf a shove from behind. She made the small leap over the lower half of the head-lock gate and hopped through, trotting forward with a dazed look and a half-felt bawl. In the corral, the mothers all converged, lowing, snuffling her to see if she was their baby.

Spider climbed into the smaller corral and waded into the blanket of red backs. The calves cried, their tongues hanging low, dripping saliva, their eyes wide with fear and anger and the first sense of weaning.

Months after all the other local ranchers had done their branding, the men were now doing the same job on Tom Butcher's stock, which would go up for sale soon. Because they hadn't been able to get to them sooner, the calves were four months old, bigger than these men were used to handling. The calves were strong, and they were wearing everyone out. The level of concentration was high, knowing they could get hurt dealing with such big animals.

Spider grabbed one calf's tail and twisted it, coaxing the calf toward the chute. He shouted "Hey, hey, hey" to keep the calf moving, and whacked it on one flank when it veered to the side and hesitated. Finally, the calf trotted along one rail and into the tiny opening.

The calf started to bolt through the chute, toward the wide-open corral, but Junior leaned into the lever, slamming the side panel against the calf's ribs and bringing the gate down on the back of its neck. The calf bawled, its tongue splaying from the side of its mouth, and saliva arched through the air, darkening the dry ground.

A pickup pulled into Spider's drive and bounced along the dirt path toward the scene.

"There he is," Junior said. "I knew he'd show up sooner or later."

"Mostly later." Arnie cackled at his own joke, and Spider laughed too. But Lester seemed annoyed. Lester's stern glare did not escape Arnie's notice either, and a look of desperation began to sneak into Arnie's eyes. A panic.

The pickup stopped. Carl stepped out and trotted toward the chutes.

"Sorry I'm late," he muttered.

"Not half as sorry as we are," Arnie said.

Carl shot him a hard look and seemed about to say something. But his lips puckered, plugging the words in his mouth instead.

"Where do you want me, Lester?" Carl asked.

"Well, we need someone to run the pen," Lester said.

"Okay." Carl crawled up onto the rails and into the corral, where the calves milled.

Spider moved back over to the branding irons and got set to lay a Lazy B on the flank of the calf they'd just captured.

"This one's a bull," Arnie announced.

Spider applied the brand, and the calf cried out.

"So how you doin', Carl?" Junior shouted over the calf's complaints.

"I'm all right," Carl said with a forced optimism. "Those kids of mine give you any problems last night?"

Junior laughed. Roger and Julie had spent the night at the Kirby house because Carl would have to leave the house hours early that morning. "They were nothing but trouble," Junior said, and Carl smiled.

"Must run in the family," Arnie said. Spider chuckled, but by now he must have noticed the cool reception Arnie's jokes were getting, as his laugh wasn't natural.

"Hey, Arnie..." Lester had just notched the car of the bull calf and was looping his lasso around the calf's neck so that they'd be able to get him down and nut him when the chute opened.

"Yeah?" Arnie looked over at Lester, his eyes bulging, hopeful.

"Why don't you shut the fuck up?" Lester said. The words just barely escaped his throat, coming out in a choked sort of cough.

Arnie laughed at first. But a moment later, the sides of his mouth went slack. His eyes showed a hurt that went deep.

"Better yet," Lester said, his voice slightly stronger now, although it shook like hell, "why don't you tell Spider here, and Junior, too, how come Carl was late this mornin'. You want to do that, Arnie? Or would you rather I did?"

Spider had finished branding the calf, and Junior yanked the lever down, shouting, "Here he comes!"

Lester braced himself, spreading his feet wide, and Spider and Junior rushed around the chute and grabbed the calf, tackling him, then getting a grip on his hind legs and kneeling on his ribs to keep him down.

Arnie wandered over, his face still slack. He knelt down next to the bull, took his buck knife, and sliced the sack open. He squeezed the testicles from inside the scrotum, sliced them off and tossed them aside, into the dusty straw of the corral. The calf, now a steer, mawed loudly.

"Okay," Arnie muttered, and after Lester pulled the lasso from around the steer's neck, they let him go.

As the morning passed, and the men pushed the calves through, Arnie became more and more animated in his discomfort. He wiped his nose repeatedly; he adjusted his collar; he hitched his pants and coughed up several mouthfuls of phlegm, spitting dark spots into the cocoa dry dirt. Finally, Arnie cleared his throat and said, in a voice weak with fear, "You know, Lester, I got to apologize, but I just remembered…uh…I just remembered that Molly asked me…well, she asked me if I'd run into town. I can't believe I forgot about it, but, well, I…"

"Go on, Arnie," Lester said. "Go on. Go on."

"Yeah," Arnie said, and he looked as if he was about to cry as he turned and slumped away to his pickup. He ducked into the cab like a guilty kid hiding in his bedroom, then revved up the engine and took off without so much as a glance in their direction.

"What the hell was that about?" Junior asked Lester.

Lester looked sideways at him, still angry. He tilted his head toward Carl. "Ask him," he said.

Junior studied Carl, who was obviously uncomfortable. Carl pushed his way through the calves and began trying to guide one of them toward the chute, ignoring the others' questioning eyes.

"It's no big deal," he finally said.

"Yeah it is," Lester said. He spoke through his teeth, his voice grinding. "You let him do that once, he'll just keep on doin' it. I oughta know."

Carl forced a calf into the chute, and Junior hit the lever, squeezing the calf into place.

"What the hell are you guys talking about?" Junior asked.

Spider applied the brand. The smoke filled the air. Lester, who was just getting set to notch the calf's ear, stopped and looked at Junior as if he hadn't given an ounce of effort into figuring things out for himself.

"Think about it, Junior," Lester said. "Why do *you* suppose Carl was late this morning? How long have you known Arnie?" Lester turned back and gripped the calf's ear.

"What didn't he do this time?" Spider asked.

"Exactly," Lester replied. "Carl told him to cut the hay in that goddam south meadow on Tuesday."

"Ah." Junior nodded.

Lester checked the calf's sex. "Let her go," he said.

Junior shoved the lever.

"Son of a bitch thinks I'm going to hire him to work for me when I get Tom's ranch," Lester muttered. "He's got another thing coming."

•

For the remainder of the morning, Lester, Carl, Spider, and Junior combined in a sort of graceless cowboy ballet. Without words, they followed the familiar choreography of many years of rehearsal. They performed this set-piece in the midst of a panorama of hot dust, accompanied by the music of mournful, frightened calves, with the audience, their mothers, watching nervously, sounding their own fear and anger.

Spider jerked and juked his way from one task to the next. Lester moved around with his boot-jaw set, his eyes nearly closed, impatient with every little thing that impeded their progress. Junior slogged forward in his own heavy but steady way. Carl was the most graceful of them, his athletic body bending and flexing and leaning as he held a calf still, or applied a brand, or ran the chute.

They concentrated on their tasks, which demanded that kind of attention but did not prevent them from thinking of other things. And they did, their minds focused on the same topic that everyone had been worrying over for weeks now.

CHAPTER TWENTY-FOUR

HALF OF THE POPULATION OF Slack School stood on the grainy concrete sidewalk leading up to the main building.

"Midnight Ghost!" A voice echoed from the back of the building, and the dozen children took off running, rounding the first corner of the building, their senses alive for any sign of the predator children waiting to clutch them in their grasp.

Roger lingered in the middle of the pack, plotting his strategy to wind through the herd of "ghosts" waiting to capture those who were still alive. When the children tired of soccer, they chose this game as the next activity for recess. The rules were simple. One child started out as the Midnight Ghost and hid somewhere in the back of the building, while the others began at the front and tried to run all the way around without getting tagged. Whoever was tagged also became a ghost and was recruited to capture the runners on the next round, until there was one player left, who then became the next ghost. Roger liked Midnight Ghost. He was fast, and nimble, and was often the last one captured.

The living children took a wide berth around the second corner of the building, and Roger spotted the first of the ghosts, who raced out from behind the old outhouse and captured Craig Kirby. Roger darted to his left, closer to the building. He was a mule deer, breaking free from the herd, his ears rotating, searching for sounds. He knew that moving closer to the building was a risk, with the chance of being trapped against the back wall, so once he passed the first ghost, he darted back toward the perimeter again, until Bobby emerged from the bushes to his right. Roger picked up speed, bounding past Bobby, and then between two of the smaller ghosts, who waved frantically at his narrow hips.

Roger broke ahead of the pack and escaped easily, cutting the last corner so close that his sleeve brushed the white stucco. He leapt onto the sidewalk and did a pirouette, jumping into the air and turning around to see who else had survived. There were only two others— Larry Janko, who was the tallest boy in the school, and Scooter. The three boys stood looking at each other, their breath racing.

"Why don't you let someone else win this time, Roger?" Larry asked.

Roger smiled. "What do you have in your lunchbox, Larry?" he asked. "What's for dessert today?"

"Oh no," Larry said. "You're not getting my chocolate chip cookies."

"Then no deal," Roger said. "How about you, Scooter? You got something good?"

Scooter didn't smile. "I'll beat your ass just like your dad beat Tom Butcher."

Roger's head snapped back. "What?"

"Come on, Roger. We all know."

"Midnight Ghost!" sang out over the rooftop, and the three boys took off like their feet were on fire.

Scooter and Roger were both faster than Larry, and they burst past him, running side by side. As they rounded the first corner, Roger's elbow nudged Scooter. Scooter flung his arm out, pushing Roger off balance. He didn't fall, but he had to reach down and touch the ground to prevent it.

The ghosts had devised a strategy of forming a solid line across the yard, and when the boys rounded the second corner, their capture seemed inevitable. But while Scooter tried to fake and dodge his way through the line, Roger cut to the far outside of the yard and plunged headlong into the bushes that surrounded the playground. He ran with his arms up, elbows out, shielding his face from the branches, and he barged through the thick brush while Scooter was captured.

Someone had raced in after him, and he could feel them getting close. Roger cut to one side and leapt over a large clump of chokecherry bushes.

When he found himself in a clearing, he ran. Roger ran for his father. He ran for his mother. He didn't know it, but he ran for Tom Butcher, and Hazel Moses, and Babe Ruth, and even Arnie Janko. He ran for Rosa Parks and Chief Joseph and Eli Weisel. He ran for Medgar Evers and Martin Luther King. He ran for every woman who had her feet bound, and every man who felt a noose around his neck, and every person who was forced to wear a yellow star, and every girl who was snatched from the street and whisked away. He ran for the centuries of human beings who had felt different and alone, trying to escape from the discerning looks and the condescending tones and the lash of persecution, his breath racing through him like a gust of wind. And even when he got to the sidewalk, where the game ended, where he had won, he kept right on running.

•

That evening, Roger lay in bed trying to sleep. The phone rang, and he heard his father answer. Roger crept from his bed.

"Where you going, Roger?"

"Go back to sleep, Julie."

He opened and closed the bedroom door as quietly as possible and sat on the stairs, where he could hear his father's side of the conversation.

"Please, honey. I know I need to talk to you more."

A pause.

"Yes, I know I've told you so many times that I'll change. I know I keep saying it, but this time I *mean* it."

Roger was shocked to hear his father crying. He had never heard him cry before.

"Laurie, I don't think I can get through this without you. And what about the kids? This isn't easy for them either."

There was another long pause.

"Yes, the Kirbys have been great, but everyone else treats me like a leper."

Roger couldn't listen anymore. He covered his ears and went back to bed, where he lay thinking about his father crying in the kitchen. And wondering how anyone could possibly think that his father would ever kill someone.

And he knew it was time to stop trying to escape.

CHAPTER TWENTY-FIVE

ALTHOUGH THE AIR BEGAN TO cool with the promise of another Montana winter, the phone lines along Paradise Valley generated their own heat wave. People grew tired of keeping their thoughts and suspicions to themselves, and rumors began to flow through the wires in great rushes. In that sense only, things were back to normal around Paradise Valley.

One evening, just as Junior was settling into a quiet night at home, his own phone rang. Carl had come by to get Roger and Julie around dark. After two weeks in Billings at her sister's, Laurie had come back, but her return only lasted a week, and she and Bradley were gone again, this time off to her parents' ranch in eastern Montana.

When Junior picked up the phone, he was surprised to hear the voice of Peter Kenwood.

"What's up, Peter?"

"Well, we've got a bit of a situation here. I'm over at Lester's place. I think maybe you and Angie ought to come over."

"What happened?" Junior asked.

"Why don't you and Angie just come by?"

"We'll be right there."

The boys were just climbing into bed, so Junior went over to the Cayleys and asked Sharon to come over until they got back.

"What's going on?" Angie asked on the drive over.

"Peter didn't say," Junior told her.

Angie sighed. "What's happening out here?"

•

Peter greeted them at the door, his face grave. He took Junior's arm and placed his other hand gently in the small of Angie's back.

"Lester's gone," Peter explained. "He disappeared early this evening. And Babe is drunk. She called about an hour ago."

"Is that you, Junior?" Babe's thin, shaking voice echoed from the kitchen.

Junior let Angie go in first.

"Angie." Babe immediately started crying. She stood and threw her arms around Angie. "Where's Tom?" she asked. "Tom's gone."

Angie nodded, putting a hand to Babe's head and holding it against her shoulder. "Tom's gone," she confirmed. "That's right. But now we need to worry about Lester, honey. You need to think about your husband."

Babe sobbed, and Angie looked up at Kenwood. "Why did you call us?" she asked.

Peter nodded toward Babe. "She asked for you."

This was not the answer Junior wanted to hear. He caught a quick, sharp look from Angie before she turned her attention back to Babe.

It had been a month since Blinder's visit informing them about the necklace. Junior watched with a sort of guilty pride as Angie set aside all her suspicions and comforted the woman who was the source of so much strain. Babe sobbed for a while, then seemed to momentarily forget what she was upset about. She lifted her head from Angie's shoulder and blinked at her a few times.

"Did Bobby Kennedy really get shot?" she asked.

Angie rolled her eyes. "Yes," she said. "He's dead, Babe."

This pushed Babe back into her anguish. She threw her head against Angie, and her shoulders began to quake. Angie ran her hand up and down Babe's back, then cradled her head again, burying her fingers in the disheveled fluff of red.

"He was such a good man," Babe wailed.

Angie sighed. "Yes he was," she said absently. "He did some wonderful things."

Kenwood backed away from the scene, settling into a chair in the corner of the living room. Junior eased over next to him.

"Where do you think Lester could be?" Junior asked him.

Kenwood shook his head. "This is odd for him," he said. "He's never done anything like this before."

"No, he hasn't. I suppose you called Arnie and Spider?"

"I called everyone I could think of. Nobody's seen any sign of him."

"Where was he working today?"

"He was out in the barn." Kenwood shook his head. "He was right outside all day. I guess he disappeared right after dinner."

"She didn't see anyone else come by?"

"Not that she told me."

"I'm sorry, Angie," Babe was muttering. "I'm really sorry."

Angie said nothing, which Junior knew to be her way of saying, *Okay, that's too far.*

At that moment, the sound of tires against gravel disturbed the quiet outside. Peter and Junior went to the window. Angie also stood, gently pushing Babe away from her.

Lester's pickup pulled in the drive. Both doors opened, then slammed shut. Loud voices echoed into the night, followed by hysterical laughter. Two shadows rounded the hood of the pickup, then came together, arms wrapped around each other. Although it was a very dark night, one of the figures had the unmistakable, sinewy build and long narrow jaw of Lester Ruth.

"Who is that with him?" Junior asked.

"Harlan," Kenwood said.

"Oh."

"I didn't even know he was around," Kenwood mused, almost to himself.

"They look pretty drunk," Junior said.

"Seems to be going around," Angie said, her voice harder than usual.

The revelers rattled the back door, and Babe suddenly woke up to the circumstances.

"Is he here?" she asked, sitting up.

"Hello!" A cheerful, boisterous greeting filled the kitchen.

Babe stood up. "Is that you, Lester?"

Lester appeared in the doorway, his eyelids drooping, his cheeks blood red. His lipless smile stretched like a string from one earlobe to the other. Babe rushed over and wrapped herself around him. They both nearly fell over.

"Peter!" Harlan Glider shouted as he entered behind Lester. "What the hell are you doing here?"

"What are *you* doing here?" Kenwood asked. "Don't you have a meeting with the attorney tomorrow morning?"

"Aw, Lester here just needed some company, is all." Harlan's hair, which was normally slicked against his skull, hung in a great swoop across his forehead. "I'll be there. You know I never miss one of those precious goddam meetings. I love those fucking meetings."

"Why don't you mind your language there, Harlan," Junior reminded him.

Harlan looked over at him, smiling like a mischievous teenager until he noticed Angie.

"Oh, I'm sorry, Angie. I didn't see you here."

"Fuck you, Harlan," Babe said.

"Now, Babe." Lester wrapped his arms around his wife, who seemed to be readying herself to go after Harlan. "He's just joking. You know Harlan. He's our pal."

"Yeah, Babe," Harlan said, holding his arms out wide. "You know I'd never say anything bad about someone as pure and sweet as you."

"All right," Kenwood said, stepping forward with purpose. "Why don't we break up this little party and get some sleep."

"Where have you been, honey?" Babe said, looking up at Lester. She took his face in her hands. "Why didn't you tell me where you were going?"

Lester laughed. Junior had never seen him so animated, even under the influence.

"What's so funny?" Babe asked. "Why are you laughing? I was worried about you."

Lester laughed again, not quite as hard this time. "Worried, huh? That's funny. Suddenly you're worried."

"Maybe we should go," Angie whispered behind Junior's ear.

Junior hesitated, fighting a sense of responsibility to be available if things went a bad direction. But he was also curious.

"Yeah, what makes you so worried all of a sudden?" Harlan said, his eyes twinkling with mischief.

"It's just because she doesn't have someone else to worry about anymore," Lester said.

Babe stepped away from him, pushing at the same time. "You better shut your mouth right now, Lester. You better shut up before you say something…"

"Sure," Lester said. "Yeah. I'll shut up. It's the only thing I do right anymore. It's the one thing I'm good at. Not like *Tom*." The name exploded from his mouth in a burst that made everyone in the room jump backward. Angie stepped on Junior's foot as she tried to regain her balance.

"Don't you do this, Lester," Babe said, bursting into tears. "Don't you bring this up again."

"Tom, Tom, Tom, Tom, Tom…" Lester chanted quietly. He lifted his arms and walked, beginning a circle around the living room. Then Lester suddenly transformed himself into Tom Butcher—he hunched his shoulders and blew up as if he had suddenly gained 50 pounds. "Hey, buddy, how you doin'? How's it goin'?" He walked up to Kenwood. "Tom Butcher, local troublemaker. I hear you're planning on killin' me off…that true? You got it in for me?"

Babe tottered after him, trying to put a hand over his mouth. Everyone in the room tried to grab one or the other of them—all but Harlan, who stood by smiling.

"What was so great about Tom, anyway?" Lester asked, suddenly turning, his arms still raised. "How did this guy become such a saint?"

"He was a great guy!" Harlan declared, waving his arms, palms up. "He was great!"

"You stay out of this, you obnoxious bastard!" Babe shouted, pointing at Harlan.

"Yeah. All right," he said, still amused, still smiling.

"Let's go home," Angie said to Junior, louder this time.

"All right," he agreed. "We're going to take off!"

"Ah, come on," Lester said. "We're just getting goin' here."

"That's enough," Kenwood said impatiently. "Come on, Harlan."

"All right, Dad," Harlan said, still smiling.

Kenwood was not amused. "Well, I'm going. I don't give a damn what you do."

"No," Lester suddenly declared. "I don't want you to go." Lester started an almost mechanical, goon-like progression toward the door. "I don't want none of you leaving." Besides his drunkenness, this effort was hindered by the fact that Babe did not let go of him. As Lester rocked back and forth toward the door, she clung to him like one of those life-sized dancing dolls.

"We haven't had enough fun around here lately," Lester decided. "You all need to stick around and have a few drinks with us—have some fun." But Lester's manner had become too disturbing, too dark, to indicate the promise of anything like fun.

"We need some music," Babe announced, finally detaching herself from Lester. He lost his balance and braced himself against the door frame.

Babe staggered admirably toward their record player, showing enough danger of falling that Peter and Junior both stepped toward her. But she made it across the room, acting as if this off-kilter gallop was the way she always walked. She began digging through their small album collection.

"Who wants a drink?" Lester asked loudly. He backed toward the kitchen, widening his stance as if to make sure everyone stayed put. "Let's celebrate my inheritance." Then he started laughing wildly. "Here's to Tom!"

"Oh, yeah," Harlan said, matching Lester's volume. "To Tom." He started laughing, and Kenwood shook his head.

"This is absurd," Kenwood mumbled.

After much fumbling, Babe dropped the needle somewhere in the middle of *Roger Miller's Greatest Hits*. "You Can't Roller Skate in a Buffalo Herd" blared in tinny lines across the room.

"Listen." Kenwood straightened his back, clearing his throat, tilting his head quickly to one side to pop a tight vertebrae in his neck. "Lester, Harlan—I'm willing to forget this whole night if we can just end it right here, right now. It's getting very late, we're all tired…"

"No!" Lester shouted, stepping back into the living room.

Harlan started laughing again, Kenwood's shoulders tightened up around his neck. The building tension seemed to energize Lester. He took three more steps, toward Kenwood.

"No," he repeated, at a lower volume. "You been telling me when to do this and when to do that for too long. I got my own ranch now. Or I will when you stop fucking with me."

Kenwood looked down at the floor and shook his head.

"Why can't you just let me go?" Lester said, and the pleading in his voice was painful to everyone. Even Peter seemed disturbed, looking down at the floor.

"Now, Lester," Babe said, careening toward him, her voice cheery and oblivious. "You're just talking silly."

"Shut up," Lester said quietly.

She stopped dead, her face falling like a child's.

"Jesus," Angie said quietly.

"You been telling me what to do for too long," Lester said again, pointing at Kenwood. His voice was quiet in a high energy, frightening way. "Why you have to fuck with me one last time? Why can't you just do what Tom wanted?"

"All right," Junior said. "That's enough."

But before anyone had the opportunity to put an end to things, Harlan busted out laughing again. The minute the first guffaw escaped his throat, Lester negotiated the two strides between them like a batter out of the box. His fist caught Harlan flush in the face. Harlan's hands flew to his nose. Blood gushed between his fingers, staining his shirt and then the floor.

Peter and Junior grabbed Lester just as he cocked his arm for the second punch. He struggled for a moment, but his condition impaired the effort.

Junior had his eye on Harlan, thinking that once he got himself together, he would retaliate. But Harlan kept his head down, holding his palm cupped over his nose. Angie ran to the kitchen and returned with a wet cloth. She held it out to him tentatively, at an arm's length.

Harlan wiped his face, then held the cloth to his nose. He lifted his head and looked at Lester. He looked at him with no hint of anger. He looked at him as if he knew exactly how he felt. As if he wished he could have done the same thing. He held the look for just a moment, waiting for Lester to see it. And then he turned without a word and walked out.

Lester stirred. "Where the hell does a guy get off? Where the hell does *that* guy get off?"

"You hit *him*, Lester," Babe said.

"That's not what I'm talking about, dammit. I thought I told you to shut up."

"There's no need to take anything out on anyone else," Kenwood said.

"Why don't you take him to bed," Angie suggested.

"Nobody needs to take him anywhere," Lester said, finally regaining control of his limbs. He jerked free of Junior and Peter's grip and headed up the stairs, grumbling to himself. Halfway up, he stopped, turned, and shouted, "Tom Butcher is dead, goddamn it. *I'm* in charge now!"

CHAPTER TWENTY-SIX

DECEMBER OF 1968 WAS A cold one in Paradise Valley. An early snow had fallen just after Thanksgiving, covering the valley with a blanket of light, fluffy down. The next morning had the soft, twinkling look that makes you forget the problems snow can bring.

The temperature did not rise for the next two weeks, and the snow began to gather dust and hay and tracks and smells of work. A week later, it was no longer pretty, no longer soft, no longer charming.

The Kirby and Logan kids were in the yard, taking advantage of the heavy snowfall to build a snowman, when Scooter and Susan came running over from their house.

Roger eyed Scooter, who gave him a nod, which he returned. Scooter and Susan started helping with the snowman, but when it became too crowded with six kids on one snowman, Susan suggested they start another one.

Roger helped the Kirby boys dig some rocks from under the deep snow, and they started poking them into the snowman's head to form a mouth. He kept a close eye on Scooter. Julie couldn't reach the head, so she went over to help the Cayley kids, scooping armfuls of snow up and packing them into the base they'd rolled.

Scooter rolled a second big snowball and lifted it up to put it on top of the base just as Julie moved to pat another armload onto the same spot. They collided, and Scooter pushed her out of the way, dropping the snowball.

"Hey!" Julie said.

"Leave her alone," Roger said.

Scooter stopped what he was doing. "Or what?"

"All right, you two," Bobby said. "Don't start."

"Or what?" Scooter repeated, coming toward Roger. Bobby stepped between them, but Scooter pushed him aside and came right at Roger, who didn't hesitate. He punched Scooter in the side of the head, and before anyone could respond, the two boys were locked in a battle. They fell to the ground, throwing punches and trying to roll each other over as the others gathered in a circle around them.

"You kids about ready for dinner?"

Roger caught the lumbering figure of Junior Kirby walking toward the house, far enough away that they could barely hear him. Bobby waved to him, and Junior went on, not noticing Roger and Scooter locked in a scuffle. Roger felt his face get numb from punches and snow. Although he tried to hit Scooter in the face, they were both tired enough that most of their punches missed.

"You guys need to stop," Bobby finally said.

"Not until he apologizes to Julie," Roger said.

"As if," Scooter said. "She's a brat. A crybaby."

Julie started crying, as if on cue.

"Tell her you're sorry," Roger said, and the anger that coursed through him was enough that he was able to roll on top of Scooter and get a solid hold on his collar. He pulled him up by the coat and pounded him back into the ground.

•

When Junior first returned to the house from a long, cold day in the saddle, he didn't pay much attention to the kids playing in the yard. He told them to come in for supper, then went inside and took off his boots, warming his frozen feet by the fire until Angie told him supper was ready, and he pulled his boots and coat back on and went out to get the kids. That's when he realized that there was a fight going on.

Roger and Scooter were both lying on the ground, arms around each other, trying to land punches. He lifted them up by their collars and pulled them apart, setting them on their feet.

"What's going on here?"

None of the kids spoke. They looked at their feet and held their arms behind their backs. Scooter squirmed in Junior's grip.

"What happened?" Junior asked, looking from one small face to the next, then the next, until he'd gone around the circle. He settled on Scooter, the only one who was looking directly at him.

Finally, Julie spoke up. "He started it." She pointed at Scooter, who turned his glare on her. "Scooter pushed me down." Julie bent over and tried to roll her pantleg up to show Junior an injury on her leg. But her pants were too tight, and her tiny fingers couldn't budge the tight fabric.

"Scooter, Susan, go on home," Junior commanded, controlling a guilty urge to slap some regret into Scooter's eyes. Junior wondered what it was about a kid who suffered so much violence that always seemed to encourage more. It was almost as if Scooter expected to be punished for everything that happened, whether he had anything to do with it or not. As if he was daring Junior to hit him.

He let go of Scooter, but he held his bulk between him and Roger. "Go on," Junior said. "That's enough. You kids go home."

Susan grabbed her brother by the arm and started leading him toward the house. Scooter kept his face turned back toward Roger as they walked away, and once they were out of hearing range, Roger started to whimper, just a little. He lowered his head and put a hand over his mouth, trying to stifle it.

"Let's go eat," Junior said, letting go of Roger. Julie was still wrestling with her pantleg. As the rest of them started for the house, Roger stopped and bent down to help his sister.

Junior walked toward the house with a sick feeling in his gut, wondering how a person could possibly save a kid like Scooter, wondering how his parents couldn't see what they were doing to this child, and wondering, again, what kind of man would let this go on without doing something—anything.

They sat at the table. Roger had washed the blood and snow off his face, but one look at him still made Angie gasp. His eyes were puffed and red, his lower lip swollen around a small cut.

"What happened?" Angie asked.

"They had a fight," Junior told her. "Scooter and him."

Angie had the good sense not to embarrass Roger any further. He ate quickly, looking down at his plate, his face showing a great shame.

Junior thought back to the day Roger had run off into the mountains, about his claim of seeing the mysterious man up there and cutting him with a knife. Like most of the community, Junior had written this story off, attributing it to the tired hallucinations of a scared kid. But the more time he spent around Roger, the more Junior was convinced that it really happened.

•

When Carl came to pick up his kids that evening, Junior pulled him to the side.

"Roger and Scooter got into it again," he told him. Concern filled Carl's eyes. "Roger was sticking up for his sister."

Carl nodded. "That sounds like him."

"I'll try and make sure they don't hang around the Cayley kids so much."

Carl frowned. "Well, we can't keep these kids away from every goddam thing that *we're* scared of, can we? I can't keep him out of school."

Junior asked him about Laurie. Carl shrugged.

"Any word on whether she's thinking of coming back?"

Carl looked up quickly. "Do you want me to see if someone else can watch the kids for a while?"

"No, no. Hell no. I'm just asking. I've just been wondering whether it's hard for you to get by without her, with all that's going on. I don't mean to pry, but you haven't been yourself."

Carl looked down at the floor. He didn't say anything for a good long while.

"I'm beginning to wonder if I'm doing right staying here, Junior." He looked up at Junior. "I'm putting everyone through a lot."

"It's tough. You leave, everybody's going to assume you're running."

Carl nodded. "That's a big part of it," he said. "But Laurie doesn't see it that way."

•

Junior didn't have to worry about keeping Scooter and Roger apart, as they didn't see Scooter for several days after that. But Junior did discover a dead mouse in the barn, with a pencil jabbed into its brain through one ear.

"Has Scooter been at school the last few days?" he asked Bobby that evening.

Bobby nodded. "Yeah. He's been there."

"Have you noticed anything off about him?"

Bobby frowned, then his eyebrows jumped halfway up his forehead. "You mean the limp?"

"Limp?"

"Yeah. He's been limping pretty bad the last few days."

Junior nodded, trying to keep his brain moving, trying to breathe. An anger coursed through him, and he felt his face turn red, as if his head was swelling.

After sitting for a few seconds and breathing through it, Junior snatched his coat and hat and stomped off to the Cayley house, ignoring his wife's questions.

"Evening, Junior," Gordon said, filling the doorway. His voice was polite but strained.

Junior pushed right past him and walked directly over to Scooter, who was sitting at the dinner table.

"What the hell do you think you're doing?" Gordon asked, following Junior. But he was too startled to respond as Junior stood Scooter up, undid his jeans, and yanked them to his ankles. What he found was too horrible to describe, an image that would stay with him always.

"You have one week to get the hell off my place," Junior told Gordon, pulling the boy's pants back up. Scooter did not even flinch, although it must have been unbearable to have the hard denim slide up his raw leg.

Sharon walked in from the back of the house. "What's going on?" she asked.

"One week," Junior repeated, holding up a single digit, barely breathing. Then he stood and made for the front door.

"Maybe you better think twice 'bout that," Gordon said.

"I've thought more than twice about it already," Junior said. "I've thought it through a hundred times. You do what you have to do. I'm doing what I have to do. I can't live with this on my ranch. And you can bet you'll be hearing from the authorities."

Junior left, slamming the door harder than he needed to, still feeling an intense anger coursing through his veins. He shook his head, trying to forget what he'd seen. But he also felt good. He felt as good as he had in a long time.

•

Sitting on the bed, shoulders slumped, Junior said, "I fired Gordon."

"You did what?" Angie turned from the mirror, where she was brushing her hair.

"I gave him a week's notice."

She walked over to the bed, where Junior had just slid under the covers. "Why on earth did you do that?"

Junior explained what had been going on with Scooter. He didn't go into detail, but even so, Angie sank to the bed.

"My God," she muttered breathlessly. "I had no idea." She mulled over the revelation, her eyes fixed on a spot somewhere on the bed. "How could we not know?" she asked, speaking downward. "That poor child. No wonder he's so angry."

"It explains a lot," Junior agreed. "Except what to do about it."

"Why didn't you tell me sooner?"

He shook his head. "I wasn't sure what to do. I gave Gordon a warning, a few weeks back. I thought I'd give him a chance to prove that he could be a better man…" Junior shook his head again, taking a deep breath. "Maybe that was a mistake. I don't know."

Angie looked down. "Oh, God, it's so hard…so hard to know," she said. She looked at him, finally, and laid a hand on his forearm. It was the first time she had touched him with anything like tenderness for a month. And it felt as good as a warm wind sweeping across the pasture and lifting away winter's persistent chill.

•

That night Junior knew that he'd done the right thing. He felt as if he'd been given a reprieve from a sentence of righteous pride. For the first time in weeks, he had a measure of hope—for the community, for his own peace of mind—for a return to the way things were before Tom was killed.

But the victory was a hollow one. Because after his wife turned off the light and slid under the covers, they lay there in the dark, not touching. And the longer they lay there, not touching, the more Junior was reminded of how they would usually spend a night like this, how Angie would wriggle until she melded against him, her front to his back, and how their skin would absorb each others' warmth, and how her hand would snake its way around his waist, then up to his chest, where she would play with the curly hairs that covered his ribs. And they would lie that way for an hour sometimes, talking, but more than that, simply sharing in the feeling of the day, whatever it was, whether it was frustration or joy, disappointment or accomplishment. The feeling didn't matter. What mattered was that they shared it.

On this night, as Junior lay there wide awake, listening to Angie's breath get slowly heavier, he felt a hollowness. Junior was no longer afraid of what would happen if Gordon told Angie about Babe. He was ready to live with the consequences. He missed that hand against his heart.

So Junior rolled over and placed his palm on Angie's shoulder. He squeezed it slightly and whispered her name.

"Hm?" She started, just a brief twitch of her muscles, then she rotated halfway onto her back. "What is it? Is something wrong?"

"I've got to tell you something, honey."

There was a short pause, while Angie came awake. Then she sat up and reached over, turning on the bedside lamp. And when she took a deep breath and looked at him, Junior could see from her eyes that she knew exactly what was on his mind. "Give it to me straight," she said.

He rose to one elbow. "She kissed me," he said. "We kissed. That was it."

Angie's hand slammed against Junior's face with a force he didn't know she had, one he hoped to never experience again.

She left the room. Junior sat alone, half under the covers, and the pain spread from the outside in, filling him like a liquid, right up to the lip. But it did not feel wrong. It felt as if it was exactly what he'd earned. Just as much as he deserved—no more, no less. But even more, it felt, finally, as if it was going to end. The anxiety and fear was going to go away.

After only a few minutes, Angie came back. She stood just inside the door for a moment, and although she still looked angry, her face had softened. She stared at Junior, measuring him. He smiled at her.

"I'm sorry," Junior said.

That was all. She walked over to the bed and sat down carefully, and when she wrapped her arms around his head, he leaned against her, reveling in her heat as weeks of anxiety and guilt and the most absurd imaginings came to a sweet, quiet end.

CHAPTER TWENTY-SEVEN

"LAURIE, IT'S SUCH A BEAUTIFUL machine!" Angie bent down low, nearly touching Laurie Logan's shoulder, watching as Laurie hunched over the smooth white plastic body of a brand-new Elna sewing machine. The machine hummed, and the needle bobbed in a furious rhythm as a length of plaid cotton fabric bunched up behind the body.

"I can't believe how many stitches this thing has," Angie said, carefully running a finger along its lever.

"You want to try it?" Laurie asked, lifting her foot from the pedal and standing.

"Okay." Angie nodded. "You sure it's all right?"

"Of course!" Laurie said. "Sit down."

"You two quit fighting," Junior said, and the women laughed.

Carl stood next to Junior, beaming, his face berry-red with excitement and pride. It was Christmas Day, and Carl had managed to put enough money together to buy his wife this state-of-the-art machine.

The week before Laurie and Bradley came home, Carl had been unable to talk about anything else. In his quiet way, he was so damn excited that he couldn't think. The Kirbys found it very charming.

"So you like it, honey?" he asked Laurie for the fourth time since the Kirbys had arrived.

Laurie smiled at him. "Will you stop, Carl? I told you..."

Carl laughed. "I can't help it," he said.

Upstairs, the kids were doing their best to break the Logans' new Christmas toys. Thumps and laughter rang from the bedroom, adding to the optimistic, joyful feeling that swept through the house.

The Kirbys had been touched by the Logans' invitation to join them for Christmas dinner. It seemed only natural that they would want to spend the day alone. But they insisted, to thank the Kirbys for their help with the kids. It didn't matter how many times Junior told them how little trouble they were.

Junior was pleased to see that the Logans had a good Christmas. It had been a good holiday for the Kirbys as well. The Cayleys were gone, and this was the only complaint Junior could muster for that week. Fortunately, the Kirbys' cows were finished calving, but there was still a lot of work to do, and Junior hadn't had much rest in the two weeks since Gordon and his family pulled out without saying goodbye.

"Hey, Junior. Why don't you come outside for a second," Carl said. "I got something to show you."

The two men walked out to the shop, the cold air burrowing in under their heavy coats. Carl stopped for a moment, looking out at the pasture behind the house.

"What is it?" Junior asked.

"Oh, I just sewed the hide onto that little calf there when his mamma died, and I wanted to see if the new mamma was taking to him."

The two men watched the calf suckle away, and they exchanged a nod. "Good work," Junior said.

"So how's it going without Gordon?" Carl asked.

"It's been tough, but I'm gettin' by. I'll need to find someone soon, though."

Carl nodded. "I was surprised. He seemed like a good worker."

"He was the best I ever had. But…well, I might as well tell you, Gordon was treating that kid of his badly. Very badly."

"Scooter?"

Junior nodded. "I couldn't have that. If something happened…" He just looked down and shook his head. "I found out where he's working now and I let the authorities know down in Laurel. I wouldn't want that on my conscience, you know?"

"Makes sense to me." Carl flipped on the light in the shop and headed for the back of the building. There was a door in the far corner, which led to another part of the shop, a big garage where Kenwood usually stored his swather.

"It's none of my business, but it sounds like you did right, Junior."

"I hope so. It's hard to know."

When Carl led Junior into that room and turned on the light, there was the frame of an old flatbed truck. The chassis had been stripped and rising up around it was an angle-iron frame.

"Are you building a stacker?" Junior asked.

"That's right."

Junior walked around it, studying the welds and the design. The rack in front was missing its teeth, but otherwise, the hay stacking machine was almost complete. "You've done this before, looks like."

Carl nodded. "Haven't I told you that? How do you think I bought that sewing machine?"

Junior looked at him. "You built another stacker? There's no possible way you'd have time to build a stacker."

Carl chuckled. "You're right. I built it over the summer, before we came here. I've been storing it at a place down by Livingston, a guy I used to stack for."

"You going to sell this one, too?" Junior asked.

"Yeah. Hopefully." Carl walked up beside the machine, running his hand up along what would eventually be the lift. "Actually, I'm hoping Kenwood will buy it."

Junior almost said the first thing that came into his head, but he held his tongue. With his construction business, Kenwood could get whatever he wanted, built to his own specifications. Junior also knew that Carl could get a lot more for this machine from just about anyone than Kenwood would pay. But there would be time to tell Carl all of that later. No point putting a damper on his enthusiasm.

"You do good work," Junior told him. He examined the even, steady welds at every joint. "You could sell a lot of these if you had the time to build 'em."

"You think so?"

"Absolutely."

At that moment, they heard the door into the shop slam shut.

"Must be time for dinner," Carl said, winking. "We're coming, honey," he shouted.

But as Carl reached for the light, Kenwood appeared in the doorway.

"Mr. Kenwood!" Carl said. "I thought you were in Omaha."

"Yeah, well, something came up." Kenwood looked at the floor, burying one fist in his pocket. "Howdy, Junior. Merry Christmas to you." He shook Junior's hand.

"Same to you, Peter. Everything all right?"

"Oh, yeah. It's nothing major." Peter looked up. "Well, what have we here? This isn't ours, is it?" He started to walk around the machine.

"No, it's not," Carl said. "I've been building a stacker. I hope you don't mind if I use this space. I put the swather in the barn. It should be all right."

"Oh, sure. That's okay. I don't mind." Peter studied a few welds. "I just hope this isn't getting in the way of you doing the job I hired you for."

"Oh no, sir. No. I'm working on this on my own time—on Sundays, or at night."

"I believe you, Carl." Kenwood looked at Carl with a bemused, patronizing look, and for a moment, Junior really hated the son of a bitch. "You don't have to get so jumpy. I was only kidding."

"Of course, Mr. Kenwood."

They stood in an awkward silence for a moment, Junior watching Carl wait for Kenwood to reveal the nature of his visit. But Kenwood seemed distracted.

Carl started for the door. "Well, I think we need to get on inside. Laurie's probably just about got dinner ready."

Kenwood looked up, as if being awakened, and nodded. "It smelled like she had something good cooking in there."

Carl killed the lights, and they ducked into the main shop, where Junior suddenly spotted Lester standing in the corner, leaning against a bench. He looked like absolute hell. As if he hadn't slept for a week.

Lester's appearance was so disturbing, and so unexpected, that for a brief moment Junior had the horrible notion that he was there to hurt somebody. Carl looked uncertain, too. But when Kenwood saw Lester and didn't acknowledge him, Junior realized they must have come together.

"Merry Christmas, Lester," Junior said.

"Same to you," he said, not quite looking up. "Merry Christmas, Carl."

"Thanks," Carl said. "Hope you have a good one yourself."

"Speaking of Christmas..." Kenwood walked over to Carl, reaching inside his coat. He pulled out an envelope, put it in Carl's hand, and patted him on the shoulder. "You folks have a good holiday."

He started for the door, with Lester following.

"Thanks, Mr. Kenwood," Carl told him. "Are you guys in a hurry? You want to come in for some coffee, maybe a little food?"

The men all stepped out into the brittle cold.

"No, no," Kenwood said. "We got our own dinner we have to get back to."

"You sure?" Carl asked.

"Yes. We need to get going."

Kenwood climbed into his pickup, and Lester followed, barely able to climb all the way up into the cab. They couldn't tell whether Lester was hurt, or sick, or what. The two men slammed their doors and waved before driving off. Junior and Carl watched Kenwood turn to the right, away from his house. They looked at each other, both asking the same question with their eyes. Junior decided to voice it.

"Wonder where they're going."

Carl shrugged.

"You know what's wrong with Lester?"

Carl shook his head. "No idea. I saw him a couple of days ago, and he looked fine then."

"Hope he's all right."

Carl nodded. He was still clutching the envelope in his gloved hand. He held it up and studied it for a second, then ripped one end open and made a clumsy effort to spread the two sides and retrieve the contents. It was too cold to take off even one glove, so it took him a while. But he finally got a grip on the slip of paper and pulled it out. He took one look at it and his face went slack. His hand fell to his side. Junior couldn't tell if he was overcome with gratitude or grief.

"You all right?" Junior asked. Carl took a deep breath, then held the check out to him. When Junior took it from him, Carl turned and walked right back into the shop. Junior watched him go inside, then looked at the check. It was made out for a grand total of twenty dollars.

"Son of a bitch," he muttered.

Junior decided not to follow Carl into the shop, thinking he might need a minute or two alone. But soon after he went in there, Junior heard a noise—a loud metallic bang. His breath stopped, and he broke for the shop at a dead sprint.

Then he heard the noise again. And again. Junior barged into the shop and shouted Carl's name. Junior rushed to the back garage and flung the door open in time to see Carl take a violent swing. His back flexed, his arms whipped upward from his waist, past his shoulders, and forward. A metallic glint flashed in a graceful arch above Carl's head. And when the head of a huge sledgehammer connected with the angle-iron of Carl's stacker, the clang was deafening.

"The guy is a goddamn millionaire," Carl muttered. "He's a goddamn millionaire."

He swung again, and the sound exploded, then echoed through the shop, vibrating in the walls. He went into another swing, and his face tightened, fist-like. The strain brought a crimson shade to his skin. He let out a vicious shout with each swing.

"Take it easy, Carl," Junior said.

Carl not only did not slow down, but he began to swing harder. His eyes looked glassy, glazed. He didn't hear a word Junior said. He pounded and pounded, and Junior began to worry that he might tear a muscle.

"Carl." Junior raised his voice. "Carl, hey. Come on, Carl. Let's go eat."

Carl kept pounding until he exhausted himself. Even then, when he barely had enough strength to lift the massive head of the hammer, he took one more swing.

Junior finally felt it was safe to approach. He eased up behind Carl, not wanting to shock him out of his trance. He put a hand on one shoulder. Carl didn't flinch, or resist, or even respond. Carl's body deflated, folding in on itself. He lowered his head until it rested on the butt of the sledgehammer's handle. He took in deep, tired breaths— loud gusts of air rushing from his slack mouth.

"Are you all right?"

Carl didn't respond immediately, but after a long pause, he rolled his head to the side, looking at Junior. A weak smile came to his face.

"I guess I'll live," he breathed. "I don't know about this poor machine, though. I might have killed him."

Junior chuckled. "You gave him a pretty good beating."

"Better check his pulse."

Junior placed a palm against the angle-iron. "It's weak, but it's there."

"Good," Carl said, still breathing heavy. "Good. I wouldn't want that on my conscience." He shook his head. "Goddamn. I haven't been that pissed in a long time."

"Well, I can see why." Junior held up the check. "This is a goddamn insult."

Carl just looked at him, still almost smiling, still working hard to get his breath back. "I don't know anything anymore, Junior. You know what I mean? I feel like nothing makes sense anymore. Nothing makes sense." He shook his head again.

"Well, there's one thing I do know."

"What's that?" Carl asked.

"I know for a damn fact that there's a big turkey waiting for us in there, and Laurie will be heartbroken if we let it go cold."

•

Carl made a remarkable transformation in the walk from the shop to the house. By the time they sat up to a table, he had regained his joyful enthusiasm. He smacked his palms together and rubbed them furiously, surveying a perfectly browned turkey, a massive bowl of mashed potatoes and another with mashed yams, stuffing dotted with roasted pecans, a gravy boat, and platters of fresh-baked bread.

They had set up a table in the living room for the kids, and sounds of laughter and teasing rang out from their table as the adults dug in.

Junior kept a close eye on Carl. His eyes shone, and he smiled even while he chewed. The disappointment of an hour earlier became ancient history.

"How are Spider and Hazel doing?" Laurie asked, looking around the table.

"They seem to be doing okay," Angie answered. "We haven't seen much of them lately."

"What about that lawsuit Kenwood filed to keep Lester from taking over the Butcher place?" Laurie asked.

Junior shook his head. "Kenwood's been dragging that thing out as long as he can, just so he won't lose Lester. He's filed every appeal he can come up with."

Carl looked at him. "Why doesn't Lester just quit working for him? I've never figured that one out."

Angie swirled her fork through her potatoes. "There are some people who are comfortable where they are, no matter how miserable they might seem to everyone else. The whole idea of changing is too much for them."

"Kenwood sees that," Junior added. "Maybe that's why he never promoted him to manager."

Carl frowned. "You really believe that?"

Junior nodded. "I do."

The conversation was interrupted by the jangling ring of the telephone. Laurie got up and answered it in the kitchen.

"Oh, hello, Hazel," she said. "I'm good. Fine. We were just wondering how you and Spider are doing...yes, Merry Christmas to you, too." Then, after a short pause, they heard a small gasp. "She is? What for?" And after another beat. "Well...gosh, thanks for calling. Is there anything we can do?"

They all stopped eating.

Finally, Laurie said, "Okay, well, if you think of anything, just let us know. Just call. Okay?" Another pause. "Yes. Thanks for calling, Hazel. Really. I appreciate it."

Everyone expected she would hang up, but there was no sound of the receiver being replaced, and another short silence followed.

"Yes. Just a few days ago. Well...I don't know, actually."

They all looked down at their plates, trying to pretend they didn't know what Laurie was dodging, the question of how long she'd be staying.

"Yes," Laurie continued. "It would be very nice to see you. I'll call you in a couple of days. Thanks again."

Laurie appeared in the doorway, a frown wrinkling her forehead. "Babe's in the hospital," she said.

"Oh," Angie uttered.

"What happened?" Carl asked.

Laurie bowed her head. "Apparently, she..."

She never finished the sentence, but everyone present knew what she meant. And it brought the meal to a standstill. They all sat silent, their heads bowed.

CHAPTER TWENTY-EIGHT

Junior Kirby couldn't bear the thought of spending New Year's Eve anywhere besides Tom Butcher's big living room. It would have felt all wrong, as if the old year never ended at all—as if 1968 was going to go on and on and on. That prospect alone was enough motivation for Junior to propose that they throw a party at Tom's house.

This idea, when he first mentioned it to Angie, was greeted with the kind of look generally reserved for suggestions like running naked through a rodeo ground (he was drunk) or painting the barn blue (he was kidding). But Junior lobbied hard, arguing that the entire community had avoided any social gathering since Tom's funeral. It seemed that they could go on forever avoiding each other, ignoring what had happened, if something wasn't done.

Junior got permission from Lester. He also talked to Sheriff Blinder, who assured him the authorities were long done with Tom's house.

Because the idea came late, invitations had to be issued by phone. Junior was pleased to find that almost everyone said yes. Only Arnie and Molly Janko flat out refused to come. "Are you inviting the Logans?" Arnie asked. When Junior answered "Of course," Arnie responded, "We won't be coming then. Aren't you worried something could happen?"

This had occurred to Junior, but he'd reached the point where he thought even an all-out county brawl would be better than the frost which had settled over their community, every family in silent, self-imposed exile. Hazel Moses said she thought it was brilliant idea, which pleased Junior.

He decided it was important to create an atmosphere as much like the original as possible. And as he made arrangements with the band from Livingston, the butcher in Bozeman, the liquor store, and talked to Kenwood's cook about preparing some of her specialties, Junior came to appreciate how much effort Tom had put into the event every year. And Tom had done it without anyone's help. Junior had Angie. The thought of planning it alone, year after year, while still running Tom's huge place, seemed overwhelming.

•

Junior was surprised how nervous he was on December 31, 1968, like a young kid trying to live up to his older brother. He arrived at Tom's house early, taping the last paper streamers to the walls. He'd gone to Woolworth's and bought all the cheap decorations he'd always scoffed at—the streamers, the party hats and banners with Happy New Year spelled out in glitter, the noisemakers, balloons by the dozens. The room was an explosion of bright colors and shapes, the streamers swooping from the peak of the ceiling in red, blue, purple, and yellow.

Angie and the boys had gone to Bozeman to pick up the booze, and Kenwood's cook was due to arrive in an hour with the food. Others had volunteered to cook the meat—two hams, half a beef, a dozen chickens, and several pounds of deer sausage.

Alone, waiting, Junior stood in the middle of the massive room, hearing the echo of his own breath. He turned in a circle, then another, studying everything. He walked to the kitchen, where he turned in several more circles. Then back to the living room, and another rotation. He finally settled with the thought that there was nothing more to do. Junior sank into the big stuffed sofa and crossed his legs at the ankles.

A minute passed, with the silence spreading out behind and ahead and above him. He stared at his feet and tried to imagine years of this same silence, this aloneness. He wondered how a man like Tom Butcher, a man who enjoyed the company of other people so much, managed to live like this. He thought briefly about exploring the upstairs bedrooms for evidence of Tom's fetish, but the thought made him uncomfortable.

Junior remembered Tom talking about the land, or the *fucking dirt*, as he called it, and he realized that in Tom's own, almost resentful way, his relationship with the land had been far more intimate than Junior's would ever be, because it was not complicated by a wife and children. The land was Tom's only love, and it was probably for this very reason that he also hated it. Because it held him so tightly, making his secret so much more powerful. He must have felt trapped, alone with that secret.

Junior stood and went searching for a bottle, hoping that a drink would help him relax. He found a lone bottle of whiskey tucked into the far corner of the dusty liquor cabinet. He wiped the bottle clean, found a glass, and fixed himself a ditch, with four parts whiskey and one part water.

As he settled back into the sofa, people began to arrive—first Kenwood's cook, with her husband helping, and then Angie. Due to Junior's nerves, he was in rare, authoritarian form. Angie recognized this and put herself in charge. The food and liquor were laid out, and Angie demoted Junior to setting up the card tables and folding chairs.

Others arrived, but the room stayed quiet. People entered almost sideways, as if they weren't sure they were at the right party. They stood awkwardly, hands buried in their pockets or fiddling with drinks or plates of food.

Spider and Hazel were among the early guests. Spider looked as if he would rather be anywhere else. His eyes darted around the room as though he expected to see a ghost. Hazel gave both Angie and Junior big, solid hugs, her smile wide and relaxed. It was the happiest Junior had seen her since her wedding day.

"This was such a marvelous idea, you two," Hazel said, and Junior was grateful to hear this again. "We need something to bring us all together." She held out her arms. "We need to gather, you know. It's what country people do."

Junior thanked her and gripped her hand harder and longer than he realized. She finally put her other hand on top of his and gently pulled away.

When the Logans arrived, Junior was happy to see Laurie was still around. Carl had his hand wrapped around her upper arm, as if he was afraid she might disappear. They surveyed the room with quick, darting glances. Kenwood arrived soon after the Logans, without his wife, who was in Omaha. He brought Harlan Glider instead.

Kenwood wore a pair of brand new snakeskin boots, smoky gray, with a matching belt. His denim pants were stiff with starch, as was his white western shirt. And he wore a sport coat with leather shoulders. He looked sharp. Although Harlan's outfit was less western than Kenwood's, he was wearing cowboy boots for the first time that Junior could remember.

"We decided not to wear our tuxedoes this year," Kenwood said, winking.

"I appreciate you coming down to our level," Junior said. "Almost."

Soon after that, Junior was surprised to see Arnie and Molly walk in, and the way they looked around the room like gawking children made it obvious that the idea of missing out was too much to bear.

Guests drifted into the house in a steady stream, and Junior was pleased to see faces from past years, people who lived a long ways from Paradise Valley. Word had spread quickly, and Junior couldn't help but wonder how many of these people were here out of morbid curiosity. Whatever the reason, there was a huge crowd by nine-thirty.

Junior circled the room, greeting each guest with a hearty hello, though he realized that, even as a memory, Tom outshone him by a mile. There were a few surprised looks from people who recognized what Junior was trying to do, but no one said anything. Except his wife.

"Don't you think you're overdoing it a bit, Junior?" Angie wrapped her arms behind his neck, looking up at him with a combination of concern and amusement. "It's not up to you to make sure everyone has a good time, you know."

Junior tried to dismiss her insight, but she had read him perfectly. And in the end, Junior did *not* want this party to take its own course. He saw this party as the standard by which the rest of the next year, and the rest of their lives, would be measured. He wanted to take control of this night, to grip it by its throat and point it in the right direction. He wanted to give their little world a chance to recover from this tragedy, and to rediscover the sense of community they had built their lives around.

The Kirbys had agreed that the one thing they could not risk was running out of liquor. If ever there was a night when social lubrication would be essential, this was it. So they filled the liquor cabinet with shining brown, green, and clear gallon bottles. A full keg of beer sat in a tub of ice in the kitchen, with another on the back porch.

Predictably, the bar and the keg proved to be the two places where everyone gathered. People loosened up, their faces red and shiny, and the volume became a persistent roar, echoing through the big room. People shouted jokes, and loud, raucous laughter rattled the windows.

Junior was in the kitchen, asking Carl whether he'd had time to do any more work on his stacker, when a noticeable buzz began to vibrate through the crowd. Junior and Carl glanced into the living room. As they made their way through the thick gathering of warm, sweating bodies, they heard several voices mutter the name *Babe*.

No, Junior thought. *It's not possible.* But as he and Carl moved closer to the front door, they saw Lester's slicked black hair, parted neatly, and then, just to his right, floating like an orange cloud, the luminescent red hair of Babe Ruth.

"Babe," Junior shouted, unable to contain himself. "What are you doing here?"

Babe looked hurt. "What do you mean?" she asked. Babe looked up at her husband. "Weren't we invited, Lester?"

"Of course you were," Junior replied, laughing it off. "I meant, why are you out of the hospital? Are you okay?"

"Oh, that." Babe waved a hand. "I'm fine," she said. "It wasn't serious."

An awkward pause followed.

"What?" Babe said, looking around at all the blank faces. "What's wrong?"

Lester spoke up. "What the hell is everyone looking at? You never seen someone who was in the hospital? Jesus."

"Forget it," Junior said. "You want something to drink? You know where the bar is, right?"

"Absolutely," Lester said, moving forward with purpose. His irritation was clear in the narrow slits of his eyes.

But Babe was not ready to be led. She stopped, looking up at Junior, ignoring Lester's effort to keep their momentum going. She tugged her arm loose. "Junior, I just want you to know how happy I am that you did this," she said with a smile. "It's nice to be back in this house."

Lester jerked her arm. She stumbled after him to the bar, where he fixed each of them a drink. Babe tilted against the counter, surveying the crowd with an odd grin. A sort of impenetrable bubble seemed to form around her. Nobody approached her, or even stood nearby. But suddenly, a streak of silver moved through the crowd, and penetrated. Angie grabbed Babe, holding each of her shoulders gently in her hands and looking her in the eye with an earnest, pleading expression. She asked her something, and Babe answered, still sporting the dreamy smile.

Lester noticed Angie and made a quick move around the bar. But Angie gave Lester a stern look and asked him something, and when she didn't like his answer, she grabbed him by the arm and led him out of the room, off to Tom's study.

Junior wanted to join them in the worst way. He could just hear the firm scolding Angie was delivering. He could imagine exactly what she would say, and he probably would have missed by only a few insignificant words. Something about him not having the common sense of a sheep to bring his wife out to a party just a few days after she tried taking her own life, and just how could he think so little about her welfare.

But when Angie and Lester emerged from the study, Angie did not have a look of righteous indignation at all. Instead, she was pale, as if she had just come out of a coma. She scanned the big room, and Junior started toward her, hoping that she was looking for him. Sure enough, when she saw him, she started weaving her way through the crowd.

"What the hell is going on?" Junior asked her.

She shook her head. "You're not going to believe this, Junior." She pulled him closer to her and whispered. "Babe did *not* try to kill herself."

"She didn't?"

Angie shook her head again. Her eyes surveyed the crowd, scanning the room as if she was searching for a culprit. "It's a vicious goddam rumor," she said. "Somebody made it up."

"Well, she was in the hospital though, right?"

"She *was* in the hospital. Because she fell. She fell and knocked herself out."

Junior looked at Babe and sighed. "Jesus."

Angie took a deep breath, holding it for a long time and closing her eyes. And when she finally did let it escape, she muttered, "I'm not going to let this get to me. I'm going to enjoy the evening anyway."

"Good," Junior said. "Let's go get a drink."

•

The band arrived around ten and took fifteen minutes to set up. Then they kicked into their swinging array of country favorites. After months of keeping their heads down, the crowd was ready to dance. By the second song, the partygoers stirred up the sawdust spread across the hardwood floor. The dust stuck to them, mixing with their sweat to give them a light yellow sheen.

They whooped and shouted, clapped and swirled, forgetting the recent past and remembering the distant one—a time when nights like this were frequent and unhampered by unspoken suspicions. For the next two hours, the crowd forged ahead without restraint, and Junior's uncertainty about the whole idea drifted away on a feathery bed of whiskey and slide guitar.

The levels in the bottles inched downward. The keg spit the last of its foam into Hazel Moses's paper cup. "We need to tap the other keg!" she demanded.

Even those who generally didn't drink filled their glasses to the brim. Carl declared loudly that anyone who didn't have a stain on their shirt wasn't having enough fun.

Carl also slapped Junior on the back time after time, sometimes hard enough to irritate him. But each time he turned to see Carl beaming at him, showing his teeth with a goofy buck-toothed expression, Junior laughed. And Carl also laughed, as if it was the first time anyone had ever thought to do such a thing. Laurie tottered unsteadily after him, dancing on soft feet with knees like water.

Junior knew the party hit a new level of decadence when Kenwood took off his jacket and didn't even notice that it landed on the floor. Harlan Glider's shirt came out of his pants, and the tails flew with each spin. It was the first time anyone had ever seen him dance. Spider and Hazel, who were excellent dancers, cut an elegant path through the chaos, despite Spider's flailing knees and elbows.

In the middle of all this, showing no regard for rhythm or order, taking no notice when one song ended and another began, Babe performed her own quiet, dreamy pirouettes, bumping into whoever happened to be in her way. Occasionally someone tried to dance along with her, even putting an arm around her waist. Sometimes she moved along with them for a few beats, but the music playing in her head inevitably threw her body away from that person. In a strange way, she seemed to be only one who wasn't out of control.

•

It would be curious to know whether the course of the lives of the people in Paradise Valley would have taken a different turn had this not been a New Year's Eve party. What would have been different if these people had continued as they were, dancing with abandon, until they were all danced out?

Several minutes before midnight, the band stopped playing and announced that 1969 was just minutes away. Everyone broke out the champagne and filled cheap plastic glasses.

Not only did they count down the final minute of 1968, but they counted down the final *five* minutes of 1968, shouting the numbers loudly, right up in each other's faces, trying to hurry the process, to put this horrible year behind them. They shouted until it seemed their faces might burst, their teeth shining pearly white in the pale light, their eyes wild with drink and the shared desperation to reach that stroke of midnight.

Then the second arrived, and the band fell into a ragged version of "Auld Lang Syne," and the whole crowd sang along, repeating the only verse they knew over and over. And finally, Hazel Moses barged up to the stage, as if she couldn't stand another bar. She grabbed the microphone from the startled singer and held it close to her mouth, like an apple, and waved her other hand in the air. "Quiet, please. Quiet. Can I have your attention for just a minute or two? Please!"

Hazel kept her hand in the air, her elbow bent slightly, as if the weight of her fingers was almost more than she could bear. She bowed her head for a moment, arranging her thoughts, and when she lifted her face to the crowd, she straightened her shoulders, and lifted her chin an inch, and suddenly she looked very professorial. There was still some slight rustling among the more inebriated, but for the most part the big room was almost as quiet as it had been when Junior Kirby was there alone.

"I just want to say a few words about Tom Butcher," Hazel said, and the silence became complete.

"I did not know Tom as well as many of you, so maybe I'm not the right person to speak about him. But I feel as if I knew him well enough to know that nobody could inspire such strong feelings of both contempt and admiration. Probably half the people in this room can say that they have been angry enough to think about killing Tom at one time or another." She cast a slow look across the silent crowd. "Now that he's gone, I for one have to live with the knowledge that there were times, even though they were small moments, when I wished Tom Butcher was dead."

She lowered her eyes.

These were not people who were accustomed to speeches, especially from one of their own. So the speeches they did hear generally had a power over them. But if it was possible to pinpoint a moment when the liquor—which until then had loosened their sorrow and allowed them to break out and laugh again—turned on them, it was after what Hazel said next. Her eyes narrowed as she lifted her head and scanned the crowd again, her expression twisting from melancholy to bitter anger.

"But there is only *one* person…" Hazel said, and the consonants exploded into the microphone. "…only *one* who has to live with his death. And it disgusts me that this person is here among us, and it disgusts me that this person has been able to live as long as they have with this secret, as every day their life becomes more and more of a *lie!*"

The silence that followed was profound, but short.

"As long as we're talking about lies…" a voice cried out, "…how about explaining why your husband lied to the sheriff about me. How about starting there?"

Everyone turned to see Carl Logan pushing toward the front of the room. Laurie tugged at his sleeve, trying to hold him back. But he jerked himself free.

"Why did you tell them I got into an argument with Tom?" Carl barged toward Spider, who looked around him, trying to back up, but trapped by the crowd.

"He didn't tell them that!" Hazel shouted. "I was there. He didn't say that."

But Carl didn't hear this, or maybe he didn't believe it. "Why did you put all this suspicion on me?" Carl closed in on Spider, whose eyes grew. A few people tried to hold Carl back, but his anger made him strong. "You're going to break up my family. You've made our life a living hell." He jabbed his finger at Spider, again and again, his arms pulling him through the crowd as if the people around him were water.

"He didn't say that!" Hazel climbed down from the platform. "Spider was upset," she said. "That deputy rattled him. He kept saying, 'Did they fight? Did Carl and Tom have an argument?' He wouldn't let up, and Spider finally said yes because he knew that's what the guy wanted to hear."

But Hazel's explanation was drowned out as the rest of the crowd began murmuring, moving closer in anticipation of where this confrontation would go. Carl drove through the last of the crowd. He wrapped his fist up in Spider's shirt and dragged him to the floor. And Hazel followed, plunging on top of Carl.

The transformation from the initial wrestling match to an all-out scuffle took only a matter of seconds. Suddenly it wasn't two people, three people fighting it out. It was a hundred people. It was all of them. Where they'd had music, now the only noises were the sounds of violence—shouting, the dull thuds of fists landing against bone, bone against floor, shouting, muffled screams, clothes tearing, bottles breaking. Someone had an arm wrapped around Junior's neck, and he reacted by instinct, landing an elbow to their ribs. When he turned to see who it was, there was Babe's surprised, grimacing face. But she recovered quickly, landing a weak right cross to Junior's jaw.

"Jesus!" Junior shouted, holding a hand to his bloody lip. "We're all going crazy!"

"Yeah," someone shouted. "Isn't it great!"

The violence was short-lived, providing an outlet for months of suspicion and nervous energy. But it didn't take long for people to realize that the face they were staring at as they threw the next punch was a longtime neighbor, someone they had known most of their lives. Soon people were holding each other up, apologizing, or wiping blood from each others' faces.

But two men did not stop. Two men fought with a vigor fueled by years of growing tension.

After years of tolerating Arnie Janko's lies and laziness, Lester Ruth jumped on this opportunity, and after everyone else was done fighting, he and Arnie silently pounded on each other. The crowd gathered around them, transfixed by the silent struggle. Their arms flailed, their faces turned red, they fell, they scrambled to their feet, they grunted, they bled and tears ran down their faces. Months of suspicion and anxiety played itself out between these two men. Nobody made a move to intervene. The band laid down their instruments and joined the circle.

Finally, after a half hour, the fight stopped, with both men seated, legs straight out in front of them, heads bowed, propping themselves up with their hands behind them. They didn't look at each other. They didn't speak.

There was no movement for a time, as everyone tried to catch their breath and assess what they'd just witnessed.

Just as everyone began to stir, a quiet moan rose from the middle of the crowd. And then it grew and took the shape of a word, repeated over and over.

"No, no, no, no, no." A figure emerged from within this mass of humanity. It was Carl again. He moved forward like a boxer who'd just beaten the ten count, then he crouched down, resting his elbows on his knees. He grabbed Lester and began to shake him.

"Not you," he said. "Not you."

People crowded in closer.

And they all started asking questions. "What are you doing, Carl?" "What's the matter?" "What are you talking about?"

"It's him," Carl said, looking up with a glazed expression.

"What's him?" Junior asked.

Carl had his hands tangled up in Lester's collar. With his chin, he nodded at Lester's arm, where his shirt sleeve had been torn away in the scuffle. Crossing Lester's upper arm at an angle was a jagged scar. It had healed ugly, as if it had never been treated. And it was recent.

"How did you get that, Lester?" Carl asked.

Lester's boot of a jaw began to work. It gnawed, pushing and twisting around his tongue, swirling and juggling whatever words were inside, but still holding them. His eyes, always so tiny, looked smaller than ever.

"Tell us what happened," Angie said.

"What are you all talking about?" someone asked.

Babe crawled over to Lester, wrapping her arms around his shoulders. Lester's jaw stopped for a moment. He blinked quickly, several times, and dropped that long narrow chin to his chest. His tiny eyes closed.

"He was killing you, Babe," he said, his voice as small as a child's.

"No, Lester." Babe shook her head. "No."

But Lester just said it louder. "He was *killing* her," he told everyone. Babe pushed her head against his shoulder. "No, Lester."

"I didn't plan on killing him," Lester muttered. Then he shook his head again and buried his face into the bosom of his wife and never emerged. They stayed in that position until someone called Sheriff Blinder to come and pick him up.

And so it was that a wide variety of lives came together, in this county, on this ranch, in this big living room. Every life, whether it had risen up from generations of ranchers, or stumbled upon this little valley by accident or by love, came together to watch Babe Ruth rest her hand tenderly against the face of her husband in the very room where he had killed a man months before. In the haze of cigarette smoke and the thick aromas of spilled liquor, the residents of Paradise Valley saw this lasting image of a tragedy that they would not comprehend or understand for many months after. There in that big living room, they saw how sad and twisted love can become.

CHAPTER TWENTY-NINE

RURAL PEOPLE ARE A STUBBORN lot, including those who live in the ranchlands of Montana. It was stubbornness that brought their ancestors west in the first place—a stubborn, idealistic belief that they could carve a life out of a place that showed very little promise. It was stubbornness that kept a handful of those homesteaders alive, despite the cruel winters, and years without rain, and land that betrayed them, drying up like a bone in the sun. And it was stubbornness that kept people there despite the quiet loneliness of being miles from their nearest neighbor. As most people knew by now, the romance of the West was pure bullshit. It was a hard, isolated, brutal life with little time for anything but work.

Those who are still there are the offspring of the most stubborn of the stubborn—the ones who were too mean to die and too determined to prove everybody wrong to leave.

It was stubbornness that kept Tom Butcher alone on his massive ranch for so many years, hiding a secret that must have made his loneliness that much more isolating. And it was stubbornness that brought Carl Logan to Paradise Valley and kept him around even when staying might cause him to lose his family. It was stubbornness that sent Babe Ruth running back to Tom, hoping to convince him to love her, even after she knew his secret, or maybe more so then. And it was stubbornness that kept her husband at her side, just as it was stubbornness that kept Lester under Peter Kenwood's thumb for so many years, showing a singular devotion that was never earned.

It was stubbornness that convinced Gordon Cayley that a good beating didn't do his son any harm, despite all evidence to the contrary. And it was stubbornness that kept Junior from telling his wife about one small incident, allowing it to grow into something bigger than it ever should have been. After the Cayleys left Paradise Valley, the Kirbys heard from a mutual friend that Scooter had ended up in the hospital after another beating from his father, and Junior decided to alert the authorities about what they'd seen. Junior had been worried ever since about the consequences of that.

But as is often the case, peoples' greatest weaknesses can also be their greatest strengths.

In Tom's case, his stubborn insistence on being himself and speaking his mind, no matter what anyone thought of him, was what many admired most about him. And it was Carl's stubbornness that prompted Junior to offer him the job that Gordon Cayley left vacant. Junior had marveled at Carl's work ethic, all while he was fighting the demons of an entire community's suspicions, and Arnie Janko's laziness, and Laurie's indecision, and Kenwood's lack of support.

Laurie Logan, too, came from homestead stock. Her stubbornness confounded people for a time, even though they were not completely unsympathetic to her position. When Carl went to work for the Kirbys, moving into the Cayley house, and when Laurie took Bradley and went to live with her sister in Billings, there was a lot of nasty talk.

But over the next several months, Laurie and her sister expanded a small business of custom-made clothing—mostly wedding dresses— into a successful venture. Laurie's sister had been doing this for several years, but having children got in the way. With the two of them sharing the workload, as well as childcare, they built a strong reputation in a short time. It went so well that Laurie was able to do most of her work at home. And once she established that, she decided that she wanted her home to be with Carl. She made the trip to Billings once a week to keep up with the business.

•

But most things don't work out so tidily. Two weeks after Lester's confession, Junior and Angie were sitting in front of a fire in a rare moment of quiet. The boys were over at the Logans'. The phone rang, and when Angie answered, she listened for a moment, and Junior watched her cover her eyes with one hand and shake her head.

"Okay," she said. "Thanks for calling, Peter." She stayed rooted in the same spot after she hung up.

"What is it?"

"Babe's in the hospital again."

Junior sighed. "What now?"

"She overdosed."

Babe was admitted for treatment, not allowed visitors for several weeks, so the Kirbys went to see her two months later. When they walked into her room, they were surprised to see her looking better than she had in years. Her face showed some color in the midst of her frizzy red hair.

"You look great, Babe," they both said at once.

She waved them away. "Stop."

"You really do," Angie said.

Babe sighed, and a tear dribbled from the corner of one eye. "Well, I guess it makes sense."

The Kirbys sat. "Why?" Angie asked.

"Well, they've been cleaning out my system since I got here."

"Cleaning it out?"

"Getting me off all the pills."

Junior and Angie looked at each other. "Pills?" she asked.

Babe shook her head, and she started crying. She wept silently for several minutes, then made a concerted effort to compose herself, and after taking several deep breaths, she was able to speak, although the tears continued to seep from her eyelids. "You two have known me for a long time, right?"

They nodded.

"Please tell me you didn't really think I was capable of behaving the way I have…not without being very sick."

Junior and Angie dropped their eyes. An uncomfortable few seconds of silence followed. "Of course not, Babe," Angie finally said.

"So you've been taking pills?" Junior said.

Babe sighed, shaking her head. "Oh God, yes. Everything under the sun. Happy pills, sad pills, whatever I could get my hands on."

"Where did you get them?" Junior asked.

Babe looked at them, pulling her mouth to one side. "Tom. Tom had an ex-girlfriend who's a nurse…right here in this hospital, actually."

"But why would he do that?" Angie wondered.

Babe lowered her chin. "Well…he tried to get me to stop when it got bad. He tried to get me in here. Remember the night he hit me?"

Angie sat forward. "That was Tom?"

Babe nodded. "I wouldn't go. He was so angry with me." Babe shook her head. "And I started calling him names. About something I had on him…a secret."

The Kirbys exchanged a look, and Babe sat up.

"You know?"

Neither of them were able to look Babe in the eye.

"How did you know?" Babe asked.

"The necklace," Junior said. "Daryl Blinder had to explain what happened with the necklace."

Babe threw herself back against her pillow. "Oh god, that was stupid. What was I thinking?" Her head rotated slowly toward them. "I'm so sorry."

"But how did *you* find out about Tom?" Angie leaned forward in her chair. "I can't imagine Tom telling you that."

Babe pulled her mouth to one side. "Actually, he did. I think he expected it to scare me away. But it just made me love him more." She started crying again. "There was something so sad and sweet about it." She turned to look at them. "Oh, I know it sounds crazy. It *is* crazy." Babe covered her eyes. "Please don't hate me. I've messed up so many lives."

"Of course we don't hate you, Babe. How could you even think that?" Angie said.

But in the end, it didn't matter whether anyone else hated her. Babe hated herself a lot more than anyone else possibly could. Without the benefit of the pills, she couldn't live with herself, so she didn't. After battling her addiction for almost a year, she put an end to her misery with one last bottle.

●

Six months after Tom's murder, Junior rounded a corner of the barn late one evening, after dark, and a month of sunrises flashed before his eyes. He heard a blast, and when he fell, he thought lightning had knocked him over. But a sharp, burning pain made him realize that he'd taken a bullet somewhere south of his head. He was still able to think, but a burning in his chest pulled his jaw tight against his teeth. Junior's eyes clenched shut.

As he lay bleeding, he heard footsteps running off into the night, and he knew it was Gordon Cayley. He wished he had the strength to get up and chase after him.

A few months before, after Junior decided to alert the authorities about Gordon's treatment of his son, they received word that Scooter had ended up in the hospital and was then placed in a foster home in Buffalo soon after that.

●

When Junior woke up in a hospital bed, Angie was asleep in a chair next to him. He thought about the night before—the look of fear on Carl's face when he found Junior, and his desperation to get him to the hospital, the rush into surgery. Although barely conscious through all of that, Junior remembered them telling him that he'd been shot through the chest.

Angie stirred, and her eyes drifted open slowly. After a glance around, she bolted upright in her chair. "Are you okay?"

Junior smiled. "I think so." He was surprised how much it hurt to speak.

Angie stood and wrapped her forearm around his head, resting her skull against his. "I was so scared, Junior."

"That was pretty scary." He rested a hand against the back of her head.

She backed away and took his face in both hands, looking down at him. "I love you."

Junior kissed her.

"Do you remember Daryl Blinder coming by last night?" she asked.

Junior shook his head.

"They caught him," she said. "They caught Scooter."

"Scooter?"

She nodded. "It was Scooter. He rode his horse from Buffalo up here. All that way."

Junior stared at his feet for the longest time, unable to comprehend this. "Good lord, that's awful."

Junior took several weeks to recover, and for years after that, a persistent ache in his chest reminded him to never underestimate the measure of love a child can feel for their parent, even when they don't deserve it.

CHAPTER THIRTY

ROGER LOGAN STEPPED INTO THE tiny trailer the first day after New Year's 1969, and every head in the room turned. The kids stared at him as if they'd never seen him before.

"What?" he said.

None of them spoke for a time, but Bobby finally piped up, saying, "So it really happened."

"What really happened?" Roger asked.

"You cut Lester with a knife."

"Oh." Roger looked down. "That. Yeah."

"Well, what was it like? Did he come at you?"

Roger sighed, sinking into his desk. "Jeez, it's hard to remember. I woke him up, so he jumped up like he was going to come after me, but I think he was mostly scared."

"And you stabbed him?" Bobby's eyes were like saucers.

"Well, I just sorta swung the knife. Blood came flying off his arm like a squirt gun."

There was a brief silence as his fellow students stared at him.

"Wow," Bobby said. "That's cool."

"It was weird, is what it was," Roger said. "I didn't know what to do next. But he ran off. I was pretty happy."

"I bet."

"And you had no idea it was Lester?" one of the other kids said.

"I'd never seen Lester before. I had no idea who he was. Plus he was all covered in stuff…blood and dirt. It was like he'd been rolling around."

The other kids couldn't seem to stop looking at him, and it made Roger uncomfortable. Thankfully, Hazel breezed into the room with her usual authority, and all heads turned to the front again, leaving Roger to ponder his new position. Ever since Scooter left, he had enjoyed a different dynamic with his classmates, and now it seemed that things had shifted even further with the revelation that the story about Roger's trek into the mountains was not just some childhood fantasy.

"Children, I have something to say," Hazel announced. She posed in front of the class, pressing her hands flat against her desk and looking at them over the top of her glasses. Just from her demeanor, they knew they were about to get a scolding, and all six heads bowed accordingly. Hazel cleared her throat. "I want to tell you kids how proud I am of you, for the way you handled the events of the past few months."

The children looked up.

Hazel stood up straight. "I really mean that. This has been a difficult time for all of us, and I know you've had your scuffles and your arguments, but mostly, you kids have done a remarkable job of treating each other kindly."

There was a long pause as Hazel bowed her head for a moment, clearly fighting some emotion.

"And I don't know if there's a way I can express this in a way that you can understand now, at this age…" She sniffed, wiped her nose, and looked up again. "But this is going to be a time that changes the way you see the world. And that's a good thing." She pointed. "You've heard a lot of rumors the last few months. Rumors about Roger's father, and rumors about me, and about Scooter, and about Tom Butcher, and Babe Ruth."

There was no acknowledgement, but they all knew it wasn't necessary.

"That's just the way people behave sometimes. It means they're trying to figure something out. They're trying to figure *someone* out. It doesn't have to be ugly, kids. Okay? It doesn't have to be ugly."

Roger felt a tear trickle from one eye, and he quickly swiped at it, hoping Craig, who sat next to him, didn't notice. But he caught Craig making the same motion.

"Just remember that no matter where you go, there are going to be people who are different, people who are easy targets, people who don't act like you. It's part of life." She pointed one last time. "And it's always going to *be* part of life."

CHAPTER THIRTY-ONE

"There he is." Carl tilted his head toward the road, and Junior turned to see Peter Kenwood's silvery-blue pickup pull into Tom Butcher's driveway.

"I guess he didn't want any of the furniture," Carl joked.

Junior laughed.

The Kirbys and the Logans had come out with most of the rest of the community, despite the undeniable pain of watching the life of their friend be scattered to the winds. Spider and Hazel had arrived late and the three couples all stood in a group, saying little.

In the background, the auctioneer offered up the last of Tom Butcher's possessions as the Montana sun baked the summer pasture. After months of legal wrangling, the last vestiges of Tom Butcher's life had been picked over and auctioned off. His livestock had been sold months before, and now all that was left was the *fucking dirt*. But the neighbors had little doubt where that would go.

"Do you want to stay for this part?" Junior asked Carl.

He shrugged. "You're the boss."

"Well, let's see whether anyone else even bids."

Peter sauntered up beside them. "Hello, folks." He wore a black leather vest stamped with palominos that put all of his other outlandish cowboy gear to shame. He turned to Carl. "Did you hear about Arnie?"

A slight smile came to Carl's face. "I did."

"I bet you wondered whether I'd gotten a divorce, huh?"

Carl chuckled.

"I actually haven't told my wife yet," Peter said. "She might divorce me when I do. But without you and Lester, I couldn't afford to keep that lazy son of a bitch around."

Carl pulled his mouth to one side, not sure what to say, and Peter said, "I know. I should have done it years ago."

Carl's head tilted to one side.

The men stood in an awkward silence for a few minutes before Peter asked, "Did you buy anything?"

Junior nodded "I bought that table where he arm wrestled half the county."

Peter nodded. "Good memory. That was quite a night."

Another awkward silence followed before Peter took a deep breath and looked around at each of them.

"Listen, I know I'm not the most popular guy in this valley. The way I took advantage of Lester was…" He dropped his head. "Well, I don't feel good about it. I even wonder…"

The others stood before Peter, shocked to see him struggling with his emotions.

"Anyway, I wanted you all to know that both Tom and Lester were fine men. They deserved a better ending." Peter dropped his head and took a deep breath. He gave one last nod, a firm gesture that seemed to indicate he was done. He turned and started to walk away.

"You're leaving?" Junior asked.

Peter turned around. "Yeah…nothing here that interests me. I heard some famous writer put a big bid on the land anyway."

As Peter drove away, Angie and Carl and Junior looked at each other and shook their heads. Angie said, "Was that an apology?"

EPILOGUE

"Are you coming, Roger?"

"Sorry." Roger, brought out of his daydream, opened the passenger door of the family sedan and stepped out onto Bozeman's Main Street. He ambled behind Carl, who suddenly stopped.

"Are you okay?" Carl rested his callused hands on his hips.

"Yeah, I'm fine."

"You've got something on your mind."

Roger shook his head. "No."

What Roger was thinking about was the calf he was raising for his 4-H project. There was something wrong with the calf's leg. But he didn't want to bother his father with it. Carl had way too many other things on his mind. Roger was going to talk to one of the Kirby kids as soon as they got home, but he was worried anyway.

"Hey, Roger."

Roger looked up to see Sammy, a friend from Hawthorn School. Sammy had his hands buried deep in his pockets. His curly hair lay flat against his scalp, and one of his tennis shoes kicked up against the back of the other.

"Hey, Sammy. How's it going?"

"Good. You ready for school?"

Roger nodded. "Yeah. I guess. Summer went fast."

Carl drifted down the street to give the boys a chance to talk.

"Where you headed?"

Roger tipped his chin upward, toward a storefront. "Going to get some boots."

"Boots?" Sammy's face screwed up in confusion. "Oh, that's right. You moved out to the sticks."

Roger nodded.

"You hate it out there?"

Roger shook his head. "Not anymore. It's kind of cool."

"Don't you live close to where that guy got murdered?"

"Yeah. Just down the road."

"So you knew him?"

Roger shook his head. "I never met him. He got killed right after we moved out there. But Dad met him." Roger tilted his head toward Carl.

"Really? Wow."

Roger stubbed his worn boot along the sidewalk. "Yeah."

And then the boys stood, their heads bowed, lips pushed up toward their noses. "Well, take care," Sammy said.

"Yeah. You too."

Sammy nodded. "Sure."

Roger watched him walk away, then turned to see his father smiling at him. "You ready?"

Roger nodded, then followed after his father, his movements and his walk very much like a boy's.